Chokher bali

Rabindranath Tagore

Chokher bali

TRANSLATED BY RADHA CHAKRAVARTY

RANDOM HOUSE INDIA

Published by Random House India in 2012

1

Copyright © Radha Chakravarty 2012

Random House Publishers India Private Limited
Windsor IT Park, 7th Floor
Tower-B, A-1, Sector 125
Noida 201301, UP

Random House Group Limited
20 Vauxhall Bridge Road
London SW1V 2SA
United Kingdom

978 81 8400 304 8

Typeset in Garamond by R. Ajith Kumar

Printed and bound in India by Replika Press Private Limited

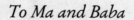

To Ma and Baba

INTRODUCTION

'The literature of the new age seeks not to narrate a sequence of events, but to reveal the secrets of the heart. Such is the narrative mode of *Chokher Bali*.' In these words from his Preface to *Chokher Bali*, Tagore announces the arrival of the modern Indian novel. Emphasizing psychology above plot and external action, *Chokher Bali* marks a radical break with literary tradition, a bold and self-conscious attempt at steering the novel form in new, uncharted directions.

Chokher Bali was serialized in the periodical *Bangadarshan* from 1902 to 1903. In 1903, it was published as a book. The novel was long in the making: Tagore had been working on it as early as in 1898 or 1899. He completed the draft version in his notebooks in 1901. Tagore's letters suggest that he had earlier used the working title *Binodini*, changing it to *Chokher Bali* shortly before its publication in *Bangadarshan*. When the novel first appeared as a book, Tagore deleted certain passages from the original serialized version. Several of these excised passages were restored, with Tagore's approval, in the first edition of *Rabindra Rachanabali* (1941) and some more in the independent Visva-Bharati edition of 1947.

The first English translation of *Chokher Bali* appeared in *The Modern Review* in 1914. Translated by Surendranath Tagore, this version was named *Eyesore*. In 1959, the Sahitya Akademi published Krishna Kripalani's translation, titled *Binodini*, which was based on the earlier book version with all its excisions. The present translation includes the restored passages of the revised Visva-Bharati edition. Of particular interest is the restored ending, which carries the narrative beyond the scene in which Rajalakshmi forgives her son and sees domestic harmony restored between Mahendra and Asha. Although Tagore's novels did not lend themselves readily to dramatization, *Chokher Bali* was recast as a play first performed at the Classic Theatre on November 26, 1904. The play was probably scripted by Amarendranath Dutta, who also enacted the role of Mahendra in the first performance. Subsequent stage and screen adaptations of the novel testify to the interest it continues to generate.

Though published in the early twentieth century, *Chokher Bali* is set in a slightly earlier time. From the details of female education provided in the novel, readers surmise that the action of the novel takes place somewhere between 1868—when it was still customary for Englishwomen to be engaged as teachers for female pupils—and 1883, when the university produced its first female graduate. This was also a period of sweeping economic changes that resulted in the emergence of a new middle class in Bengal. Between 1875 and 1941, the bhadralok or gentlemanly class, earlier rooted in the economics of the zamindari system, had begun to move from the country to the city in search of new professions such as medicine, law, engineering, education and government service. Mahendra in *Chokher Bali* studies medicine; Bihari joins him at medical college after dabbling briefly in engineering. They clearly belong to a social world where a professional qualification is desirable, but not financially necessary. Mahendra can combine his sporadic forays into the world of medical training with a dilettantish lifestyle in an affluent Kolkata household. Bihari gives up medical college to set up a charitable hospital in a garden estate acquired for the purpose.

While the male characters in *Chokher Bali* pursue a professional degree, the education of women remains a domestic matter. Binodini's father engages a 'mem' or white woman to educate his daughter. The subjects taught would normally include some works of literature, mathematics, and the history of Bengal. Along with needlework, a basic knowledge of English was also considered desirable. Bengali remains the dominant language: although Binodini recognizes Bihari's name and address on a letter inside a glass display case at the railway station, her expertise lies in Bengali literature rather than in English. She leaves volumes of Bankimchandra and Dinabandhu in Bihari's room during their early acquaintance at Barasat. Asha, meanwhile, is virtually illiterate at the time of her marriage to Mahendra; even under her husband's tutelage, her education does not extend much beyond the primer *Charupath*. Yet, even this limited education invites the wrath of Asha's mother-in-law Rajalakshmi, who is clearly not highly educated herself, although she comes from a good family.

The complex forces of tradition and modernity, Hindu orthodoxy and British liberalism create a strangely contradictory social milieu. New systems of knowledge jostle with the old—when Rajalakshmi sends for the family astrologer to seek advice on Mahendra's predicament, her son, a man of science, feels exasperated at her blind faith in horoscopes and magic. In *Chokher Bali*, there are only passing references to caste, as in the mention of Kayet Thakrun, Rajalakshmi's friend and confidante; yet the novel conveys the sense of old hierarchies and attitudes that remain in place even as new socio-economic forces threaten to destabilize them. On these issues, Tagore's position remains ambivalent. The protagonists in *Chokher Bali* belong to a Hindu social framework, but the Brahmo element, traceable to

Tagore's own upbringing, is evident in many contextual details.

Although Tagore was reared in a large family, he had sensed by the late 1890s that the joint family system was on the decline. *Chokher Bali* presents a small, compact family with a single male head. In Mahendra's household, Asha, the new bride, is expected to be subservient to her widowed mother-in-law Rajalakshmi; dependents, such as Annapurna or Binodini, remain short-term visitors. By 1911, nearly two-fifths of the urban population of Bengal lived in Kolkata and Howrah. In keeping with these changing demographic patterns, the city, too, was striving for a modern lifestyle. *Chokher Bali* presents an impressionistic image of life in Kolkata in this period of transition.

In this time of flux, the position of women was a hotly debated issue. Although Keshab Chandra Sen had presented his wife in public in 1862, it would take many years for women in larger numbers to shed the purdah, and participate actively in the Swadeshi and Non-cooperation movements. *Chokher Bali* is set in the interim period, when elite households still kept women segregated. The novel also refers to the oppressive effects of the dowry system. In part, the disastrous trajectory of Binodini's life is due to her lack of dowry, because her father spends too much on her education. It is significant, though, that Mahendra marries Asha, a dependent orphan, without any dowry: the Brahmo influence is clearly visible here. Orthodox society in Tagore's time still disapproved of widow remarriage, in spite of the Widow Remarriage Act, which legitimized it. Some readers feel that *Chokher Bali* should have ended with Binodini's marriage to Bihari. The novel, however, suggests another reason for Binodini's rejection of Bihari: knowing her reputation to be tainted by her association with Mahendra, she is unwilling to let the social stigma affect Bihari.

At the time of the novel's publication, notions of 'originality' and individual authorship had not yet gained wide currency in the Indian literary establishment. Yet Sureshchandra Samajpati, a contemporary critic, accused Tagore of plagiarizing the work of Panchkori Bandyopadhyay whose novel *Uma* (1901) was about a promiscuous widow named Binodini. As modern commentators point out, however, Tagore's novel, unlike its alleged original, is neither self-consciously sensational, nor a cautionary tale trapped in a rigid morality, but a probing analysis of the inner psyche of its protagonists. In the characterization of Binodini, we see Tagore's attempt to question contemporary gender stereotypes, and his recognition of the conflict between women's need for freedom and the pressure of social constraints. The complexity of the character of Binodini is matched by the representation of Bihari in the novel. A landowner without materialist aspirations, a dabbler in different trades who is neither an idler nor a dilettante, Bihari is the product of a particular historical moment. Yet Tagore's handling of Bihari's character is distinctly modern in its psychological subtlety. Morally upright, with an acerbic tongue and a stringent sense of personal and social responsibility, Bihari could well have remained an uninspiring ethical emblem, but his fallibility, his inner torment and his susceptibility to love provide shades of gray that preclude conventional moral stereotyping.

While *Chokher Bali* demonstrates Tagore's familiarity with *Bishabriksha* (1873) and *Krishnakanter Will* (1878), novels by his Bengali literary predecessor, Bankim Chandra Chatterji, Tagore's nuanced writing also carries overtones of the nineteenth-century European novel. The historical moment, coupled with his own upbringing, enabled Tagore to straddle two literary worlds, synthesizing features of both to create a narrative mode both uniquely his own and a signal of things to come. To this mingling of approaches, the critical establishment responded with mixed feelings. Accusing Tagore of writing an English novel in the Bengali language, Prashantakumar Pal conceded: 'But it is a masterpiece.'

A century after its publication, *Chokher Bali* continues to surprise readers with its startlingly modern approach. Of its time, yet in many ways ahead of its time, it confirms Tagore's position as a world novelist, a facet of his genius not yet sufficiently recognized. Translating

Introduction

Chokher Bali for twenty-first century readers has proved both a challenge and a reminder of the need to look afresh at texts that have changed the course of our literary history.

Radha Chakravarty

1

Binodini's mother Harimati appealed to Mahendra's mother Rajalakshmi to consider a match between their children. The women had once been childhood playmates in the same village.

'Baba Mahin,' Rajalakshmi urged Mahendra, 'we must rescue this poor girl, a poor man's daughter. I hear she is very beautiful, and has even been educated by a memsahib—that would suit your modern sensibilities.'

'Ma, there are plenty of other modern young men, besides me,' said Mahendra.

'That's the problem with you, Mahin, one can't mention the subject of marriage.'

'Ma, since there's no dearth of other subjects to talk about, it's not a fatal shortcoming.'

Mahendra had been fatherless since childhood. His behaviour towards his mother was somewhat unconventional. Although he was almost twenty-two-years old now, and had started studying medicine, when dealing with his mother, there was no end to his moods, whims and fancies. Like a baby kangaroo that lives in its mother's pouch even after birth, he had grown accustomed to the shelter of his mother's protective care. He depended on her for all his needs, be it food, entertainment, rest or leisure.

Now, when his mother insisted that he should consider marrying Binodini, Mahendra consented. 'Very well, let me go and see the girl once,' he said.

But on the appointed day, he protested, 'What purpose would going to see her serve? It is pointless to weigh the pros and cons when I am marrying only to please you.'

There was a hint of anger in his words, but Rajalakshmi expected Mahendra's sharp tone would soften after the shubhadrishti ritual—when the bride and groom see each other for the first time—for then her son was bound to approve her choice.

With a carefree mind, Rajalakshmi fixed the date for the marriage. As the day approached, Mahendra grew more and more anxious. 'No, Ma, I just can't go through with it,' he finally declared, a few days before the wedding.

Mahendra had enjoyed every possible indulgence from his childhood; hence his desires were unchecked. He could not tolerate the pressure of other peoples' expectations. Because he felt coerced by his own pledge and the requests of others, his inexplicable distaste for the proposed match grew very pronounced, and as the event drew near, he utterly rejected the idea of marriage.

Bihari was Mahendra's close friend; he used to address Mahendra as 'Dada', his elder brother, and Mahendra's mother as 'Ma'. Rajalakshmi considered him a beast of burden to serve Mahendra's needs, like a trailer tethered behind a steamboat, and hence she also felt a maternal tenderness towards him.

'Baba, it is you who must fulfil this duty,' Rajalakshmi appealed to Bihari, 'or else this girl, a poor man's daughter . . .'

Joining his hands in supplication, Bihari said, 'Ma, that's the one thing I cannot do. At your request, I have often eaten the sweetmeats rejected by Mahendra, but when it comes to a prospective bride, that would be intolerable.'

'As if Bihari would ever marry!' Rajalakshmi thought to herself. 'He is devoted only to Mahendra; the idea of bringing home a wife hasn't even occurred to him.' The thought enhanced the pity mingled with tenderness that she felt towards Bihari.

Binodini's father was not particularly wealthy, but he had employed a missionary memsahib to train his only daughter in literary and creative skills. The daughter would soon be past marriageable age, but he was not conscious of the fact. Finally, after his death, the girl's widowed mother was driven to desperation looking for a match. There was no money, and the girl was also too old.

Finally, Rajalakshmi got Binodini married to the nephew of a fellow-villager from her birthplace, Barasat.

Not long after, the girl became a widow.

'Thank goodness I didn't marry her,' laughed Mahendra. 'Had my wife been widowed, I wouldn't have survived an instant.'

One day, about three years later, mother and son were talking to each other. 'Baba, it's me people blame.'

'Why, Ma, what harm have you done them?'

'They say I'm not getting you married for fear of losing you to your bride.'

'You should be afraid, indeed. Had I been a mother, I would never be able to bring myself to get my son married. I would accept people's criticism with bowed head.'

'Just listen to what this boy is saying,' Rajalakshmi laughed.

'A wife takes over a man's whole life upon arrival. Then the mother who has lavished so much care and affection on her son is forced to step aside; even if you like this state of affairs, I don't like it at all.'

Rajalakshmi was inwardly delighted. 'Listen, Mejobou,' she said to Annapurna, her widowed sister-in-law, who had just entered. 'Just listen to what Mahin is saying. He doesn't want to marry for fear that his wife will supersede his mother. Have you ever heard such an outrageous thing?'

'My boy, this is rather extreme on your part,' declared Mahin's kaki. 'It behoves you to act in accordance with your age. It's time to let go of your mother's aanchal and set up house with your wife; it seems shameful for you to still behave like a little boy.'

Rajalakshmi did not find these words pleasing, and what she said in response, though simple, was not sweet. 'If my son loves his mother more than other boys love theirs, why should you feel ashamed, Mejobou? You would know what it means to have a son if you had one of your own.'

Rajalakshmi thought this sonless woman envied a mother like herself, fortunate enough to have a male child.

'It was you who spoke of finding a bride, Didi,' replied Mejobou Annapurna. 'Else, what right would I have to speak of such things?'

'If my son does not bring home a bride, why does it offend you? I have spent all these years raising my son, and can look after him even now. There is no need for anyone else.'

Mejobou left in tears. Mahendra was inwardly hurt, and returning early from college, he went to his kaki's room.

He was certain that there was nothing but affection in what his kaki had said to him. He also knew that the childless widow had an orphan niece, whom she hoped to wed to Mahin, thus finding a pretext to keep her bonjhi, her own sister's daughter, close to herself, and see her happy. Though averse to marriage, he nevertheless found his kaki's secret desire natural and extremely moving.

When Mahendra went to Annapurna's room, the day was waning. She was sitting by the open window of her room, her head resting against the iron grill, her face wan and dejected. In the next room, her rice lay untouched.

Tears tended to spring to Mahendra's eyes at the slightest reason. Seeing his kaki now, his eyes grew moist. 'Kakima!' he called gently, coming close.

'Come, Mahin, sit down,' said Annapurna, trying to smile.

'I'm very hungry. I want some prasad, food blessed by your touch.'

Seeing through Mahendra's guile, Annapurna checked her brimming tears with difficulty and after her own meal, she fed him.

Mahendra's heart was filled with pity. After the meal, wishing to console his kaki, he said impulsively, 'Kaki, this niece of yours you spoke about, won't you let me see her once?'

The moment he uttered these words, he grew frightened.

'Is your mind inclined towards marriage, then, Mahin?' smiled Annapurna.

'No, I am not asking for myself, Kaki,' Mahin declared

hastily. 'I have persuaded Bihari to agree. Please fix a date when the girl can be seen.'

'Oh, could she be so fortunate? Can a boy like Bihari really be part of her destiny?'

On his way out of his kaki's room, Mahendra bumped into his mother at the door.

'Why, Mahendra, what were you discussing for such a long time?' demanded Rajalakshmi.

'We were not discussing anything. I came to get some paan.'

'But your paan has been prepared and kept in my room.'

Mahendra left without offering any further explanations.

Seeing Annapurna's tear-swollen eyes as she entered the room, Rajalakshmi immediately jumped to her own conclusions. 'Why, Mejothakrun! Were you after my son?' she hissed, like a serpent, and swept out of the room without waiting for a reply.

2

Mahendra had almost forgotten about going to
see the prospective bride, but Annapurna had not.
To fix the date for the meeting, she wrote to the girl's
jyatha—her father's elder brother and her guardian—at
his Shyambazar address.

'Why did you act so fast, Kaki?' protested Mahendra,
when he heard that the date had been fixed. 'I have not
even told Bihari yet.'

'What's to be done, Mahin?' Annapurna replied.
'What will they think if we don't go to see the girl now?'

Mahendra sent for Bihari and told him everything.
'Just come along,' he insisted. 'If the girl is not to your
liking, you can't be forced into marrying her.'

'I'm not so sure about that. After going to see her,
I won't have the heart to say that Kaki's bonjhi is not
to my liking.'

'That's very magnanimous of you.'

'But it was unfair of you to have done this, Mahinda. To travel light yourself, you should not have placed the burden on someone else's shoulders. It will be very difficult for me to hurt Kaki's feelings.'

Offended and rather embarrassed, Mahendra asked, 'What do you wish to do, then?'

'Since you have raised her hopes on my behalf I shall go through with the marriage. There is no need to make a pretense of going to see the girl.'

Bihari revered Annapurna as if she were a goddess.

Ultimately, Annapurna herself sent for Bihari. 'How is that possible, my boy?' she demanded. 'Getting married without seeing the bride is out of the question. I insist; you must not consent to the marriage if the girl does not please you.'

On the appointed day, Mahendra returned from college and said to his mother, 'Please take out my silk shirt, and the dhoti from Dhaka.'

'Why, where are you going?'

'Something urgent has come up, Ma. Just give me my clothes; I'll tell you about it later.'

Mahendra could not resist grooming himself for the occasion. Even if it is for somebody else, the very idea of viewing a prospective bride impels a young man to add a slight curl to his hair, a dash of perfume to his shawl.

The two friends set out to see the bride.

With his self-gotten wealth, the girl's jyatha, Anukulbabu of Shyambazar, had built a house—a three-storey structure that towered above the rest of the neighbourhood—with a garden.

After the death of his impoverished brother, Anukulbabu had brought his orphaned niece to live in his own house. 'Let her stay with me,' the girl's mashi, her mother's sister Annapurna, had suggested. That would indeed have diminished his expenditure, but for fear of losing his prestige, Anukul had not agreed. In fact, he never even sent the girl to her mashi's house on a social visit, so particular was he about his own social standing.

Eventually, it was time to think of getting the girl married, but in today's world, when it comes to marrying off a girl, the thought alone is not enough. Along with the thought of marriage, one also requires money. But whenever the question of dowry arose, Anukul would say, 'I have daughters of my own, after all. How much expenditure can I bear by myself?' And so the days passed by. It was at this juncture that Mahendra entered the scene, all dressed up and perfumed, with his friend in tow.

At the end of a warm Chaitra day, it was almost time for sunset. The south-facing second-floor veranda was paved with fine tiles of patterned porcelain. Arranged at one end of the veranda for the two visitors were fruits and sweets on silver plates and iced water in silver glasses frosted over with droplets of moisture. Rather embarrassed, Mahendra sat down to this repast, with Bihari beside him. Downstairs, the gardener was watering the plants with a hose. Laden with the tender fragrance of moist earth, the southerly Chaitra breeze stirred the end of Mahendra's white, perfumed, pleated shawl. Through the slatted doors and windows around them came sounds of suppressed laughter, whispered words, and the tinkle of jewellery.

When the meal was over, Anukulbabu glanced towards the interior of the house. 'Chuni, bring us some paan,' he called.

After a while, a door at the rear opened hesitantly and a young girl came and stood near Anukulbabu, holding the box of paan in her hands, her entire body stiff with embarrassment. 'Why are you so shy, my girl! Place the paandaan over there, before those gentlemen,' he instructed.

Hands trembling, the girl bent to place the paandaan on the floor, beside the seated visitors. From the western end of the veranda, the glow of the setting sun illuminated her shy face. Mahendra took this opportunity to inspect the pitiful face of this shivering young girl.

As she was about to depart, Anukulbabu stopped her—'Wait a bit, Chuni,'—and turned to his visitors. 'Biharibabu, this is the daughter of my younger brother Apurbo. He is no more; now she has nobody but me,' he sighed.

Mahendra's heart was smitten with pity. He glanced once more at the orphaned girl.

Nobody would clearly declare her age. 'She'd be about twelve or thirteen years old,' her relatives said. In other words, fourteen or fifteen seemed more likely. But because she had been brought up on other people's charity, her budding adolescence had been checked, or suppressed, by an air of diffidence and timidity.

'What is your name?' asked Mahendra, moved by compassion.

'Speak, my dear, tell him your name,' urged Anukulbabu.

Head bowed, with her habitual air of compliance, the girl answered, 'My name is Ashalata.'

Asha! It seemed to Mahendra that the name was full of pathos and that her voice was very tender. Poor orphaned Asha!

The two friends came out onto the road and set off in their carriage.

'Bihari, don't let this girl go,' said Mahendra.

Without offering a direct answer, Bihari remarked, 'The girl reminds me of her mashi. I think she will be just as sweet-natured as her aunt.'

'The burden I have placed on your shoulders probably doesn't seem so heavy anymore.'

'No, I'll probably be able to bear it.'

'Why suffer needlessly?' Mahendra said. 'What if I take your burden onto my own shoulders? What do you say?'

Bihari looked gravely at Mahendra's face. 'Mahinda,

do you mean it?' he asked. 'Tell me for certain; it's not too late. If you were to agree to the marriage, Kaki would be much happier, for she would be able to keep the girl with her always.'

'Are you mad? If that were so, it would have happened long ago.'

Bihari departed without raising too many objections. Mahendra, too, left the direct route for a longer one, and went home slowly, after a long delay.

His mother was busy frying luchis at the time. His kaki had not yet returned from her bonjhi's house.

Alone, Mahendra walked up to the terrace, spread out a mat and lay down. On this seventh night of the lunar cycle's bright quarter, the crescent moon was silently spreading its exquisite magic over the clustered roofs of the grand edifices of Kolkata. When his mother announced dinner, Mahendra declared lazily, 'I'm quite comfortable, I can't get up now.'

'Why don't I bring your meal here?'

'I won't have any more to eat today, I have dined already.'

'Where did you dine?'

'That's a long story. I'll tell you later.'

Offended by her son's unusual behaviour, Rajalakshmi turned to leave without replying.

Instantly pulling himself together, an apologetic Mahendra said, 'Ma, please serve my food here.'

'Why eat if you're not hungry?'

After mother and son sniped at each other in the same vein for some time, Mahendra had to sit down to a meal once again.

3

Mahendra did not sleep well that night. Early the next morning, he arrived at Bihari's doorstep. 'My friend,' he said, 'I've thought things over and it seems to be Kakima's heartfelt desire that I should marry her bonjhi.'

'There was no need to think things over all of a sudden. She has expressed this desire in many different ways.'

'That is why I think that if I don't marry Asha, there will remain an unfulfilled desire in Kakima's heart.'

'That is indeed possible.'

'I think that would be very wrong of me.'

With somewhat unnatural enthusiasm, Bihari exclaimed, 'That's wonderful! If you consent to the marriage, there's nothing more to be said. If only this sense of duty had dawned on you yesterday!'

'If it has dawned a day later, where's the harm in that?'

Once Mahendra had allowed his mind to dwell on matrimony, it became impossible for him to remain patient. He began to think, 'It's better to go through with the ceremony instead of prolonging our deliberations.'

He went to his mother and announced, 'Very well, Ma, I shall heed your request. I am ready to get married.'

'Now I understand why mejobou suddenly went to see her bonjhi the other day, and why Mahendra went out looking so well-groomed,' Rajalakshmi thought to herself.

The fact that Annapurna's ploy had succeeded where her own repeated pleas had failed roused her ire against the whole universe. 'I shall look for a suitable girl,' she promised.

'But the girl has been found.'

'Let me tell you, my boy, that girl will not do.'

Controlling himself, Mahendra responded mildly, 'Why, Ma, the girl is not unsuitable.'

'She has nobody in the world; if you marry her, I will have no prospect of enjoying a relationship with your in-laws.'

'I will not regret the lack of social interaction with my in-laws, but I do like the girl, Ma.'

Her son's obstinacy further hardened Rajalakshmi's heart. She accosted Annapurna reproachfully: 'Would you turn my only son against me by marrying him to an ill-starred girl whose father and mother are dead? What an evil ploy!'

Weeping, Annapurna pleaded, 'I have not discussed the subject of marriage with Mahin. Whatever he has said to you is of his own free will; I know nothing of it.'

Mahendra's mother did not believe a word. Annapurna sent for Bihari. 'The match was arranged with you in mind. Why have you turned everything upside down?' she demanded, tearfully. 'It's you who must consent to this marriage, once more. If you don't save the situation, I shall be placed in a very shameful position. The girl is extremely sweet-natured; she would not be unworthy of you.'

'Kakima, you needn't tell me that. When the girl is your niece, there can be no question of my turning her down. But Mahendra . . .'

'No, Bihari, Mahendra cannot marry her under any circumstances. To tell you the truth, I would be most relieved if you were to marry her. I am averse to the idea of her marrying Mahin.'

'Kaki, if you are averse to the idea, then there's nothing more to be said.'

He went to Rajalakshmi and announced, 'Ma, my marriage to Kakima's bonjhi has been fixed. In the absence of female relatives, I had to overcome my embarrassment and break the news to you myself.'

'Is that so, Bihari! I am very happy. She's a sweet girl, suitable for you. Don't let this girl slip out of your hands on any account.'

'Why would I let her slip out of my hands, Ma? Mahinda himself approved the match.'

All these hindrances redoubled Mahendra's agitation. Enraged at his mother and kaki, he took refuge in a shabby hostel for students.

Rajalakshmi came to Annapurna's room in tears. 'Mejobou, Mahin has left home in dejection. Please rescue him.'

'Didi, be patient, his anger will subside in a couple of days.'

'You don't know him. If he doesn't get what he wants, he is capable of anything. By whatever means, a match with your bonjhi . . .'

'Didi, how is that possible? The match with Bihari is almost fixed.'

'It wouldn't take long to cancel that!' Rajalakshmi sent for Bihari and urged him, 'My son, I'll find a good match for you, but you must relinquish this girl. She is not even worthy of you.'

'No, Ma, that's not possible. The matter has been settled.'

Rajalakshmi went to Annapurna once again and pleaded: 'Upon my word, Mejobou, I fall at your feet. If you would only speak to Bihari, the matter would be sorted out.'

'Bihari, it is very difficult for me to say this to you, but I have no choice,' Annapurna told Bihari. 'I would have felt extremely relieved if Asha had been placed in

18

your care, but you know all that has happened.'

'I understand, Kaki. It will be as you say. But you must never again urge me to marry.'

With these words, Bihari departed. Annapurna's eyes filled with tears, but she wiped them away for fear that they would bring misfortune upon Mahendra. Again and again, she tried to persuade herself that the step taken was for the best.

In this way, amidst such cruel, secret, silent exchanges between Rajalakshmi, Annapurna and Mahendra, the wedding day arrived. Lights shone brightly, the notes of the shehnai rang out melodiously, and there was no lack of sweetness in the sweetmeats prepared for the occasion.

With her beautifully bedecked body and bashful, rapt face, Asha stepped for the first time into her new home; her gentle, trembling heart never sensed the presence of a thorn anywhere in this nest. The prospect of being close to Annapurna, her only mother-substitute in the world, filled her with reassurance and joy, dispelling all anxiety or doubt.

After the wedding, Rajalakshmi sent for Mahindra. 'I think bouma, the bride, should go and stay with her jyatha for a few days.'

'Why, Ma?'

'You have your examinations now; your studies may be affected.'

'Am I a callow youth? Can I not use my own judgement?'

'It's only a matter of one more year, Mahin.'

'If my bride had a father or a mother, I would not object to her visiting them, but I can't keep her at her jyatha's house.'

'Oh, my goodness!' Rajalakshmi thought to herself. 'He's the master, and the mother-in-law's opinion doesn't count! So much sympathy after being married for just one day! We, too, were brides once, married to the masters of the house. But in those days, there was no such uxoriousness, nor such arrogance!'

'Have no fear, Ma,' declared Mahendra emphatically. 'My examinations will not suffer at all.'

4

Thereafter, Rajalakshmi showed a sudden zeal for training the bride in household duties. Asha's days were spent in the store room, kitchen and prayer room. At night, as compensation for the loss of her own relatives, Asha was made to share Rajalakshmi's bed.

After careful consideration, Annapurna thought it best to maintain a distance from her bonjhi.

Mahendra's condition was like that of a greedy boy who watches in desperation as his powerful mentor chews upon a sugarcane stick until almost all its juice is exhausted. He could not bear to watch his youthful bride's sweetness being relentlessly wrung out of her by the pressures of housework.

'Kaki, I can't bear to see the way Ma is working my wife to death,' Mahendra protested to Annapurna.

Annapurna knew that Rajalakshmi was carrying things to an extreme, but she replied, 'Why, Mahin, it's a good thing that your wife is being taught some domestic skills. Would it be better if she lived like the girls of today, reading novels, weaving rugs and leading a life of leisure?'

Agitated, Mahendra declared, 'A girl of today will be like other modern girls, whether you like it or not. If my wife can read a novel and appreciate it as I do, then I see no cause for reproach or mockery.'

Hearing her son's voice in Annapurna's room, Rajalakshmi dropped everything and came there. 'What's this!' she demanded, sharply. 'What are the two of you plotting?'

'We're not plotting anything, Ma,' insisted Mahendra in the same agitated manner. 'I can't allow my wife to labour over household chores like a slave.'

Controlling her burning fury, his mother spoke slowly, but sharply: 'What is to be done with her ladyship, then?'

'I shall teach her to read and write.'

Rajalakshmi swept out of the room without replying. She returned an instant later, dragging her daughter-in-law along. 'Here she is. Teach your bride to read and write.'

She turned to Annapurna, the aanchal of her sari wrapped about her neck in contrition, and said, with folded hands, 'Forgive me, Mejoginni, please forgive me. I was not aware of your bonjhi's prestigious position. I have stained her tender fingers with turmeric; now you

22

must cleanse and scrub her and groom her like a lady before handing her over to Mahin. Let her ladyship learn to read and write in luxury, while I slave away at housework.'

With these words, Rajalakshmi rushed into her room and slammed the door. Annapurna sank to the floor in sorrow. Failing to understand the significance of this sudden domestic upheaval, Asha grew pale with shame, fear and pain. Enraged, Mahendra told himself, 'No more of this; I must take responsibility for my own wife. It would be wrong of me not to.'

The flame of desire was instantly fanned by a sense of duty. Throwing college, examinations, demands of friendship and social obligations to the wind, Mahendra ensconced himself in his room along with his wife to strive for her intellectual improvement. He paid no heed to his work, and not the slightest attention to other people.

A petulant Rajalakshmi declared to herself, 'Even if Mahendra and his bride came to my door begging for forgiveness, I would still ignore them. Let's see how he manages with his wife, after having excluded his mother.'

The days passed, but no penitent footfalls approached her door. Rajalakshmi decided that when he came to ask forgiveness she would forgive Mahendra, or else he would be terribly hurt.

No plea for mercy was forthcoming. Then Rajalakshmi

decided that she herself would go and forgive him. If the son was sulking, ought the mother sulk, too?

In a corner of the terrace on the second storey was the tiny room where Mahendra slept and studied. During the last few days, his mother had neglected the tasks of folding his clothes, making his bed and cleaning his room. Not having performed these habitual duties of maternal love, her heart ached inwardly, like breasts overfull with milk. That afternoon, she thought, 'Mahendra must have left for college by now. I shall take this opportunity to go and set his room in order. When he returns, he will instantly detect his mother's touch in the room.'

Rajalakshmi went upstairs. One of the doors to Mahendra's bedroom was ajar; approaching it, she stopped short just outside as if suddenly pricked by a thorn. Inside, Mahendra was sleeping on the floor, and his bride, her back to the door, was gently stroking his feet. Glimpsing this scene of conjugal love through the open door in the harsh afternoon light, Rajalakshmi cringed with shame and self-contempt, and crept downstairs in silence.

5

At the onset of the rains, crops that have been shrivelled and yellowed by drought suddenly show a spurt in growth, shedding the effects of prolonged undernourishment. Casting off their feeble, drooping air, they raise their bright, shining heads unabashedly and confidently to claim their space amidst the fields of grain. So it was with Asha. With her own blood relations, she had never been able to demand the rights of kinship. But now, upon entering a strange home, when she found it so easy to claim an intimate relationship and was given undisputed rights, when her husband personally crowned this neglected orphan with the crest of Lakshmi the household goddess, she was quick to accept her prestigious position. Shedding the bashfulness and awe expected of a new bride, she basked in the glory of being a fortunate wife, unhesitatingly ascending the throne at her husband's feet.

That afternoon, after seeing this newcomer from another family seated on that throne with an air of such long-accustomed daring, Rajalakshmi descended the stairs in a state of unbearable disbelief. She went to scorch Annapurna with her own heartburn.

'Oh! Just go and see what sort of grooming this princess of yours has brought with her from her royal abode. If our husbands had been alive today . . .'

'Didi, it is for you to train your daughter-in-law and discipline her,' pleaded Annapurna sorrowfully. 'Why say these things to me?'

Like the twang of a drawn bowstring, Rajalakshmi's voice rang out: 'My daughter-in-law? With you encouraging her, would she heed me?'

At this, Annapurna went up to Mahendra's bedroom, with a noisy step, so as to alert the couple to her arrival. 'You wretched girl, to bring disgrace upon me in this fashion!' she accused Asha. 'Have you no shame, no decency, no sense of time? Would you bask in comfort here and leave your old mother-in-law to cope with all the housework? It is my misfortune that I brought you into this household!'

As she spoke, tears flowed from her eyes. Asha, too, began to weep, standing silently with bowed head, picking at the corner of her sari.

'Kaki, why rebuke my wife?' Mahendra intervened. 'After all, it is I who has held her captive.'

'Was that a good thing to have done?' demanded

Annapurna. 'She is a young girl, an orphan, with no mother to guide and train her—what would she know of right and wrong? What are you teaching her?'

'Look, I have bought her a slate, notebooks and textbooks. Even if people malign me, even if it offends all of you, I am going to educate my wife.'

'But must you educate her all day long? An hour or two of tuition in the evening would be more than enough.'

'It's not so easy, Kaki, studies take a little time.'

Exasperated, Annapurna left the room. Asha began to follow her, but Mahendra stood obstructing the door, refusing to yield to the plea in her moist, sorrowful eyes. 'Wait,' he commanded, 'we must make up for the time we have wasted in sleep.'

For the express information of any grave, venerable readers foolish enough to imagine that Mahendra had wasted hours meant for studying on sleep, it is necessary to point out that no school inspector would endorse the way in which education was imparted under Mahendra's supervision.

Asha had trusted her husband. Although learning to read and write was difficult for her on several counts, she had taken it to be her bounden duty as decreed by her husband. Hence, she strove to control her restless, distracted mind, sitting very seriously at one end of the divan on the bedroom floor, bent low over her books and papers, swaying her head rhythmically as she tried to memorize her lessons. At the other end of the bedchamber, his medical books open on a small table, the teacher sat on a chowki, casting an occasional sidelong glance at his pupil to check her level of concentration. Watching her, Mahendra suddenly closed his medical textbook and addressed Asha by her pet name: 'Chuni!' Startled, Asha raised her head to look at him.

'Bring the book here,' he ordered. 'Let's see what you're reading.'

Asha was afraid that he might test her. She had little hope of passing the test. Her rebellious mind refused to be tamed by the charms of the primer *Charupath*; the more she tried to learn about anthills, the more the letters of the alphabet crawled across her field of vision like a row of black ants.

Hearing the examiner's call, Asha crept timidly like a culprit to stand beside Mahendra's chowki with her book. Imprisoning her by firmly wrapping one arm around her waist, Mahendra took the book in his other hand and said, 'Let's see how much you read today.' Asha indicated to him the lines that she had glanced at. 'Oh! Were you able to read thus far?' asked Mahendra testily. 'Do you want to see how much I have managed to read?' He pointed to the title of a chapter in his textbook of medicine.

'Then what were you doing all this while?' enquired Asha, her eyes wide with surprise.

Grasping her chin, Mahendra replied, 'I was thinking

of someone, but that heartless person was immersed in the extremely entertaining account of termites in *Charupath*.' Asha could have offered a suitable retort to this baseless complaint, but alas, out of sheer bashfulness, she had to silently concede unfair victory to her adversary in this romantic encounter.

Clearly, Mahendra's school did not follow the rules of any educational institution, accredited or private.

Some day, for instance, Asha would take advantage of Mahendra's absence to concentrate on her lesson, when Mahendra would appear unexpectedly, cover her eyes with his hands, then snatch away her book, and demand, 'O cruel one, don't you think of me in my absence? Do you simply remain busy with your studies?'

'Do you want me to remain illiterate?'

'Thanks to you, my own education is not making much headway, either.'

Asha was hurt. Ready to leave the room at once, she asked, 'How have I hindered your education?'

'You won't understand,' Mahendra responded, grasping her hand. 'I can't study as easily in your absence as you can in mine.'

This was a grave accusation. Naturally, it gave rise to a round of tears like an autumn shower that soon evaporates in the sunshine of love, leaving behind only a glow of moisture.

When the teacher himself was a major obstacle in the path of education, how could the helpless pupil find her way through the forest of knowledge? Sometimes, when she recalled her mashi's sharp rebuke, she would feel perturbed; she realized that her studies were merely a farce, and cringed with shame when she saw her mother-in-law. But her mother-in-law never assigned her any tasks, nor offered any advice. If Asha tried to help with the housework without being instructed to do so, Rajalakshmi would grow agitated and object. 'What are you doing? Go to your bedroom, you are neglecting your studies.'

Ultimately, Annapurna rebuked Asha. 'I can see the kind of education you are receiving. Now won't you even allow Mahin to take his medical examinations?'

Hearing this, Asha hardened her heart and told Mahendra, 'You are not studying properly for your examinations. From tonight I shall live downstairs, in Mashima's room.'

Such a harsh vow of abstinence at such a tender age! Banishing herself from her own bedroom and moving into Mashima's room! Uttering this cruel vow brought tears to her eyes; her delicate lips began to tremble uncontrollably and her voice almost broke.

'Very well, then,' declared Mahendra. 'Let's go to Kaki's room. But in that case, she will have to move into our room upstairs.'

Having made such a serious, large-hearted proposal, Asha was angered by such mockery.

' Better that you personally keep a constant vigil over

me,' Mahendra told her. 'You can see if I memorize my lessons for the examinations or not.'

The matter was very easily settled. It is needless to offer a detailed account of the manner in which a constant vigil was maintained. Suffice it to say that Mahendra failed his examinations that year, and despite the detailed descriptions provided in *Charupath*, Asha's ignorance about polyps persisted.

It can't be said that this extraordinary process of teaching and learning was accomplished entirely without hindrance. Sometimes, Bihari would come and create a tremendous disturbance. 'Mahinda! Mahinda!' he would call out, rousing the entire neighbourhood. He would not be content until he had dragged Mahin out of the shelter of his bedroom. Thereupon, he would subject Mahendra to prolonged scoldings for neglecting his studies.

To Asha he would say, 'Bouthan, food swallowed whole can't be digested; it must be chewed first. Now you are swallowing all your rice in a single mouthful, but after this you won't find a pill to aid your digestion.'

'Chuni, pay him no attention,' Mahendra would order. 'Bihari is jealous of our happiness.'

'Since happiness is within your grasp, enjoy it in a way that would not arouse jealousy in others,' Bihari would retort.

'But there is pleasure in being the object of other people's envy,' Mahendra would reply. 'Chuni, I narrowly escaped surrendering you to Bihari like a fool.'

'Quiet!' Bihari would exclaim, flushing.

At such times, Asha inwardly felt very annoyed with Bihari. It was because Bihari had once been proposed as a match for herself that she harboured a certain hostility towards him. Bihari sensed this, and Mahendra would joke about it.

Rajalakshmi would send for Bihari and express her grief. Bihari would tell her, 'Ma, when the worm weaves a cocoon there is not much to fear, but when it breaks out and flies away, it is hard to make it return. Who would have thought he would break free of his bond with you in such a manner?'

At the news of Mahendra's failure in his examinations, Rajalakshmi exploded in anger like a sudden summer blaze, but it was Annapurna who bore the brunt of her fury. She was unable to eat or sleep.

6

One cloudy evening resonant with early monsoon showers, Mahendra entered his bedroom in a happy frame of mind. He wore a soft, fragrant shawl on his shoulders and a jasmine garland around his neck. Intending to surprise Asha, he made sure his shoes made no sound. Looking around the room, he saw rain-laden gusts of wind coming in through the open window to the east, the lamp snuffed out, and Asha lying prone upon the divan, weeping silently.

Rushing to her, Mahendra asked, 'What is the matter?'

The girl began to cry in earnest. It took Mahendra a long time to obtain the answer to his question—finding the situation unbearable, Mashima had left for her paternal cousin's home.

'Did she have to ruin such an exquisite monsoon evening by her departure!' Mahendra thought to himself in annoyance.

Ultimately, all his rage was directed towards his mother. She was the source of all this unpleasantness, after all.

'We shall follow Kaki, wherever she has gone,' declared Mahendra. 'We'll see who Ma quarrels with, then.'

Making an unnecessary noise and fuss, he began packing his things and shouting for porters.

Rajalakshmi understood everything. She slowly came up to Mahendra and asked in a calm voice, 'Where are you going?'

At first, Mahendra offered no reply. After the question was repeated two or three times, he answered, 'I shall go to my Kaki.'

'The two of you need not go anywhere. I shall bring your Kaki back to you,' vowed Rajalakshmi.

So saying, she immediately mounted her palanquin and went to Annapurna's house. Wrapping the aanchal of her sari round her neck in a gesture of supplication, she said, with folded hands: 'May you be happy, Mejobou. Please forgive me.'

Flustered, Annapurna touched Rajalakshmi's feet and implored, 'Didi, why are you making me feel so guilty? I shall do whatever you say.'

'Because you have left, my son and daughter-in-law are preparing to leave home too.' As she spoke, Rajalakshmi burst into tears of wounded pride, anger and shame.

The two sisters-in-law returned home. It was still

raining. When Annapurna went to Mahendra's room, Asha's tears had abated, and Mahendra was saying all sorts of things to make her laugh. The rainy evening had not been entirely ruined, after all.

'Chuni, you won't let me remain at home, nor will you leave me alone if I go away. Is there no peace for me anywhere?' demanded Annapurna. Asha started like a stricken doe.

'Why, Kaki, what harm has Chuni done to you?' Mahendra protested, annoyed.

'I left because I could not bear to see such brazenness in a bride,' Annapurna replied. 'Why has the wretched girl forced me to return by reducing her mother-in-law to tears?'

That his mother and aunt would prove such a hindrance to this romantic chapter in his life was something Mahendra had not anticipated.

The next day, Rajalakshmi sent for Bihari. 'My boy, please tell Mahin that I have not visited Barasat, my native place, in a long time. I would like to go there now.'

'Since you haven't been there in a long time, you might as well not go at all,' Bihari said. 'Very well, I shall try telling Mahendra, but he is unlikely to agree under any circumstances.'

'Well, the desire to visit one's birthplace is understandable,' was Mahendra's response. 'But it is not advisable for Ma to remain there long. The place is not too comfortable during the monsoons.'

Bihari was annoyed at Mahendra's ready acquiescence. 'If Ma travels alone, who will look after her? Why don't you send Bouthan with her?' he said with a faint smile.

Offended by Bihari's subtle rebuke, Mahendra demanded, 'Do you think I can't?'

But the matter did not progress any further.

In this way, Bihari would alienate Asha, and the thought of her annoyance seemed to afford him a sort of dry amusement.

Needless to say, Rajalakshmi was not very keen to visit her birthplace. Just as a boatman uses a plumbing rod to ascertain the depth of the water when the river shrinks in summer, similarly Rajalakshmi was testing the depth of the mother-son relationship at this critical time. But she had not anticipated that her proposal to visit Barasat would be approved so quickly and with such ease. She told herself, 'There is a difference between Annapurna's departure and mine. She is a sorceress well versed in magic, while I am simply a mother. It is better that I leave.'

Annapurna understood Rajalakshmi's suppressed feelings. 'If Didi leaves, I can't stay on either,' she informed Mahendra.

'Do you hear this, Ma?' Mahendra asked Rajalakshmi. 'If you leave, Kaki will go as well. Who will manage the household, then?'

'Do you plan to leave, Mejobou?' asked Rajalakshmi,

full of venomous envy. 'But that is impossible. How would we manage without you? You *must* stay.'

Rajalakshmi did not tolerate any further delay. The next afternoon, she was ready to depart for Barasat. Neither Bihari nor anyone else had doubted that Mahendra would escort his mother on her journey. But at the time of departure, it was discovered that Mahendra had arranged for an attendant and a bodyguard to accompany Rajalakshmi.

'Mahinda, why aren't you ready yet?' asked Bihari.

Sheepishly, Mahendra replied, 'I must attend college, after all . . .'

'Very well, you remain here,' said Bihari. 'I shall return after escorting Ma to her destination.'

Mahendra was secretly incensed. 'Really, Bihari has started going too far,' he protested to Asha in private. 'He wants to show that he cares more for Ma than I do.'

Annapurna was forced to stay behind, but she remained withdrawn out of shame, grief and annoyance. His kaki's aloofness angered Mahendra. Asha, too, grew sulky and peevish.

7

Rajalakshmi arrived at Barasat, her birthplace. Bihari was supposed to return after escorting her there, but seeing the situation, he stayed on.

Only a couple of aged women still remained at Rajalakshmi's ancestral home. The deep forests and bamboo thickets all around, the green waters of the pond and the call of foxes in broad daylight drove Rajalakshmi to desperation.

'Ma, this may be your birthplace, but I cannot, on any account, describe it as heaven on earth. Let's return to Kolkata,' proposed Bihari. 'It would be unconscionable for me to abandon you here.'

Rajalskhmi was also tired of the place. At this juncture, Binodini appeared on the scene, to offer and to seek refuge.

Binodini was introduced right at the beginning of the

story. She had once been considered as a prospective bride for Mahendra or, alternatively, for Bihari. The man she was destined to eventually marry had a spleen that was larger than all his other internal organs. It was due to the excessive weight of his spleen that he did not survive very long.

Like a single garden vine planted in a jungle, Binodini, since her husband's demise, had led a listless existence in the dreary environment of the village. Today, this orphaned woman came to respectfully touch the feet of Rajalakshmi, her paternal aunt by marriage, and devoted herself to the lady's service.

And such wonderful service it was. Not a moment of lassitude. Such neat work, such wonderful cooking, and such sweet conversation!

'It's late, my girl, go and have something to eat,' Rajalakshmi would say.

Binodini would refuse to obey. Until she had fanned her pishima to sleep, she would not get up.

'But you'll fall sick if you go on like this, my girl.'

Displaying utter unconcern for herself, Binodini would respond, 'Sickness does not touch unfortunates like me, Pishima. You have come to your birthplace after such a long time, but what do we have to offer you here, what can I pamper you with?'

In no time, Bihari became the leader of the neighbourhood. People would come to him for medicine to treat their ailments, for legal advice, to request him to find employment in some office for their sons, or to write applications for them. From gatherings of old men playing cards and chess, to the toddy-drinking sessions of the lower caste Bagdis, he went everywhere, carrying with him his good humoured curiosity and natural warmth. Nobody considered him an outsider; yet he commanded everyone's respect.

Behind the scenes, from the seclusion of the inner quarters of the house, Binodini would try to mitigate the suffering of this young man from Kolkata who found himself exiled to this godforsaken place. Every time Bihari returned from his wanderings in the neighbourhood, he would find that someone had cleaned and tidied his room, arranged a bunch of flowers in a brass tumbler, and placed volumes of Bankim and Dinabandhu beside his mattress. In the flyleaf of each book, inscribed in a firm yet feminine hand, was Binodini's name.

Such care was rather different from the forms of hospitality customary in rural areas. When Bihari pointed this out admiringly, Rajalakshmi would be full of reproach. 'And you boys slighted such a girl!' she would remind him.

Bihari would smile. 'We did not act wisely, Ma, we were deceived. But it is better to be deceived without being wed; being deceived after marriage can cause a real problem.'

'This girl could have become my daughter-in-law,'

Rajalakshmi would think. 'Why didn't that happen?'

Rajalakshmi had only to mention the subject of her return to Kolkata and Binodini's eyes would grow moist. She would plead, 'Pishima, why did you come just for a few days? When I did not know you, the days would somehow pass. How will I live without you now?'

In an outburst of emotion, Rajalakshmi would exclaim, 'My dear, why did you not become my daughter-in-law? For then I could have kept you close to my heart!'

Embarrassed, Binodini would get up and go away on some pretext.

All this while, Rajalakshmi was awaiting a distressed, beseeching letter from Kolkata. Since his birth, her Mahin had never stayed apart from his mother for so many days. Surely, by now his mother's absence would have made him restless! Rajalakshmi thirsted for a letter from her son, begging her indulgence even as it revealed his hurt feelings.

Bihari received a letter from Mahendra. Mahendra had written, 'Ma must be very happy to be visiting her birthplace after such a long time.'

'Ah, Mahendra has written this out of wounded pride,' Rajalakshmi thought. 'Happy? As if this unfortunate mother could live happily anywhere in Mahendra's absence!'

'O Bihari, what has Mahendra written next? Why don't you read it to me, my boy?'

'There's nothing more, Ma.' Bihari crumpled the letter in his fist, placed it inside a book, and hurled the volume into a corner of the room with a thud.

Rajalakshmi could not remain calm after this. Mahendra's letter must have been so reproachful towards his mother that Bihari refused to read it to her.

As a calf nudges the cow's udder to stimulate the flow of milk and maternal love, so Mahendra's rage prodded Rajalakshmi into expressing her stifled maternal affection. She forgave Mahendra. 'Mahin is happy in his wife's company. So let him be happy—let him be happy by all means. I shall not trouble him about his wife anymore. Poor Mahin is angry with his mother, because she who could not live without him for a single hour has abandoned him!' Again and again, tears welled up in her eyes.

That day, Rajalakshmi repeatedly pleaded with Bihari: 'Go baba, go and take a bath. Your habits have grown very irregular since you came here.'

Bihari seemed to have no inclination to bathe or dine that day. 'Ma, wretches like me are better off in an unkempt state,' he said.

'No, my boy, please go and bathe,' Rajalakshmi pleaded.

Finally, after a thousand persuasions, Bihari went to bathe. As soon as he left the room, Rajalakshmi quickly extracted the crumpled letter from within the book.

Handing the letter to Binodini, she said, 'Take a look, my dear, see what Mahin has written to Bihari.'

Binodini began to read aloud. Mahendra had begun by writing about his mother; but that was very brief, not much more than what Bihari had already told her.

Immediately after, he had written of Asha. Mahendra had written as if intoxicated by the delights of love, its mystery and its joy.

After reading out just a bit, Binodini paused in embarrassment. 'Pishima, you wouldn't wish to hear any more of this!' she faltered.

The expression of eager affection on Rajalakshmi's face froze instantly into a rock-like hardness. 'Let it be!' she said, after a short silence, and left without reclaiming the letter.

Carrying the letter, Binodini entered her room. She locked the door from within and, sitting down on the bed, began to read.

What emotion the letter evoked in Binodini only she knew. But it was not amusement that she felt. As she read the letter over and over again, her eyes began to burn like sand in the glare of the afternoon sun. Her breath grew fiery like the hot desert wind.

What was Mahendra like, what was Asha like, and what was the nature of their amorous relationship?—this was the sole question that incessantly tormented her. Leaning against the wall, with her legs outstretched, the letter in her lap, she sat for a long time, staring straight ahead of her.

Bihari never found Mahendra's letter again.

That afternoon, Annapurna suddenly arrived on the scene. Fearing bad tidings, Rajalakshmi's heart suddenly began to quake; she did not dare ask any questions, just gazed at Annapurna with a pale face.

'All is well in Kolkata, Didi,' Annapurna assured her.

'Then what brings you here?'

'Didi, please take charge of your own household once again. I have no interest in worldly matters anymore. I have set out on a pilgrimage to Kashi. That is why I have come to seek your blessings. Whether knowingly or unknowningly, I have committed many misdemeanours; please forgive me. And as for your daughter-in-law, she is young and motherless.' As she spoke, her eyes grew moist and tears began to flow. 'Guilty or innocent, she is yours.' She could say no more.

Rajalakshmi busied herself with arrangements for Annapurna's bath and dinner. Hearing the news, Bihari came running from Gadai Ghosh's chandimandap, the Ghoshs' family shrine for the annual Durga Puja. Reverently touching Annapurna's feet, he protested, 'Kakima, how is this possible? Could you be so cruel as to abandon us?'

'Bihari, don't try to make me return,' pleaded Annapurna, controlling her tears. 'May all of you live happily. My absence will make no difference.'

Bihari sat in silence for a while. Then he said, 'It is Mahendra's misfortune that he has caused your departure.'

'Don't say such things!' cried Annapurna, startled. 'I am not at all angry with Mahin. Unless I leave, good fortune will not visit the household.'

Gazing into the distance, Bihari sat in silence. Annapurna undid the knot in the aanchal of her sari and extracted two thick gold bangles. 'Baba, please keep this pair of bangles. When you marry, give them to your bride with my blessings.'

Reverently touching the pair of bangles to his forehead, Bihari rushed to the adjoining room to stem his tears.

When it was time to leave, Annapurna said, 'Bihari, look after my Mahin and my Asha.' Handing a piece of paper to Rajalakshmi, she said, 'In this document, I have transferred my share of the property, my father-in-law's legacy, to Mahin. Just send me fifteen rupees every month.'

She prostrated herself, and touched Rajalakshmi's feet. Taking her leave, she set out on her pilgrimage to the holy land.

8
❧❦❧

Asha was frightened. What was happening! Ma had gone away, and now Mashima had left as well. It seemed as if the conjugal bliss of the newlyweds was driving everyone away. As if it would be her turn next. In the empty, abandoned household, their playful, amorous antics began to strike her as rather excessive.

As a flower plucked from a tree gradually droops and shrivels, love that avoids the harsh realities of practical life cannot thrive on its own resources. Asha, too, began to secretly notice that a jaded, weary note had crept into their constant togetherness. Every now and then, their mutual passion would show signs of fading; without the firm support of the world of everyday duty, it was difficult to keep up this fervour. Unless love is rooted in purposeful activity, its delights are neither fulfilling nor lasting.

Defying hostile disapproval, Mahendra, too, tried to

make a great show of celebrating their conjugal bliss in the ominous atmosphere of the empty home by summoning all the amorous resources at his command.

'Chuni, what's the matter with you nowadays?' he taunted Asha. 'Why are you so morose about Mashi's departure? Don't all other forms of love find their culmination in our love for each other?'

Wounded by his remark, Asha thought, 'There must be something lacking in my love, then. After all, I think of Mashi often, and I feel afraid because my mother-in-law has gone away.' And so she tried her utmost to compensate for the crime of loving all these other people.

Now, the housework did not proceed smoothly, as the servants had taken to shirking their duties. One day, the maidservant reported sick and the cook vanished somewhere in a state of inebriation.

'What fun, let us cook for ourselves today,' Mahendra proposed to Asha.

Mahendra went by carriage to New Market to shop for groceries. Having no idea what was required and in what quantity, he came home joyfully carrying a few packages. Asha, too, was not sure what was to be done with these items. Two or three hours went by in experimentation. Mahendra felt greatly amused, having produced a variety of novel, inedible dishes. However, Asha could not join in Mahendra's merriment; she felt ashamed and hurt at her own ignorance and lack of expertise.

Things were in such disarray in all the rooms that nothing could be found when required. One day, Mahendra's surgical instrument was banished to oblivion in the garbage after being used for chopping vegetables, and his notebook, having served its purpose as a hand-held fan, now rested in the ashes of the kitchen.

Mahendra's amusement knew no bounds in the face of such unimaginable domestic turmoil, but Asha continued to find it distressing. To this young girl, there seemed to be something horrifying in the way they were drifting along blithely, after drowning the entire household in a flood of unrestrained willfulness.

One evening, the two of them were lounging on a bed laid out in the covered veranda. Before them lay the open terrace. After the rains, the Kolkata skyline, a row of palatial domes extending across the horizon, was flooded with moonlight. Her head bowed, Asha was stringing a garland of wet bakul blossoms plucked from the garden. Trying to provoke her unnecessarily, Mahendra kept tugging at the garland, hindering her work and making critical remarks. If Asha began to scold him for such unreasonable disruptive behaviour, Mahendra would cover her mouth, nipping her admonitions in the bud.

Suddenly, they heard the call of the caged koel next door. Mahendra and Asha immediately glanced up at the cage suspended above their heads. Their own koel could never silently endure the cooing of the bird next door. Why was she not responding today?

'What is the matter with the bird today?' asked Asha anxiously.

'The sound of your voice has put her to shame.'

'No, don't joke, please see what has happened to the koel,' begged Asha.

Mahendra lowered the cage. Removing the cover, he saw that the koel was dead. After Annapurna's departure, the attendant had gone away on leave, and nobody had taken care of the bird.

Asha's face grew pale. Her fingers refused to move; the flowers lay neglected. Although Mahendra was shaken, he tried to laugh off the matter lest their amorous mood be dispelled in an untimely manner. 'It's all for the better; it would have plagued you with its cooing while I was away practising medicine.' With these words, Mahendra enfolded Asha in his arms and tried to draw her towards him.

Slowly disengaging herself, Asha shook out the bakul blossoms from her aanchal. 'No more of this!' she cried. 'We should be ashamed. Go quickly and bring Ma back.'

9

Just then a voice from the first floor called: 'Mahinda, Mahinda!'

'Who is it? Come in, come in!' Mahendra replied. Hearing Bihari's voice, Mahendra's heart grew cheerful. After the wedding, Bihari had sometimes seemed an obstacle to their happiness, but today, he was a welcome intrusion.

Asha, too, felt relieved at Bihari's arrival. Covering her head with her aanchal, she quickly rose to her feet. Mahendra said, 'Where are you going? It's only Bihari.'

'Let me go and organize some snacks for Thakurpo.' At the prospect of doing some work, Asha lost some of her lethargy. Head covered, she stood waiting to hear news of her mother-in-law. She still did not speak directly to Bihari.

'What a disaster!' Bihari exclaimed as soon as he entered. 'I have interrupted such a romantic scene! Have no fear, Bouthan, please remain seated. I'll be off.'

Asha glanced at Mahendra's face.

'Bihari, what news of Ma?' he asked.

'Why speak of mothers and aunts today, my friend? There will be plenty of time for all that,' said Bihari, adding, in English, 'Such a night was not made for sleep, nor for mothers and aunts!'

With these words, Bihari prepared to depart, but Mahendra dragged him in and forced him to sit down. Bihari pleaded, 'Bouthan, I am not at fault, as you can see. He has forcibly dragged me here; do not curse me for a sin that Mahinda has committed.'

Because she could not offer a retort, Asha was extremely annoyed by such remarks. Bihari was teasing her deliberately.

'I can see the condition of the house,' he observed. 'Isn't it time to bring your mother back?'

'By all means,' replied Mahendra. 'We are waiting for her.'

'It would take very little time for you to write a letter informing her of this, but it would make her extremely happy. Bouthan, I beg you, you must give Mahinda a couple of minutes' leave to perform this task.'

Asha went away in anger. Tears began to flow from her eyes.

'The two of you must have met at such an auspicious moment!' said Mahendra. 'Nothing can reconcile you; you get at each other all the time.'

'Your mother has spoilt you, and now your wife is all set to spoil you as well. It's because I can't bear to see it happen that I make a few remarks when I get the chance.'

'What difference does that make?'

'Very little where you are concerned, but to me, it does make a slight difference.'

10

Bihari personally supervised the letter Mahendra wrote to his mother. Carrying the letter with him, he departed the very next day to fetch Rajalakshmi. Though Rajalakshmi realized that this letter had been written at Bihari's instance, still, she could not keep away any longer. With her came Binodini.

Observing the condition of her house upon her return—unscrubbed, filthy, topsy-turvy—the lady of the house felt even more hostile towards the bride.

But what a change had come over her daughter-in-law! Asha would follow her like a shadow; unasked, she would come forward to help her at work. Flustered, Rajalakshmi would say, 'Let it be, let it be, you will ruin everything. Why interfere in a task that you don't know how to perform?'

Rajalakshmi concluded that it was Annapurna's departure that had brought about such an improvement in her daughter-in-law. But she thought, 'Mahendra will think when his aunt was here, he could live in unhindered bliss with his bride, but as soon as his mother arrived, he was separated from his beloved. This will only prove that Annapurna is his well wisher, while I am an obstacle to his happiness. Why let this happen?'

Nowadays, if Mahendra sent for Asha in the daytime, she would hesitate, but Rajalakshmi would scold her, saying, 'Should you ignore Mahin when he calls you? This is what happens ultimately when you are too pampered. Go, there is no need for you to help with the vegetables.'

Again the false games with slate, chalk and *Charupath*. Hurling baseless romantic accusations at each other. Groundless yet tumultuous arguments on the relative measure of their love for each other. Turning monsoon days into nights and moonlit nights into daylight hours. Forcibly warding off fatigue and lassitude. Habituating each other to a situation where even momentary freedom from the bonds of sexual union seemed a fearsome prospect, even when togetherness failed to bring any joy to their enervated hearts. Their conjugal bliss was reduced to ashes, yet they felt no urge to seek a change of activity. It is the terrible curse of self-indulgence that the joy of it is short-lived but the bondage grows insurmountable. In the meantime, Binodini came to Asha one day, placed her arms around her neck, and said, 'My friend, may your good fortune last forever, but does my unhappy situation not merit a single glance?'

Reared in relatives' homes as an outsider, Asha had developed an innate diffidence in her manner towards people in general. She was afraid of being rejected. When Binodini appeared on the scene, with her arched eyebrows and penetrating gaze, her flawless face and youthful voluptuousness, Asha did not have the courage to approach her.

Asha noticed that Binodini had no reticence in dealing with Rajalakshmi. Rajalakshmi, too, seemed to make much of Binodini, especially for Asha's benefit. Every now and then, she would burst into effusive praise of Binodini, particularly in Asha's hearing. Asha saw that Binodini was well versed in all kinds of domestic skills. Mastery came naturally and easily to her; she had no qualms about setting the domestic staff to work, rebuking them or ordering them about. Observing all this, Asha felt that she was utterly inferior to Binodini.

So when this paragon took the initiative and sought her friendship, the diffident Asha was overwhelmed with joy. Like a magic tree conjured up by a sorcerer, the seeds of their affection sprouted, grew green, and blossomed, all in one day.

'Come, my friend, let's create a ritual bond of friendship,' Asha proposed.

Binodini smiled, 'What name would you give to our bond of friendship?'

Asha named Ganga water, bakul blossoms, and several other auspicious items.

'All that stuff is outdated; these terms of affection are no longer admirable.'

'What name would you like?'

'Chokher bali. A constant irritant, like a grain of sand in the eye,' laughed Binodini.

Asha was more inclined towards a name that would be melodious to the ear, but upon Binodini's advice, she accepted this abusive term of endearment. 'Chokher Bali!' she repeated, throwing her arms round Binodini's neck. Then she collapsed in giggles.

11

~~~~~

Asha was in acute need of a companion. Even a celebration of love requires more than two participants—a few ordinary spectators are needed to savour the sweetness of the romance.

Like a drunkard thirsting for fiery spirit, Binodini, starved of love, began avidly devouring the history of the newly wedded bride's first flush of love. Her mind was intoxicated, her blood on fire.

In the stillness of the afternoon, when Ma slept; when the household staff vanished into the resting-room on the ground floor; when Mahendra, prodded by Bihari, went to college for a short while; when, occasionally, the shrill cry of a kite could be heard very faintly from the sun-scorched blueness of the far horizon—at such times, Asha would recline on the floor of the secluded bedchamber, her hair spread out on a pillow, and Binodini would lie on her stomach, her bosom resting on another pillow, listening to the murmured narrative with rapt attention. And as she listened, her ears would turn red, and her breathing would grow rapid. Binodini would ask questions to ferret out even the most inconsequential details. She wanted the same things repeated over and over again, and when the tale was finished, she would resort to fantasy: 'So, my friend, what if things had happened thus, and what would you have done if matters had taken a different course?' Asha, too, would enjoy prolonging their discussion of her marital bliss by pursuing these improbable, fanciful lines of thought.

'Now, my dear Chokher Bali, what if you had been married to Bihari Babu?' Binodini would wonder.

'No, my dear, don't say such a thing. For shame! I feel very embarrassed. But it would have been nice if he had married you; there was such a proposal, after all.'

'Many people proposed many things to me. If they didn't materialize, it's for the best; I am better off as I am.'

Asha would argue with her. How could she accept that Binodini's situation was better than her own? 'Imagine what it would have been like, my dear Bali, for you to have married my husband. It almost happened, after all.'

Indeed, it had almost happened. Then why didn't it? This bed that was now Asha's had once lain in wait for Binodini—looking around this well decorated bedchamber, Binodini would find it impossible to forget that fact. Now, she was a mere guest in this room—here today, gone tomorrow.

In the evening, Binodini would set about dressing Asha's hair with exquisite skill, and send her off, beautifully attired, for her union with her husband. It was as if her imagination, like a veiled woman, followed the bedecked bride into the empty bedchamber, on her rendezvous with the besotted young lover. But sometimes, she would simply not let Asha go. She would say, 'Come now, why don't you sit here a while longer? Your husband will not run away. He's the pet deer of our neighbourhood, not the mythical forest deer, after all.' With such words and artful manoeuvres, she would try to detain Asha and cause a delay.

Mahendra would get very angry. 'Your friend and companion makes no move to leave,' he would complain. 'When will she return to her own home?'

'You must not be angry with my Chokher Bali,' Asha would plead anxiously. 'You have no idea how much she loves to hear about you, how lovingly she tends to my appearance before sending me to you.'

Rajalakshmi would not allow Asha to do any housework, but Binodini got her interested in domestic work. Almost all day, Binodini would work tirelessly, and she would not let Asha off, either. Step by step, Binodini created such a chain of tasks that Asha found it difficult to escape. At the thought of Asha's husband fretting and fuming by himself in a corner of the empty room on the terrace, Binodini would smile heartlessly to herself. In desperation, Asha would beg, 'Let me go now, Chokher Bali, he will be angry with me again.'

'Wait, just finish this little task,' Binodini would insist. 'It won't take much longer.'

After a while, Asha would again grow restless. 'No, my friend, this time he will be really furious. Please let me go.'

'So what if he's a little angry? Love loses its flavour unless rage is added to desire; it's just like adding chillies and pepper to spice up a vegetable dish.'

It was Binodini who truly understood the taste of chilli and pepper; she only lacked the vegetable dish to go with them. Every vein in her body seemed to be on fire. Her eyes rained sparks on whatever they beheld. 'Such a comfortable home and such an amorous husband! I could have made a kingdom of this home, a slave of this husband. Would the house have been in such a condition then, or the man of the house been reduced to such a state? And to have this babe in arms, this toy doll in my place!'

Casting her arms round Asha's neck, Binodini would ask: 'Dear Chokher Bali, tell me, what did you say to each other last night? Did you say the words I had taught you? I forget all other cravings when I hear about your mutual love.'

12

❦

$\mathscr{O}$ne day, in exasperation, Mahendra sent for his mother and demanded, 'Is this a good idea? Is it necessary to take on the added responsibility of having a young widow from another family stay with us? I don't approve: who knows what crisis may befall us?'

'But she is our Bipin's wife. I don't consider her a stranger.'

Mahendra said, 'No, Ma, it is not a good idea. I don't think it is right to keep her here.'

Rajalakshmi was well aware that Mahendra's opinion was not easy to ignore. She sent for Bihari. 'O Bihari, please try explaining to Mahendra. It's because Bipin's wife is here that I get some rest in my old age. She may belong to another family, but I have never received such devoted care even from those I call my own.'

Without answering Rajalakshmi, Bihari went to

Mahendra and asked, 'Mahinda, have you been thinking about Binodini?'

'I can't sleep nights for thinking of her,' smiled Mahendra. 'Ask your Bouthan, my preoccupation with Binodini has driven out all other concerns from my mind.'

From behind her veil, Asha silently remonstrated with Mahendra.

'What's this! A second *Bishabriksha*, another tale of adulterous love!'

'Exactly. Now Chuni is desperate to get rid of her.'

From behind the veil, Asha's eyes again showered him with rebuke.

'Even if you were to send her away, it woudn't take her long to return. Get the widow married; that will draw her poison,' Bihari suggested.

'In the story, Kunda was married off, too,' Mahendra pointed out.

'Let it be, forget that comparison. I think about Binodini sometimes. After all, she can't remain here with you forever. Exiling her for a lifetime in the wilderness that I visited would also be a very harsh punishment.'

Binodini had never come before Mahendra until now, but Bihari had seen her. Bihari had understood that she was not a woman to be condemned to the jungle. But he feared that the flame of a prayer lamp that illuminated the home could also set the house on fire.

Mahendra teased Bihari a great deal on this subject. Bihari answered him with suitable rejoinders. But he understood that this was not a woman to be trifled with, nor could she be ignored.

'Listen, my child, don't make such demands upon my daughter-in-law,' Rajalakshmi warned Binodini. 'Having grown up in a provincial household, you don't know the ways of the modern world. You are an intelligent woman, think carefully about how to conduct yourself.'

After this, Binodini made a great show of keeping Asha at arm's length. 'Who am I, after all?' she would say. 'If people in my situation don't know how to behave with dignity, who knows what might happen one day?'

Asha wept and pleaded, but Binodini remained steadfast in her resolve. Asha's heart grew full to bursting with untold confidences, but Binodini paid no heed.

Meanwhile, Mahendra's embrace seemed to have slackened, and his devoted gaze overcome with fatigue. The disorder and indiscipline that had once appeared comical to him had now begun to annoy him slightly. He was frequently exasperated with Asha's ineptness in domestic matters, but he would not say so directly. But even though he did not express his feelings, Asha knew in her heart that the glory of their uninterrupted conjugal bliss was fading. Mahendra's amorous attentions struck a false chord—part false exaggeration, part self-deception.

At such a time, there was no recourse save flight, no cure save separation. By natural feminine instinct, Asha tried to stay away from Mahendra nowadays. But where could she go, except to Binodini?

Awakening from the fevered sleep of newly wedded love, Mahendra slowly changed his position as it were, to attend once more to practical concerns and his own education. Retrieving his medical textbooks from all sorts of improbable places, he dusted them, and prepared to air the jackets and trousers he wore to college.

13

When Binodini remained elusive, Asha thought of a strategy. She asked Binodini, 'My dear Bali, why do you never appear before my husband? Why play hide and seek?'

'For shame!' was Binodini's brief but spirited reply.

'Why? Ma tells me that you belong to our family.'

'In this world, there is no such thing as belonging or not belonging,' Binodini replied gravely. 'If someone accepts you, he belongs to you—if someone regards you as a stranger, he remains a stranger, even if he is family.'

Asha knew the statement was irrefutable. Her husband was indeed unfair to Binodini; he considered her a stranger to their household and was unaccountably annoyed by her.

That evening, Asha begged her husband's indulgence, saying, 'You must get to know my Chokher Bali.'

'I must say you are very brave,' smiled Mahendra.

'Why, what is there to fear?'

'From your accounts of your friend's beauty, she seems to be dangerous!'

'Never mind, I can handle that. Jokes apart, tell me, will you meet her or not?'

Not that Mahendra was not curious to meet Binodini. In fact, lately, he was sometimes rather keen to see her. Such uncalled-for eagerness did not strike him as appropriate. When it came to matters of the heart, Mahendra had unusually rigid ideas of right and wrong. Earlier, he had never raised the subject of marriage lest it cause the slightest damage to his mother's claim over him. Since their wedding, he had become so protective about his relationship with Asha, that he would not permit his mind to entertain the slightest curiosity about other women. He prided himself on being extremely finicky and loyal where love was concerned. In fact, having declared Bihari his friend, he would not willingly grant anyone else that status. If someone made friendly overtures, Mahendra would make a great show of ignoring him, and in his mocking rejection of the hapless person, he would demonstrate to Bihari his supreme indifference towards ordinary people. If Bihari objected to this, Mahendra would say, 'You are capable of accepting others, Bihari; you have no dearth of friends wherever you go. But I can't become friends with just anyone you please.'

Now, when Mahendra found himself attracted to

this unknown woman, drawn to her by an irresistible eagerness and curiosity, he felt that he had fallen short of his own ideals. Ultimately, in desperation, he began to urge his mother to send Binodini away from their house.

To Asha, Mahendra said, 'Chuni, let it be. Where do I have the time to meet your Chokher Bali? When it is time to study, I read my medical textbooks; in my spare time I have you. There is no room in my life for your friend and companion.'

'Very well, I shall not impinge upon your time for study, but I shall give Bali a share of the time you spend with me.'

'You may be willing to give her a share of our time, but why would I permit it?'

Mahendra claimed that Asha's love for Binodini diminished her love for her own husband. He would proudly assert, 'Your love lacks the singular devotion of mine.'

Asha would never accept this; she would quarrel and shed tears over it, but could never win an argument.

Not granting Binodini the slightest bit of room to come between Asha and himself became a matter of pride for Mahendra. Asha could not tolerate such pride, but today, she admitted defeat. 'Very well, then, meet Bali only for my sake.'

Finally, having demonstrated to Asha the steadfastness and superiority of his love, Mahendra condescendingly agreed to a meeting with Binodini. But he cautioned

Asha, 'If she begins to disturb us at odd times, I shall not tolerate it.'

Early the following day, Asha went to Binodini's bed and embraced her. 'Amazing!' remarked Binodini. 'The chakori, a bird so besotted with the moon, has abandoned the moon to visit the kingdom of clouds!'

'Such poetic phrases are beyond me, my dear. Why scatter pearls in a wilderness of weeds! Why not speak these words to the person who can answer in kind.'

'Who would that interesting man be?'

'My husband, your brother-in-law. No, my friend, I am not joking; he has urged me to arrange a meeting with you.'

'Why should I rush to answer a summons issued upon the wife's insistence!' Binodini said to herself.

Binodini would not agree to a meeting. This placed Asha in an embarrassing position. Mahendra was secretly very offended. How could she refuse to appear before him? How could she consider him the same as other ordinary males? Any other man in his situation would have come up with all sorts of strategies to orchestrate a meeting with Binodini and get better acquainted with her. That Mahendra had not made the slightest attempt to do so should have sufficiently indicated his character to Binodini. Once she got to know him properly, she would understand the difference between Mahendra and all other men.

A couple of days earlier, Binodini, too, had told

herself resentfully, 'I have lived in this house for so long, but Mahendra does not even try to meet me. When I am in Pishima's room, he doesn't even enter the room on some pretext. Why such indifference? Am I an inanimate object? Am I not human? Am I not a woman? If he got to know me, he would realize the difference between Chuni and me.'

'I shall pretend that you are away at college and bring Chokher Bali to my room,' Asha proposed to her husband. 'Then you can come in suddenly. She will be trapped!'

'What offence has she committed, to deserve such harsh discipline?'

'No, I am really very annoyed. She is averse to even meeting you. I shall not rest until I have broken her resolve.'

'I am not devastated at having been denied a glimpse of your favourite companion. I don't want to meet her in such a devious manner.'

'Please,' Asha begged, grasping Mahendra's hand, 'you must, just this one time. I want to destroy her pride just once, by whatever means. After that, both of you can behave as you please.' Mahendra did not reply.

'Dearest, please grant my request,' begged Asha.

Mahendra's eagerness was growing, so he acquiesced with a show of excessive indifference.

One still, clear autumn afternoon, Binodini was seated in Mahendra's secluded bedchamber, teaching Asha how to weave carpet shoes. Asha kept glancing distractedly at the door, her errors in counting the stitches revealing her incredible ineptness.

Finally, Binodini snatched the tapestry from Asha's hands and flung it aside in exasperation. 'You can't handle this. Let me go, I have work to do!'

'Please stay. I shall not make any mistakes this time, you will see.' With these words, Asha applied herself again to her needlework.

Meanwhile, Mahendra approached softly and stood in the doorway behind Binodini. Without raising her eyes from her needlework, Asha began to laugh in a low voice.

'What have you remembered suddenly that is so amusing?' asked Binodini. Asha could contain herself no longer. Breaking into loud laughter, she tossed the piece of tapestry at Binodini and said, 'You were quite right, my friend. I can't handle it.' She twined her arms around Binodini's neck and began laughing twice as hard.

Binodini had understood everything right from the start. Asha's restlessness and her odd demeanour had revealed all. She was also aware that Mahendra had come to stand behind her. Like an utterly simple, docile creature, she allowed herself to fall into Asha's feeble trap.

'Why should I be left out of such merriment?' asked Mahendra, coming forward.

Binodini started, pulled her sari over her head and prepared to rise. Asha grasped her hand.

'Either you could stay and I take my leave, or all three of us could stay,' smiled Mahendra.

Unlike other women, Binodini did not make a great show of embarrassment by snatching her hand out of Asha's grasp, or creating a great fuss. In an easy, natural tone, she said, 'I consent to remain seated only because you request me to do so, but please don't curse me inwardly.'

'I shall curse you so you become immobilized for a long time,' declared Mahendra.

'I do not fear such a curse, because your notion of a long time is not likely to last very long. I think my time is up already.'

With these words, Binodini tried to rise to her feet once more. Asha grasped her hand. 'Upon my word, you must stay a while longer,' she insisted.

14

'Tell me truly, how did you like my Chokher Bali?'
Asha wanted to know.

'She's not bad,' answered Mahendra.

'You like nobody at all,' complained Asha, extremely
upset.

'Nobody at all, but one.'

'Well, get to know her a little better, and then we
shall see if you like her or not.'

'Get to know her better? Is it going to continue like
this now?'

'Out of politeness, if nothing else, one must interact
with people. If you were to ignore her after the very first
meeting, how would Chokher Bali feel? You are utterly
amazing, I must say. Anyone else in your place would
have begged to be introduced to such a woman, but
you behave as if you are faced with immense difficulty.'

Mahendra was very pleased to hear of this difference

between other men and himself. 'Very well, then. But why such haste? I have nowhere to escape to, and your friend, too, seems in no hurry to run away. We are bound to meet every now and then, and when we do, your husband is educated enough to observe social niceties.'

Mahendra had assumed that from now on Binodini would appear before him on some pretext or other. He was mistaken. Binodini never crossed his path, nor did she bump into him accidentally in the course of their daily activities.

Lest he betray the slightest sign of eagerness, Mahendra could not mention Binodini to his wife. Sometimes, as he attempted to suppress even the most ordinary desire for Binodini's company, Mahendra's desperation seemed to increase. And Binodini's indifference only incited him further.

The day after his meeting with Binodini, Mahendra asked Asha jokingly, in a casual conversational tone: 'So, what did Chokher Bali think of this unworthy husband of yours?'

Mahendra had been sure that he would receive an enthusiastic, detailed report on this subject from Asha. But when his patience failed to bear fruit, he broached the subject in a playful manner.

Asha was placed in a difficult position. Chokher Bali had not said anything at all. Asha had felt extremely offended by her friend's behaviour.

'You must wait,' she told her husband. 'She can only give her opinion after meeting you a few times, after all. You met her for such a short time yesterday, and you scarcely exchanged any words.'

Mahendra was somewhat disheartened at this, and it became even more difficult for him to demonstrate his lack of interest in Binodini.

In the midst of these discussions, Bihari arrived on the scene. 'Why Mahinda, what are you arguing about today?' he asked.

'Look, my friend, your Bouthan may have established a ritual friendship with some Kumudini or Promodini in the name of fishbones or ropes of hair or what have you, but does that mean I, too, must create a bond based on cigar ash or matchsticks? If that were so, life would grow intolerable.'

From behind her veil, Asha flashed silent signals of war. For a short while, Bihari watched Mahendra's face without offering any reply; then he smiled. 'Bouthan, the signs do not bode well. These are words meant to allay your fears. I have seen your Chokher Bali. I swear I would not take it amiss if I were to catch more frequent glimpses of her. But when Mahinda takes such pains to disavow it, that is a matter for grave suspicion.'

Asha took this as one more example of the vast differences between Mahendra and Bihari.

Mahendra suddenly developed a fancy for photography. He had once abandoned an attempt to learn photography. Now, he repaired his camera, purchased some spirit, and began to take pictures. He even began to photograph the servants and bearers of the household.

Asha insisted that he must take a picture of Chokher Bali.

'Very well,' answered Mahendra, curtly.

'No,' said Chokher Bali, even more curtly.

Asha had to resort to a stratagem once again, and from the start, her manoeuvre failed to deceive Binodini.

The plan was that Asha would bring Chokher Bali to her bedroom in the afternoon, and somehow induce her to sleep. Mahendra would photograph her while she slept, thus outwitting Asha's recalcitrant friend.

Binodini never slept in the afternoon, but surprisingly, when she came into Asha's room that day, she dozed off. Wearing a red shawl over her shoulder, she slept in such a beautiful posture—facing the window, with her head resting on her hand—that Mahendra observed, 'She looks as if she is deliberately posing for a photograph.'

Mahendra tiptoed in with the camera. He had to spend a long time inspecting Binodini from all sides, to determine the best angle for the photograph. In the interest of art, he even had to cautiously rearrange a lock of her loose hair, and when the result did not please him, he had to correct the position of the lock again. He whispered to Asha, 'Move the shawl to the left of her feet.'

'I can't manage it properly,' whispered the artless Asha. 'She is bound to wake up. You had better do it.'

Mahendra adjusted the shawl.

When he finally inserted a plate into the camera to take the picture, Binodini stirred in her sleep, as if at a sound, and letting out a deep sigh, she sat up, looking flustered. Asha burst into loud laughter. Binodini was furious. 'This is very wrong of you,' she declared, darting arrows of fire at Mahendra from her glittering eyes.

'Undoubtedly,' Mahendra agreed. But in stealing, yet failing to get away with the stolen goods, I have lost out on both counts. Please let me complete my misdeed before punishing me for it.'

Asha, too, pestered Binodini to agree. The picture was taken. But the first picture did not turn out well, and so the photographer refused to rest until another picture was taken on the following day. Subsequently, Binodini could not bring herself to reject the proposal that the two friends pose together for a picture that would be a permanent token of their friendship. 'But this will be the last photograph,' she warned them.

Hearing this, Mahendra made sure the picture was ruined. Thus, in the course of these photography sessions, they grew much better acquainted with each other.

15

Just as smouldering embers reignite when a fire is stirred, the intrusion of a third party renewed the fading passion of the newly-weds.

Asha did not know the art of repartee, so she took shelter behind Binodini's endless wit. She could give up the futile struggle to keep Mahendra entertained.

Within a short time after their marriage, Mahendra and Asha had almost drained their interest in each other—they had begun their marital harmony on too high a pitch. Rather than saving it like precious capital and living off the interest, they had attempted to squander the very core of their love. How could they convert this flood of lunacy into the easy flow of everyday life? How was Asha to provide the re-intoxication that an addict desires to dispel the lassitude that follows immediately after fulfilment? It was at such a juncture that Binodini became for Asha a vessel brimming with novelty and colour. Seeing her husband cheerful, Asha felt relieved.

Now she made no effort of her own. When Mahendra and Binodini engaged in repartee, she would join in their hearty laughter. When Mahendra cheated at a game of cards, Asha would resort to making piteous appeals to Binodini's judgement. If Mahendra mocked her or said something unpleasant to her, she would hope that Binodini would offer a suitable retort on her behalf. And thus, they became a threesome enjoying an intricate relationship.

But that did not cause Binodini to neglect her household duties. Cooking, supervising the housework, attending to Rajalakshmi—only after completing all these tasks would she join in the fun. Growing restless, Mahendra would complain, 'I can see you will spoil all the servants by not giving them a chance to work.'

'That is better than ruining oneself by remaining idle,' Binodini would retort. 'Go, you should go to college.'

'On such a beautiful, rainy day . . .'

'No, that won't work—your carriage is ready—you must go to college.'

'But I had dismissed my carriage.'

'I have sent for it.' So saying, she brought Mahendra the clothes he wore to college.

'You should have been born into a Rajput family,' he protested. 'In times of war, you would have dressed your kinsmen in armour.'

Binodini would never encourage him to take time

off or shirk his studies for the sake of having fun. Under her strict surveillance, the idea of unscheduled, unbridled enjoyment disappeared completely, and the evening interlude began to seem extremely romantic and desirable to Mahendra. It was almost as if his day waited to end and make way for the evening.

Before this, Mahendra had sometimes happily skipped college on the pretext that his lunch was not ready on time. Now, Binodini personally saw to it that Mahendra's meal was prepared punctually, and as soon as he had eaten, he would be informed that the coach was ready. His clothes were now folded and arranged neatly, every day. Previously, it had been impossible to ascertain without a prolonged search whether his garments had been sent to the laundry or whether they were lying undetected in some obscure part of the wardrobe.

At first, Binodini had laughingly chided Asha in Mahendra's presence about this lack of orderliness. Mahendra, too, had smiled indulgently at Asha's helpless ineptitude. Ultimately, out of friendly affection, Binodini claimed Asha's duties as her own. The household underwent a transformation.

When Mahendra's chapkan lost a button, and Asha failed to find a quick solution, Binodini swiftly snatched the garment from Asha and sewed on the button herself. One day, when a cat tasted the rice that had been prepared for Mahendra, Asha was distraught, but to her amazement, Binodini immediately went into the kitchen, and in some inexplicable way procured provisions to take care of the matter.

Thus, in his food and apparel, at work and at leisure, Mahendra began to sense Binodini's caring touch everywhere. The fur shoes on his feet and the woven fur collar at his neck enwrapped him like a delicate psychological bond. Nowadays, adorned by her friend's hands, Asha would present herself to Mahendra, looking neat and tidy, well dressed and perfumed. Part of her allure would be her own, part someone else's: in her attire, beauty and joyfulness, she seemed to have merged with her friend, like a union of the Ganga and Yamuna.

Bihari was no longer welcomed as before, nor was he sent for. He had written to inform Mahendra that on the following day, which was a Sunday, he would come in the afternoon to enjoy a meal cooked by Mahendra's mother. Realizing that his Sunday was likely to be ruined, Mahendra hastily wrote back that he would be away on urgent work that day.

Nevertheless, Bihari visited Mahendra's house after lunch, to find out how things were. He was informed by the bearer that Mahendra had not ventured forth from the house. Calling out to Mahendra from the staircase, Bihari entered his room.

'I have a severe headache,' declared Mahendra in embarrassment, and reclined, leaning his head on the pillow. Hearing this, and seeing the expression on

Mahendra's face, Asha grew agitated, and glanced at Binodini to ascertain what was to be done. Though well aware that the situation was not grave, Binodini showed great anxiety: 'You've been sitting up for a long time; lie down now. Let me fetch some eau de cologne.'

'Let it be, there's no need,' Mahendra protested.

Binodini would not hear of it. She went swiftly to fetch some eau de cologne mixed with iced water. Handing a damp kerchief to Asha, she said, 'Tie this onto Mahendrababu's head.'

'Let it be,' Mahendra begged. With a suppressed smile, Bihari watched the performance in silence. 'Let Bihari see how well I am looked after,' thought Mahendra, proudly.

Self-conscious in Bihari's presence, Asha could not tie the kerchief properly because her hands were trembling; a drop of eau de cologne trickled into Mahendra's eye. Taking the kerchief from Asha, Binodini tied it on expertly, and soaking another piece of cloth in eau de cologne, she squeezed it gently over Mahendra's brow. Covering her head, Asha began to fan Mahendra.

'Mahendrababu, do you feel some relief?' asked Binodini tenderly.

As she spoke in such honeyed tones, Binodini cast a swift, sidelong glance at Bihari's face. She saw amused mockery in Bihari's eyes. The whole matter struck him as farcical. Binodini realized that this man would be hard to deceive; nothing eluded his gaze.

'Binod Bouthan, if the patient receives such ministrations, his illness will not disappear, it will only grow more acute,' smiled Bihari.

'How would illiterate women like us know such things? Is that what your medical textbooks say?' asked Binodini.

'Indeed they do,' replied Bihari. 'Watching you nurse him, I am developing a headache, too. But unfortunates like me must cure themselves quickly, without any medical treatment. Mahinda is more fortunate.'

Putting down the piece of damp cloth, Binodini said, 'Let it be, let friends do the nursing.'

Bihari was annoyed by the scene he had just witnessed. Having been busy with his studies all these days, he had not known the extent to which Mahendra, Binodini and Asha had become embroiled with each other in the meantime. Today, he took special note of Binodini, and she, too, observed him closely.

'Quite so,' said Bihari, rather sharply. 'A friend should be nursed by friends. I was the cause of his headache, now I shall take the headache away with me. Don't waste your eau de cologne.' Turning to Asha, he warned: 'Bouthan, prevention is better than cure.'

16

'*I* must not stay away any longer,' thought Bihari. 'I must take my place amongst these people by whatever means possible. None of them will want me, but it is still necessary for me to remain here.'

Uninvited, Bihari began to invade Mahendra's protected territory. 'Binod Bouthan, this boy has been ruined,' he declared. 'Spoilt by his mother, spoilt by his friend, he is now being spoilt by his wife. Instead of joining the company, I beg of you, please show him a new direction.'

'In other words . . .?' asked Mahendra.

'In other words, people like me, whom nobody ever asks after–'

'Let them be spoilt,' Mahendra interrupted. 'It is not easy to become a candidate for spoiling, dear Bihari, it is not enough just to submit an application.'

'You must have the capacity to be ruined, Biharibabu,' laughed Binodini.

'Even if I'm born without such aptitude, my destiny might make it possible,' replied Bihari. 'Why not give me a chance?'

'It's no use being prepared beforehand, one must throw caution to the winds,' replied Binodini. 'What do you say, my friend Chokher Bali? Why don't you take charge of this brother-in-law of yours?'

Asha pushed her away. Bihari, too, did not participate in the joke.

It did not escape Binodini's notice that Bihari would not brook any jibes about Asha. It hurt her to observe that Bihari respected Asha while he took Binodini lightly.

She turned to Asha, once again: 'This beggar, your brother-in-law, has come to seek your affection, using me as a pretext. Grant him your favour, my friend.'

Asha was extremely annoyed. Bihari flushed briefly, but the very next moment, he smiled. 'When it comes to me, you would operate through other people, but with Mahinda, you deal in direct transactions.'

Binodini was left in no doubt that Bihari intended to ruin everything. She realized that she would have to arm herself against him.

Mahendra was annoyed. Blunt talk destroys the sweetness of romance. In a slightly sharp tone, he said, 'Bihari, your Mahinda doesn't engage in commerce; he is content with what he has in hand.'

'He may not do so himself,' retorted Bihari. 'But if destiny decrees, the tide of commerce may engulf him from without.'

'You have nothing in hand at the moment; but what is the direction of your tidal wave?' With these words, Binodini pinched Asha, with an oblique smile. Annoyed, Asha got up and left. Defeated, Bihari fell into an angry silence. As soon as he prepared to arise, Binodini said, 'Don't leave in despair, Biharibabu. I shall send Chokher Bali to you.'

Binodini left. Mahendra was annoyed at the breakup of their company. Seeing Mahendra's displeased countenance, Bihari's suppressed agitation brimmed over. 'Mahinda, ruin yourself if you wish,' he spluttered. 'That has always been your habit. But don't destroy the simple, devoted woman who has placed her implicit trust in you. It is not too late for me to say this: don't destroy her life.'

As he spoke, Bihari's voice grew choked with emotion.

Controlling his anger, Mahendra replied, 'Bihari, I can't understand what you are saying. Tell me clearly, don't speak in riddles.'

'I shall speak clearly. Binodini is deliberately dragging you into sin, and like an ignorant fool, you are venturing down the wrong path.'

'A pack of lies!' roared Mahendra. 'If you regard a well brought up woman with such unjust suspicion, then you should not step into the private quarters of the house.'

At this moment, Binodini smilingly brought a plate of sweets and placed it before Bihari.

'What's this? I'm not hungry,' protested Bihari.

'How is that possible? You must taste some sweets before you leave.'

'It seems my plea has been granted. This is the beginning of all the spoiling I shall receive,' smiled Bihari.

With an extremely oblique smile, Binodini said, 'As the husband's younger brother, you have a special position of kinship. Why beg where you can demand your rights? You can snatch affection by force. What do you say, Mahendrababu?'

Mahendra was speechless.

'Biharibabu, is it due to embarrassment or anger that you refuse to eat? Must someone else be summoned?' asked Binodini.

'There is no need. What I have received is more than enough.'

'Such mockery? It's impossible to keep up with you in this. Even sweets are not enough to silence your tongue.'

At night, Asha told Mahendra how upset she was with Bihari. Mahendra did not laugh it off as on other days; he was in complete agreement with her.

At dawn, immediately upon awakening, Mahendra went to Bihari's house. 'Bihari,' he said, 'Binodini is not quite a member of our own family, after all; she seems rather irritated if you appear in her presence.'

'Is that so? Then it's not a good idea. Since she objects, I might as well avoid appearing before her.'

Mahendra was relieved. He had not imagined that this unpleasant task would be accomplished so easily. He was afraid of Bihari.

That very day, Bihari went to the private quarters of Mahendra's house and spoke to Binodini. 'Binod Bouthan, you must forgive me.'

'Why, Biharibabu?'

'I heard from Mahendra that you are annoyed by my presence in the private quarters of the house. I am here to beg your forgiveness and leave.'

'How is that possible, Biharibabu? I am here today, gone tomorrow; why would you leave on my account? Had I known there would be such complications, I would not have come here at all.

With these words, a dejected Binodini hurried away, as if to control her tears.

For an instant, Bihari thought, 'I have injured Binodini's feelings by my false suspicions.'

That evening, Rajalakshmi came to Mahendra with a troubled expression. 'Mahin, Bipin's wife is determined to go back home,' she said.

'Why, Ma, what discomfort does she suffer here?'

'No discomfort. Bahu says people will cast aspersions on her character if a young widow like her remains for too long in someone else's home.'

Offended, Mahendra said, 'Is this home someone

else's then? Not her own?' He cast an accusing glance at Bihari who was sitting nearby.

'There was a hint of criticism in my words yesterday,' thought Bihari, penitently. 'Perhaps that is what has hurt Binodini's feelings.'

Both husband and wife adopted a reproachful attitude towards Binodini. One asked, 'Do you consider us strangers, friend!'

'After all these days, to call us strangers!' protested the other.

'My friends, would you hold me captive forever?' demanded Binodini.

'Would we dare do such a thing?' asked Mahendra.

'Then why did you steal our hearts in this fashion?' said Asha, accusingly.

That day, nothing was decided. 'No, my friends,' insisted Binodini, 'it's better not to develop such attachments when they are only temporary.' With these words, she cast a desperate glance at Mahendra.

The next day, Bihari came to her. 'Binod Bouthan, why do you speak of going away? Is it to punish me for some offence that I have committed?' he asked.

Slightly averting her face, Binodini replied, 'The fault is not yours; my destiny is to blame.'

'If you go away, I shall always feel that you left because you were angry with me,' said Bihari.

Binodini looked beseechingly at Bihari, and asked: 'You tell me, would it be appropriate for me to stay?'

Bihari was caught in an awkward position. How could he say that it was appropriate for her to stay? He answered, 'You would certainly have to leave, but what is the harm in staying a few days longer?'

Lowering her eyes, Binodini said, 'All of you are asking me to stay. It is difficult for me to ignore your requests, but it is very wrong of you all.' As she spoke, enormous teardrops fell from beneath her long, dark eyelashes.

Unable to bear this flood of silent tears, Bihari exclaimed, 'In the few days since your arrival, you have captivated everyone with your talents. That is why nobody wants to let you go. Please don't mind, Binod Bouthan, but who would willingly part with such a wonderful lady?'

Asha had been sitting in a corner with her head covered. She began to wipe away her tears with the corner of her aanchal.

After this, Binodini did not speak of leaving.

17

To wipe out the memory of this recent unpleasantness, Mahendra proposed, 'Let's go on a picnic to the orchard at Dumdum this Sunday.'

Asha was very excited. But Binodini would not agree to the plan. Mahendra and Asha were extremely downcast at Binodini's objections. 'Nowadays Binodini seems rather remote,' they thought.

In the evening, as soon as Bihari arrived, Binodini complained, 'Look at this Biharibabu! Mahinbabu wants to go to the Dumdum orchard on a picnic, but because I am reluctant to accompany them, the two of them have been sulking since morning.'

'Their anger is not uncalled for. If you don't accompany them, their picnic would be the kind of disaster that one would not wish upon one's worst enemy.'

'Why don't you come with us, Biharibabu? If you

come along, I am willing to join the party, too.'

'An excellent suggestion. But we must do as the master decrees. What does the master say?'

Both husband and wife were secretly offended at Binodini's partiality towards Bihari. Half of Mahendra's enthusiasm evaporated at the prospect of taking Bihari with them. Mahendra wanted to impress upon his friend that Binodini found his presence unpleasant at all times. But after this, it would be hard to hold Bihari back.

'Well then, it's a good idea,' said Mahendra. 'But Bihari, you never fail to create a disturbance wherever you go. Perhaps you will get all the boys of the locality to gather at the venue, or get into fisticuffs with some white man—who can predict what you might do?'

Inwardly amused at Mahendra's heartfelt dismay, Bihari declared, 'That's the fun of living in this world: it's impossible to predict how one thing may lead to another, or what problems may crop up at any juncture. Binod Bouthan, we must leave at dawn; I shall be here on time.'

At dawn on Sunday, a third-class carriage was hired for the attendants and all the equipment, and a second-class carriage for the family. Bihari arrived on time, bringing with him an enormous box.

'What's that you have brought?' asked Mahendra. 'There is no room left in the servants' carriage.'

'Don't worry, Dada, I shall take care of everything.' Binodini and Asha entered the carriage. Mahendra hesitated a bit, wondering what to do with Bihari. Hoisting his load onto the roof of the carriage, Bihari quickly climbed onto the coachbox.

Mahendra heaved a sigh of relief. He had been thinking, 'There's no saying what Bihari might do, he might even seat himself inside the carriage.'

Anxiously, Binodini asked, 'Biharibabu, you won't fall off, will you?'

'Have no fear,' Bihari assured her, 'my role in the script does not warrant falling and fainting.'

As soon as the carriage set off, Mahendra proposed, 'I may as well go and sit up there, and send Bihari to sit inside.'

Asha clutched at his wrap. 'No, you cannot go.'

'You are not used to it,' Binodini pointed out. 'What if you fall off? There's no need.'

'Fall off? Never!' In his excited state, Mahendra immediately prepared to go out.

'You blame Biharibabu, but it is you who are the supreme troublemaker,' declared Binodini.

'Very well, I have an idea,' responded Mahendra gravely. 'Let Bihari come and sit inside. I shall go in a separate hired carriage.'

'In that case, I shall go with you as well,' insisted Asha.

'And am I supposed to jump off the carriage?' demanded Binodini. On this confused note, the matter ended.

All the way, Mahendra maintained a very grave countenance.

The carriage arrived at the Dumdum orchard. The servants' carriage had set out much earlier, but there was no sign of it yet.

It was an exquisite autumnal dawn. The rising sun had dried out the dew, but the foliage glistened in the pure light of day. Against the wall were rows of shefali trees, the ground beneath them a fragrant carpet of flowers.

Released from the imprisoning brick walls of Kolkata into the freedom of the garden, Asha was exhilarated, like a wild doe. She and Binodini gathered a mass of flowers from the ground, and sat beneath the wood-apple tree munching the ripe fruit they had plucked from it. Together, the two friends threw themselves into the pond and enjoyed a long bath. The dappled shade beneath the trees, the waters of the pond and the flowers and leaves of the arbour were infused with a joyous spirit by the playful spontaneity of these two women.

Returning from their bath, they found that their attendants' carriage had not yet arrived. Mahendra sat on a chowki placed on the veranda, with an extremely sour expression, reading the advertisement for a British store.

'Where is Biharibabu?' asked Binodini.

'I don't know,' replied Mahendra curtly.

'Come, let's find him.'

'There is no fear of his being abducted. He will be found even without being sought.'

'But he may be dying of worry about you, lest a

precious jewel be lost. Let us go and reassure him.'

Beside the pond was an enormous banyan tree, with a paved area around its base. Bihari had taken out a kerosene stove from his box and was now heating up some water. As soon as everyone arrived, he displayed great hospitality, seating them on small raised platforms built for the purpose and serving them individual cups of tea and sweetmeats arranged on small dishes.

Binodini remarked, again and again, 'Thank goodness Biharibabu had arranged to carry all the required items! Imagine Mahendrababu's condition if tea had not been available.'

Though the tea had brought him great relief, Mahendra complained, 'Bihari always goes to extremes. We have come here on a picnic, but even here, he has made such elaborate arrangements. There's no fun in it.'

'Very well, my friend, then return your cup of tea,' retorted Bihari. 'Go and have fun without food, I shall not stop you.'

The day grew long, but the attendants did not arrive. All kinds of eatables kept emerging from Bihari's box. Rice and dal, vegetables, and even ground spices in tiny bottles were discovered there.

'Biharibabu, you have outdone all of us,' exclaimed Binodini in amazement. 'Without a woman to keep house for you, how did you learn all these things?'

'I learnt in order to survive. I have to take care of

my own needs.' Bihari spoke in jest, but Binodini grew grave; her eyes showered pity on him.

Together, Bihari and Binodini applied themselves to the task of cooking a meal. When Asha made a feeble, self-conscious attempt to lend a hand, Bihari stopped her. The inept Mahendra made no attempt to help at all. Leaning against a tree trunk, his legs crossed, he fixed his gaze on the rays of sunshine dancing on the trembling banyan leaves.

When the cooking was almost done, Binodini called, 'Mahinbabu, you will never finish counting those banyan leaves. Now go and have your bath.'

At long last, the party of attendants arrived, along with all the provisions. Their carriage had broken down on the way. It was now well past afternoon.

After their meal, it was proposed that they play a game of cards under the same banyan tree. Mahendra would have none of it, and in no time at all, he fell asleep in the shade of the tree. Asha went inside the building, shut the door and prepared to take some rest.

Partially covering her head with her aanchal, Binodini said, 'Let me go to my room, then.'

'Please don't go, let's talk awhile,' urged Bihari. 'Tell me about your native place.'

From time to time, the warm afternoon breeze murmured through the leafy treetops, and every now and then, the koel called from the deep foliage of the jamun tree beside the pond. Binodini spoke of her childhood days, her parents, and her playmates. As she spoke, the covering on her head slipped off, and the shadow of childhood memories softened the fierce radiance of youth that always shone from her countenance. Until now, the piercing mockery in Binodini's sidelong glance had aroused all kinds of suspicions in the mind of the sharp-eyed Bihari, but when that dark brilliance faded into a quiet, tear-moist expression, Bihari felt he was seeing a different person altogether. At the core of this radiance was a tender heart still flooded with the nectar of love, its femininity not yet shrivelled by the fire of an unquenched desire for enjoyment, frivolity and self-indulgence. Until now, Bihari had never for a single moment tried to imagine Binodini as a modest, chaste wife, devotedly serving her husband, or as a loving mother holding her child in her lap. Today, it was as if the curtains of the stage had parted for an instant, affording him a glimpse of the beautiful scene backstage. Bihari thought, 'Though outwardly frivolous, Binodini is really a pious woman with austere habits.'

'Human beings can't recognize their own true selves,' sighed Bihari to himself. 'Only God knows such things. Outward appearances produced by the force of circumstance are taken for truths by the world at large.' Bihari did not allow Binodini's narrative to end; he kept it going by asking a series of questions. Until now, Binodini had never found a listener to whom she could say all these things in this fashion; she had never spoken to any man in such an unselfconscious, natural way. Today, as she spoke in her fluent, sweet voice of the simplest thoughts in her heart, her very nature seemed to become gentle and contented, as if bathed in a fresh shower of rain.

Tired after the effort of having risen at dawn, Mahendra awoke at five o'clock. 'Now let us prepare to return,' he ordered, irritably.

'What is the harm if we return a little later in the evening?' asked Binodini.

'No, we might fall into the clutches of some drunken white man,' Mahendra replied.

By the time they packed up all the things, it had grown dark. At this moment, an attendant came to inform them, 'The hired carriages have gone; they are nowhere to be found. They were waiting outside the orchard, but two white men bullied the coachmen into driving the carriages to the station.'

The attendant was sent to fetch another carriage.

'This day has been ruined, to no purpose,' Mahendra muttered to himself in annoyance. He could no longer conceal his impatience.

From a horizon entangled in a web of branches, the moon in its bright quarter arose gradually, ascending the open sky. The still, silent orchard seemed etched in a shadowy light. Tonight, in this magical world, Binodini felt a strange, exquisite self-awareness. Tonight, when she embraced Asha in the arbour, it was not from a pretence of love. Asha saw tears streaming from Binodini's eyes. Concerned, she asked, 'Why, my dear Chokher Bali, why do you weep?'

'It's nothing, my friend, I am fine. I have really enjoyed this day.'

'What was it you enjoyed so much, my friend?'

'I feel as if I have died and entered the afterworld; as if here, in this place, everything is mine for the asking.'

Bewildered, Asha understood nothing of what she said. Saddened by the mention of death, she protested, 'For shame, dear Chokher Bali, do not speak of such things.'

A carriage was found. Bihari again ascended the coach-box. Binodini gazed in silence at the scene outside— frozen in moonlight, the rows of trees passed before her eyes like a deep, flowing stream of shadows. Asha fell asleep in a corner of the coach. Throughout the long journey, Mahendra sat in utter dejection.

18

After the disastrous picnic, Mahendra was eager to reclaim his power over Binodini. But the very next day, Rajalakshmi developed influenza. It was not a serious illness, but it caused sufficient discomfort and weakness. Binodini remained busy day and night, looking after her.

'If you slave like this, you will eventually fall sick yourself,' Mahendra warned her. 'I shall engage a nurse to take care of Ma.'

'Mahinda, don't be so anxious,' said Bihari. 'Let her continue to look after your mother. Could anyone else match her devotion?'

Mahendra began to visit the invalid's chamber several times during the day. That a man should remain idle, yet be constantly by her side while she was at work, was intolerable to the efficient Binodini. She frequently protested, 'Mahinbabu, what purpose does it serve for you to remain sitting here? Please go away—don't miss college for no reason.'

It gave Binodini pride and pleasure that Mahendra was following her around, but to see him behave like an abject beggar, lusting after her even while sitting beside his mother's sickbed, made her impatient and contemptuous. When a task awaited her attention, Binodini forgot all else. As long as it was necessary for her to attend to meals, look after a patient or perform domestic chores, Binodini was never known to shirk; in times of need, she could not tolerate any unnecessary complications.

Sometimes, Bihari would pay a brief visit to find out how Rajalakshmi was doing. Immediately upon entering the room, he would gauge what was required, notice what was lacking, and in an instant, he would set things in order and leave the room. Binodini sensed that Bihari viewed her devoted nursing with respect. Hence, she found Bihari's visits particularly rewarding.

Feeling rejected, Mahendra began attending college, adhering to a very strict schedule. His temper remained extremely volatile, and to make matters worse, things had changed drastically! Meals were no longer ready on time, the coach driver often disappeared, the holes in his socks grew larger and larger. Mahendra did not consider this disorderliness amusing any more; he had briefly experienced the comfort of having things beautifully arranged and ready at hand whenever required. In the absence of that comfort, Mahendra no longer found Asha's ineptitude charming.

'Chuni, how many times have I told you to fix studs on my shirt before I bathe, and to keep my chapkan-pantaloons ready for me to wear. Still, these things are never done. After my bath, it takes me two hours to fix the buttons and hunt around for my clothes.'

Asha would grow pale with shame. 'I had asked the steward,' she would say, contritely.

'Asked the steward! What is the harm in doing it yourself? If only one could get some work out of you!'

Asha was thunderstruck. She had never been scolded like this before. It did not occur to her to retort: 'It was you who hindered my training in household duties.' She had no idea that training in domestic skills depends on regular practice and experience. She would think, 'It is only due to my natural ineptitude and foolishness that I am unable to perform any task properly.' When Mahendra, forgetting himself, condemned Asha by comparing her unfavourably with Binodini, she would accept his opinion humbly and without jealousy.

Sometimes, Asha would loiter near the room where her sick mother-in-law lay; sometimes, she would come and stand at the door with an embarrassed air. She wanted to make herself indispensable to the household, she longed to demonstrate her capacity for work, but nobody wanted any work from her. She did not know how to enter the sphere of household duties, how to take her place within the domestic establishment. Shamed by her own inefficiency, she lingered on the periphery. Day after day, a pain grew in her heart, but she could not clearly understand this indistinct anguish, this unexpressed anxiety. She felt that she was ruining everything, all around her, but how the situation had been created, how it was being destroyed, and what could be done to counter the process, she did not know. Now and then, she wanted to cry out loud: 'I am utterly unworthy, extremely inept, and foolish beyond compare.'

Earlier, Asha and Mahendra would spend long spells of time together in a corner of the house, sometimes talking, sometimes in silence, in a state of complete bliss. Nowadays, in Binodini's absence, Mahendra found it hard to think of what to say to Asha when they were alone together. But to remain silent without saying anything was also awkward for him.

One day, the attendant brought a letter. Mahendra asked, 'Whose letter is that?'

'Biharibabu's.'

'Who has sent it?'

'Bahu-thakurani,' he replied, referring to Binodini.

'Let me see,' he said, taking the letter. He wanted to tear it open and read it. Turning it over in his hands a few times, and shaking it about a little, he flung it at the attendant. If he had opened the letter, he would have seen that it said: *Pishima simply refuses to take sago and barley. Should we let her have dal broth, today?* Binodini never consulted Mahendra on matters concerning medication and diet; it was Bihari she relied upon.

After pacing up and down the veranda for a while, Mahendra entered his room to find that a picture on the wall hung askew, because the loop by which it was suspended had become frayed. He rebuked Asha severely: 'You don't take note of anything; this is how all our things are ruined.' The bouquet of flowers from the Dumdum orchard that Binodini had arranged in a brass vase was still there, exactly as it was, though dried and faded. On other days, Mahendra would not even notice such things, but today, it caught his eye. 'Unless Binodini comes to discard the flowers, they will not be disposed of,' he declared. He flung the flowers, vase and all, out of the room. With a loud clanging sound, the vase rolled down the stairs.

'Why does Asha not please my taste; why does she not perform tasks to my liking; why, with her inborn slackness and frailty, does she fail to keep me steady on the marital path; why does she constantly drive me asunder?' Turning these thoughts over and over in his mind, Mahendra suddenly noticed that Asha's face had grown pale, her lips were quivering. Trembling, she clung to the bedpost, then abruptly rushed out of the room through the adjoining chamber.

Slowly, Mahendra went to pick up the vase; he returned it to its place. He sat on the chowki in a corner of the room, leaned his elbows on the study table in front, and remained like that for a long while, holding his head in his hands.

When it grew dark, a light was brought to his room, but Asha did not come. Mahendra began to pace on the terrace. By nine o'clock, Mahendra's empty room grew still and silent as if it was late night, but still, Asha did not come. Finally, Mahendra sent for her. Timidly, Asha came and stood near the door to the terrace. Mahendra went up to her and drew her close to his heart. Instantly, she burst into tears, her head resting upon her husband's chest; there was no stopping her, no end to her tears, the sound of her weeping could no longer be suppressed. Holding her tightly against his chest, Mahendra kissed her hair. From the silent sky, the stars looked down on them, mutely.

At night, when they were in bed, Mahendra told her: 'We're being given night duties more frequently in college, so I will now have to find some accommodation close to the college for a while.'

'Is he still angry?' wondered Asha. 'Is he leaving because he is annoyed with me? Am I driving my husband out of his home due to my own lack of talent and ability? Better if I were dead!'

But there was no sign of anger in Mahendra's behaviour. For a long time, he remained silent, holding Asha's face against his chest. Stroking her hair with his fingers, he undid her hair-knot. In the early days of their romance, Mahendra would loosen Asha's bound and braided hair in this way, but Asha would object. Tonight, she showed no resistance; overcome with rapture, she remained silent. Suddenly, a teardrop fell on her forehead, and turning her face upwards, Mahendra whispered, 'Chuni!' His voice choked with tenderness. Without replying in words, Asha held Mahendra close in a tender embrace.

'I have wronged you, please forgive me,' said Mahendra.

Asha stopped Mahendra's mouth with her delicate, flowerlike hands. 'No, no, don't say such things. You have done no wrong. I am entirely to blame. Discipline me as if I am your slave. Make me worthy of a place at your feet.'

As he left his bed at dawn, when it was time to part, Mahendra assured her, 'Chuni, my jewel, I shall hold you above all others in my heart; nobody can take your place there.'

At this, Asha, determined to accept all sorts of sacrifice, made only one tiny demand of her husband: 'Will you write me a letter every day?'

'Will you write, as well?'

'As if I know how to write!'

Mahendra tugged at the curl on her cheek. 'You can write better than Akshay Kumar Dutta, the author of *Charupath*.'

'Go away, don't tease me anymore.'

Before he departed, Asha sat down to pack his portmanteau with her own hands, as best she could. It was hard to fold Mahendra's heavy winter clothes, difficult to fit them into the box. The two of them somehow forced the clothes in, loading into two boxes what a single box could have accommodated. Even after this, some things were left out by mistake; these were tied into several separate bundles. Asha felt ashamed about that, but their tugging and pulling, their joking and laughter-filled mutual blaming revived the joy of their earlier days together. Asha momentarily forgot that this was preparation for parting. At least ten times, the coach driver reminded Mahendra that the carriage was ready, but Mahendra ignored him. Ultimately, he said in exasperation, 'Unbridle the horses.'

Morning gradually stretched into late afternoon, and then it became evening. Then, after cautioning each other to mind their health and extracting repeated promises to write regularly, the two of them parted with heavy hearts.

For about two days now, Rajalakshmi had been able to sit up. This evening, clad in a heavy shawl, she was playing a game of cards with Binodini. Today there was no weariness in her body. Mahendra entered the room, and without glancing at Binodini at all, he said to his mother, 'Ma, I have night duties in college, so it's not convenient for me to remain here. I have taken up lodgings near the college. I shall stay there from today.'

'Go, then,' responded Rajalakshmi, hurt. 'How can you remain here if it affects your studies?'

Although her illness was cured, at the news of Mahendra's departure, she instantly imagined herself to be extremely sick and frail. 'There, my dear child, hand me that pillow,' she asked Binodini. She reclined on the pillow. Binodini slowly stroked her back.

Mahendra felt his mother's forehead once, then examined her pulse. Pulling away her hand, Rajalakshmi said, 'Much you can tell from checking my pulse. You need not worry about me, I'm doing fine.' With these words, she turned over on her side, with a very feeble air.

Without making any gesture of farewell to Binodini, Mahendra touched his mother's feet and left.

19

'What is the matter?' wondered Binodini to herself. 'Is it petulance, or anger, or fear? Does he want to show me that he doesn't care about me? Does he plan to live in rented lodgings? Let's see how long he can stay there!'

But even Binodini began to feel restless. Deprived of her daily endeavour to subject Mahendra to different forms of bondage and to pierce him with different types of arrows, she felt tormented. The household lost all charm for her. To her, Asha without Mahendra had no appeal whatsoever. Mahendra's amorous attentions towards Asha had constantly troubled Binodini's frustrated heart; the anguish had kept her lovelorn imagination in a state of painful arousal, full of acute excitement. Mahendra had denied her the fulfilment of all her life's aspirations, ignoring a jewel such as herself to embrace a feeble-minded, poor-spirited girl like Asha. Whether Binodini loved or hated him, whether she

wanted to punish him harshly or to surrender her heart
to him, was something she herself had not understood
clearly. Whether the fire that Mahendra had ignited in
her heart was the fire of envy or passion, or a mixture
of both, Binodini could not tell. Laughing bitterly
to herself, she would wonder: 'Has any woman ever
suffered a condition such as mine? Whether I want to
die or to kill, I simply couldn't say!' But whether she
wanted to surrender to the fire or to scorch others with
it, she needed Mahendra desperately. Where else in the
world would she direct her poisoned arrow of fire?
'Where can he go?' sighed Binodini. 'He must return.
He belongs to me.'

On the pretext of cleaning the room, Asha entered
Mahendra's outer chamber in the evening. Mahendra's
armchair, stained with his hair oil, the desk strewn
with his papers, his books, his pictures—she fiddled
with all these things over and over again, dusting them
with her aanchal. By touching Mahendra's possessions,
putting them down, then picking them up again, Asha
was trying to pass her evening of separation from her
beloved. Slowly, Binodini came up and stood beside her.
Embarrassed, Asha ceased her pottering and pretended
to be hunting for something.

'What's the matter with you, my friend?' asked
Binodini, gravely.

Summoning up a small smile, Asha replied, 'Nothing
at all, dear.'

Binodini embraced Asha. 'Why, my dear Bali, why did Thakurpo go away like this?'

Binodini's question frightened Asha. Instantly on her guard, she replied, 'You know why, my friend—he has left because he has some special duties in college.'

Holding Asha's chin in her right hand, Binodini tilted her face up and gazed at it in silence, as if melting with pity. She let out a sigh.

Asha's heart sank. She knew she was foolish and Binodini intelligent. Seeing Binodini's manner, her whole world was suddenly plunged into darkness. She did not dare to question Binodini directly. She sank into a sofa near the wall. Binodini, too, sat down next to her, and held Asha pressed close to her bosom in a firm embrace. Embraced thus by her friend, Asha could contain herself no longer. Tears began to flow from her eyes. At the door, a blind beggar sang, playing the khanjani, 'O Ma Tara, my saviour, grant me shelter at your feet, so I may have a safe crossing.'

Arriving at the door in search of Mahendra, Bihari found Asha weeping and Binodini wiping away her tears, holding her friend close to her bosom. Immediately, Bihari moved away. He went into the empty room adjoining, and sat in the dark. Clutching his head in both hands, he began to wonder why Asha was crying. In the whole world, could there be a man villainous enough to hurt a girl naturally incapable of giving anybody the slightest offence? And then, recalling the way Binodini was consoling her, he told himself, 'I had misunderstood Binodini. In her devoted care of others, her powers of consolation, her selfless affection for her friend, she is a goddess here on earth.'

Bihari sat in the dark for a long time. When the blind beggar's song ended, Bihari approached Mahendra's chamber with loud footsteps, coughing as he went. Before he could reach the door, Asha ran away towards the private quarters, pulling her aanchal over her head.

'What is this, Biharibabu!' exclaimed Binodini, as soon as he entered the room. 'Are you ill?'

'It's nothing.'

'Why are your eyes so red?'

Without answering her question, Bihari asked, 'Binod Bouthan, where has Mahendra gone?'

'I hear he has rented a place close to his college because he has been assigned some duties at the hospital,' responded Binodini gravely. 'Biharibabu, please step aside, I'll take my leave.'

Preoccupied, Bihari had been standing at the door, obstructing Binodini's path. Startled, he quickly moved aside. It suddenly occurred to him that talking to Binodini alone in the evening in the outer room was likely to incur public disapproval. As Binodini departed, Bihari managed to say, 'Binod Bouthan, please look after Asha. She is very simple; she can neither hurt anybody, nor protect herself from injury.'

In the darkness, Bihari could not see Binodini's face,

on which envy flashed like lightning. Today, as soon as she saw Bihari, she realized that his heart was racked with pity for Asha. Binodini herself was nothing to him! She was born only to shield Asha, to remove thorny obstacles from Asha's path, to ensure that Asha's cup of bliss was full to the brim! Mahendrababu had wanted to marry Asha, hence fate decreed that Binodini be banished to the jungle in the company of a barbaric baboon from Barasat. Biharibabu couldn't bear to see the simple Asha weep, hence Binodini must always be ready to wipe her tears away with the corner of her aanchal. Once, just once, Binodini wanted to drag Mahendra and Bihari down into the dust and show them the difference between Asha and Binodini. What a contrast between the two of them! Prevented by adverse circumstances from conquering any male heart with her brilliance, Binodini assumed the image of the goddess of destruction, her fiery, powerful spear upraised in her hand.

'Have no fear, Biharibabu,' Binodini assured Bihari very sweetly as they parted. 'Don't inflict undue suffering on yourself by worrying so much about my Chokher Bali.'

20

Not long after, a letter in a familiar hand was delivered to Mahendra at his office. Instead of opening it in the midst of his humdrum daytime routine, he put it away in his breast pocket. Every now and then, as he listened to lectures at college or did his rounds at the hospital, he would suddenly get the feeling that love nestled in his heart like a sleeping bird. When awakened, its tender cooing would resound in his ears.

In the evening, alone in his room, Mahendra reclined comfortably on the chowki by the light of the lamp. From his pocket, he extracted the letter, warmed by the touch of his body. For a long time, without opening the letter, he studied the name inscribed on the envelope. Mahendra knew the contents of the letter would not amount to much. There was no likelihood that Asha would be able to express her feelings adequately in writing. He would simply have to infer the tender thoughts of her heart from the crooked lines of her unsteady handwriting. Seeing his name lovingly inscribed in Asha's unformed hand, Mahendra felt he was listening to the music of pure love from the intimate recesses of a devoted woman's heart.

In these one or two days of separation, all the fatigue of prolonged togetherness had been wiped away from Mahendra's mind, and the memory of his blissful love for his simple natured wife shone brightly once more. Of late, the minor discomforts of daily housekeeping had begun to irritate him, but they had been erased from his heart. He only remembered the image of Asha, suffused with the light of pure, blissful love, beyond the logic of the workaday world.

Very slowly, Mahendra tore the envelope open, and extracting the letter, he stroked his own forehead and cheeks with it. From the pages of the letter, the scent of the perfumed essence that he had once given Asha wafted up like a desperate sigh, piercing him to the heart.

Mahendra unfolded the letter and read it. But what was this? The lines were crooked, but the language was not so simple. The characters were inscribed in an unformed hand, but the contents did not match the writing. The letter said:

Dearest, why let this letter remind you of the person you have gone away to forget? Why should the binding vine you tore and cast upon the earth, shamelessly try to raise its head again? Why did it not turn to dust and mingle with the earth?

And yet, how would such a trifle harm you, my lord? So what if you were reminded of me, just for a moment? It would scarcely affect you. Your disregard of me is like a thorn embedded in my side. All day, all night, in the midst of all my work and all my thoughts, wherever I may turn, it causes piercing pain. Teach me a means of forgetting, just as you have forgotten me.

My lord, am I to blame for the fact that you loved me? I had never imagined such good fortune, even in my dreams. I belonged nowhere, nobody knew me. If you had not taken any notice of me, if I had been an unpaid slave in your household, could I have blamed you? What charms did I possess that made you forget yourself, my beloved? What did you see in me that you gave me such an elevated status? And if, today, a bolt from the blue had to strike me, then why did the thunderbolt merely scorch me, without reducing my body and mind to ashes?

In these two days, I have borne a great deal, thought a great deal, but there's one thing I cannot understand: could you not have remained at home and still rejected me? Was there any need for you to have left home on my account? Have I taken up so much space in your heart? Would I have caught your attention, even if you had cast me in a corner, or thrown me out of the door? If that was indeed so, then why was it you who *went away? Could I not have found a way out, and gone away to some other place? I had drifted into your life, and would have drifted out again.*

What kind of letter was this? Mahendra understood perfectly whose language this was. Like someone who faints from a sudden injury, Mahendra remained stupefied, holding the letter. Like a train travelling at full speed on a certain track until a head-on collision flings it off the rails, his mind seemed to lie overturned in an inert heap.

After thinking for a long time, he read the letter again, two or three times. What had been a distant hint so far now seemed to take clear shape. The comet that had appeared like a shadow in the corner of his mind's sky, today assumed gigantic proportions as its tail shone in lines of fire.

This letter was indeed Binodini's. The simple minded Asha had inscribed it, thinking it to be her own. As she wrote the letter composed by Binodini, thoughts arose in her mind that had never occurred to her earlier. The words she copied penetrated her mind from outside, implanting themselves in her heart and becoming her own. Asha could never have expressed her undefined anguish so beautifully. She wondered, 'How did my friend understand my state of mind so exactly? How did she express it so perfectly in words?' In her helplessness, Asha seemed to cling even more eagerly to her intimate friend, who possessed the words in which to express the pain in Asha's own heart.

Rising from the chowki, Mahendra frowned, and tried very hard to feel upset with Binodini, but he grew angry with Asha instead. 'Look at this! How foolish of Asha to torment her husband this way!' He sat on the chowki and re-read the letter as proof of what he felt. In his perusal, he began to feel a sense of pleasure. He tried very hard to read the letter as if it had indeed been written by Asha. But this language was in no way reminiscent of the artless Asha. As soon as he had read a few lines, a joyous, intoxicating suspicion would fill his mind and spill over, like foaming liquor. This hint of love, indirect yet explicit, forbidden yet intimate, poisonous yet sweet, given yet withheld, roused Mahendra to a state of frenzy. He began to wish that he could stab himself somewhere in the arm or leg, or do something else to break the spell and to divert his mind. Banging the table with his fist, he jumped up from the chowki. 'Away with it! Let me burn the letter!' So saying, he carried the letter close to the lamp. He didn't burn it, but read it again, instead. The next day, the servant had to dust a lot of ash off the table. But those were not the ashes of Asha's letter; they were the ashes of Mahendra's many incomplete attempts to answer the letter.

21

In the meantime, another letter arrived:

*Why did you not answer my letter? It is for the best.
The truth cannot be written down; I have sensed in
my heart what your answer must be. When the devotee
prays to the deity, does He answer in words? It seems
this unfortunate woman's prayer offering of wood-
apple leaves has been granted a place at your feet!*

*But if the devotee's prayer has disrupted Shiva's
meditation, please don't be angry, lord of my heart.
Whether you grant a boon or not, whether you open
your eyes to see me or not, whether you are aware of
my devotion or not, the devotee has no option but to
offer her prayers. Hence, even today, I am writing this
two-line letter to you. O my stone-hearted lord, please
remain unperturbed.*

Mahendra was again inspired to frame a reply. But when he tried writing to Asha, words addressed to Binodini appeared unasked at the tip of his pen. He was unable to write in a subtle, indirect manner. Having torn up many replies, and stayed up late into the night, he ultimately managed to frame an answer; but as he stuffed it into an envelope and was about to address it to Asha, he felt a whiplash on his back as it were. A voice seemed to say, 'You villain, to deceive a trusting young girl in this way!' Mahendra tore the letter into a thousand pieces, and spent the rest of the night seated at the table, burying his head in his hands, as if to hide his face from himself.

The third letter said:

Can a person devoid of pride be capable of love? How can I offer my love to you, if I cannot protect it from neglect and insult?

Perhaps I have dared because I have failed to understand your state of mind. When you abandoned me, I still took the initiative to write to you; even when you maintained silence, I revealed my innermost thoughts to you. But if I have been mistaken about you, am I to blame? Try, once, to remember everything that happened, from beginning to end, and ask yourself, was it not you who led me to believe certain things?

Be that as it may, what I have written, whether true or false, cannot be erased; what I have given I cannot retrieve: such is my regret. For shame, that a woman's destiny should subject her to such ignominy. But for that reason, don't imagine that one who loves can endlessly debase herself. If my letters are not welcome, then let it be. If you do not answer, then this is where it ends . . .

After this, Mahendra could contain himself no longer. 'I am returning home only out of extreme anger,' he thought. 'Binodini thinks it was to forget her that I ran away from home!'

It was to directly disprove Binodini's arrogant assumption that Mahendra immediately decided to go back home.

At this moment, Bihari entered the room. Seeing Bihari, Mahendra's inner rapture seemed to double. Before this, various suspicions had made him secretly jealous of Bihari; their friendship had grown strained. Today, having read the letter, Mahendra relinquished all his envy and welcomed Bihari with excessive emotion. Getting up from the chowki, he slapped Bihari on the back, and taking him by the hand, dragged him to an armchair and made him sit down.

But Bihari appeared dejected. Mahendra thought, the poor fellow must have met Binodini in the meantime and been spurned by her before coming here. Mahendra asked, 'Bihari, did you visit my house recently?'

'I am coming from there right now,' replied Bihari gravely.

Imagining Bihari's pain, Mahendra felt secretly amused. 'Unfortunate Bihari!' he thought to himself. 'The poor fellow is completely deprived of female affection.' He patted the area near his breast pocket once; the three letters rustled within.

'How did you find everybody?'

Without answering Mahendra's question, Bihari demanded, 'Why have you left home to come and live here?'

'I have frequent night duties nowadays; it's inconvenient to stay at home.'

'You have been assigned night duties before this, but I never saw you leave home for that reason.'

'Do you harbour some suspicions in your mind, then?' laughed Mahendra.

'No, this is no joke; now let's go home.'

Mahendra was already prepared to return, but hearing Bihari's request, he convinced himself that he felt no urge to go home. 'How is that possible, Bihari? Then my entire year at college would go waste.'

'Look, Mahinda, I have known you since you were very young; don't try to deceive me. What you are doing is wrong.'

'Who is the victim of my wrongdoing, Mister Judge?'

'Where is the large heartedness you have always boasted of, Mahinda?' Bihari asked angrily.

'It is currently at the college hospital.'

'Stop, Mahinda, stop! Here you are laughing and joking

with me, and there is Asha, in tears, wandering through the outer and inner chambers of your sleeping quarters.'

The mention of Asha's tears was a sudden blow to Mahendra's heart. His new intoxication had made him forget that others in this world also had their own joys and sorrows. Suddenly jolted, he asked, 'Why does Asha weep?'

'Is that something you don't know? Am I supposed to know the answer?' demanded Bihari, in fury.

'If you must be angry that your Mahinda is not omniscient, then direct your anger at Mahinda's Creator.'

Then Bihari narrated all that he had witnessed.

As he spoke, the memory of Asha's tear-wet face pressed against Binodini's bosom almost choked his voice.

Mahendra was amazed to see Bihari's acute anguish. He knew that Bihari didn't bother about matters of the heart, so when did he acquire this added quality? Was it the day he had gone to see Asha, the unwed maiden? Poor Bihari. Although Mahendra privately called him poor Bihari, he felt amused rather than sad. Mahendra was certain in the knowledge that he was the single object of Asha's devotion. 'Those precious ones, coveted by others in vain, have voluntarily surrendered themselves to me forever.' The thought made Mahendra's breast swell with pride.

'Very well, then, let's go,' Mahendra consented. 'But you must send for a carriage.'

22

Like the lifting of a fog, all suspicions instantly evaporated from Asha's mind at the sight of Mahendra's face upon his return. Remembering her letters, she was too ashamed to raise her head and look Mahendra in the eye.

Mahendra rebuked her: 'How could you write such accusatory letters?' He extracted from his pocket the three much-read letters.

'I beg you, destroy these letters,' pleaded Asha. She tried desperately to take the letters from Mahendra's hand.

Fending her off, Mahendra put them back in his pocket. He said, 'I went to answer the call of duty, but you did not understand my intentions! How could you doubt me?'

'Please forgive me this time,' Asha begged, her eyes brimming with tears. 'It will never happen again.'

'Never?'

'Never.'

Then Mahendra drew her close and kissed her.

'Give me the letters; let me tear them up,' implored Asha.

'No, let them be.'

'He is keeping the letters to punish me,' thought Asha, full of humility.

This unpleasantness over the letters made Asha somewhat hostile towards Binodini. She did not run to her friend to celebrate the news of her husband's arrival; rather, she seemed to avoid Binodini. Binodini noticed this and, on the pretext of work, maintained her distance.

'This is very strange,' thought Mahendra. 'I had imagined that Binodini would be more visible this time, but it turns out to be quite the opposite! Then what was the meaning of those letters?'

Mahendra had decided that he would not try to fathom the mystery of the female heart. 'If Binodini tries to come close, I shall still keep a distance,' he had thought. But now, he told himself, 'No, this is not going well. It's as if something has really gone wrong between us. I should dispel this stifling cloud of suspicion by talking to Binodini in a natural, jovial manner.'

To Asha, Mahendra said, 'It seems it is I who am your friend's Chokher Bali, rankling like a grain of sand in her eye. One doesn't get to see her at all these days.'

'Who knows what is the matter with her!' remarked Asha, indifferently.

Then, Rajalakshmi came to them tearfully. 'It's not possible to persuade Bipin's wife to stay here any longer.'

'Why, Ma?' asked Mahendra, trying to conceal his shock.

'Who knows, my child, but she is extremely insistent about going home now. You know nothing of the art of hospitality. Why would the daughter of a bhadralok, a girl from a genteel family, stay on in someone else's house, if she's not looked after and made to feel welcome?'

Binodini was sitting in the bedroom, embroidering a bed sheet. 'Bali!' called Mahendra, as he entered.

Binodini composed herself. 'What is it, Mahendrababu?'

'What a disaster! Since when did Mahendra become a babu?'

Fixing her lowered gaze on her embroidered bed-sheet once more, Binodini said, 'What should I call you, then?'

'The same name by which you address your friend—Chokher Bali.'

Binodini did not offer a witty retort as on previous occasions; she continued to sew.

'So is that a true relationship, not to be ritually replicated with anyone else?' Mahendra persisted.

Pausing for a moment, Binodini bit off some excess thread from the corner of her embroidery. 'How would I know? You should know.'

Then, preempting any sort of reply to that, she asked gravely, 'Why this sudden return from college?'

'How long can one go on dissecting corpses?'

Again, Binodini bit off some thread and, without raising her head, she inquired, 'Do you now require a live specimen?'

Mahendra had decided to enjoy his session with Binodini, laughing, joking and exchanging repartee in an extremely natural, easy manner. But he felt so weighed down with gravity that, try as he might, he could not summon up a light hearted reply. Seeing Binodini so rigidly remote today, Mahendra's heart was drawn to her with great force; he wanted to shake the wall that separated them until it collapsed to the ground. Instead of offering a suitable retort in answer to Binodini's verbal barb, he suddenly came and sat beside her.

'Why are you leaving us?' he demanded. 'Have we wronged you somehow?'

Moving away a little, Binodini looked up from her sewing and, fixing her enormous, shining eyes on Mahendra's face, she declared, 'Everybody has duties to perform. When you leave everyone behind to go and live close to the college, is it because someone has hurt you? Must I not go as well? Don't I have duties, too?'

Racking his brains, Mahendra could think of no suitable reply. 'What urgent duties do you have that make it essential for you to leave?' he asked, after a short silence.

Very carefully threading the needle, Binodini replied, 'My heart knows where my duties lie. Why offer you a catalogue of my responsibilities?'

With a grave, thoughtful expression, Mahendra remained silent for a long time, gazing at the top of a coconut tree in the distance. Binodini continued sewing quietly. There was pin drop silence in the room. After a long while, Mahendra suddenly spoke. Binodini started at this sudden break in the silence, pricking her finger on the needle.

'Will no amount of persuasion prevail upon you to stay?' Mahendra asked.

Sucking the drops of blood from her injured finger, Binodini answered, 'Why such persuasion? How does it matter whether I stay or go? What difference would it make to you?'

As she spoke, her voice seemed to grow heavy; bending her head very low, Binodini became deeply engaged in her embroidery; there seemed to be a hint of tears beneath her lowered eyelashes. Outside, the cold Magh afternoon was fading into the darkness of evening.

Mahendra impulsively grasped Binodini's hand, and said in a choked, tearful voice, 'If it did make a difference to me, would you stay?'

Binodini quickly pulled her hand away and moved further away. The spell was broken. The words Mahendra had just spoken began to echo in his ears like a terrible mockery. He bit his offending tongue, and fell silent.

Just then, into this room filled with silence, entered Asha. Immediately, as if in continuation of an earlier conversation, Binodini informed Mahendra, laughing: 'Since you have flattered my self-esteem to such an extent, it is my duty to honour your request. Until you bid me farewell, I shall remain here.'

Delighted at her husband's success, Asha embraced her friend. 'So that's decided, then. Now swear three times, that until we bid you farewell, you shall stay, stay, stay.'

Thrice, Binodini repeated her oath.

'Dear Chokher Bali,' said Asha, 'if you ultimately agreed to stay on, then why demand so much persuasion? In the end, you had to concede victory to my husband.'

'Thakurpo, have I conceded victory, or forced you to accept defeat?' smiled Binodini.

All this while, Mahendra had remained stupefied; he felt as if his guilt had filled the entire room, as if his whole body was enveloped in shame. How could he speak to Asha in a cheerful, natural manner? How instantly transform his monstrous loss of control into a frivolous joke? Such demonic cunning was beyond him. 'Indeed, the defeat was mine,' he declared gravely, and immediately left the room.

Not long after, Mahendra returned. 'Please forgive me,' he begged Binodini.

'What offence have you committed, Thakurpo?'

'We do not have the right to keep you here by force.'

'Where was the use of force on your part?' smiled Binodini. 'I did not notice any. You asked me affectionately, and in words that were pleasant enough. Is that using force? Tell me, my dear Chokher Bali, are force and love the same?'

'Never,' declared Asha, in complete agreement.

'Thakurpo, you want me to stay, you will suffer if I leave; this is my good fortune,' said Binodini. 'What do you say, Chokher Bali, how many such soulmates can one find in this world? If I am fortunate enough to find a friend who shares my sorrows and my happiness, why would I be eager to leave him?'

Upset at seeing her husband speechless and humiliated, Asha said, 'No one can rival you in the use of words, my friend. My husband has acknowledged defeat, now please let matters rest.'

Mahendra hurriedly left the room again. Just then, following a short conversation with Rajalakshmi, Bihari came in search of Mahendra. Seeing him at the door, Mahendra declared, 'Bihari, there's no villain like me in this whole world.' He said this with such force that his words carried into the room.

Instantly, from within, came the call, 'Bihari Thakurpo!'

'Binod Bouthan, I'll come in a little while,' answered Bihari.

'Please come and listen to what we have to say!' called Binodini.

As soon as Bihari entered the room, he shot a quick glance at Asha; the portion of her face that he could glimpse behind the covering on her head showed no sign of dejection or pain. Asha tried to get up and leave, but Binodini forced her to stay, saying: 'Tell me, Bihari Thakurpo, do you have a stepbrotherly relationship with my Chokher Bali? Why does she want to run away whenever she sees you?'

Highly embarrassed, Asha nudged Binodini.

'Because the Maker has not given me an attractive appearance,' smiled Bihari.

'Do you see, my dear Bali, Bihari Thakurpo knows how to speak guardedly; instead of finding fault with your taste, he blamed the Maker Himself. It is your misfortune that you don't know how to appreciate a brother-in-law as wonderful as Rama's brother Lakshman in the Ramayana.'

'If that makes you feel pity for me, Binod Bouthan, then I have no cause for regret.'

'When the sea is available, why does a bird like the chatak need rain to quench its thirst?' asked Binodini.

It was impossible to keep Asha there any longer. Wrenching her hand from Binodini's grasp, she left the room. Bihari, too, prepared to leave. Binodini asked, 'Thakurpo, can you tell me what the matter is with Mahendra?'

Hearing this, Bihari at once stopped short and turned around to face her. 'I have no idea,' he replied. 'Is something amiss?'

'I don't know, Thakurpo, but I don't like the look of things.'

Anxiously, Bihari sat down on the chowki, and gazed with an eager, expectant expression at Binodini's face, waiting to hear a detailed account of the matter. Without speaking, Binodini began to embroider the bed sheet very attentively.

'Have you noticed anything particular about Mahinda?' asked Bihari, having waited a while.

'I don't know, Thakurpo,' answered Binodini in a very natural manner. 'But it doesn't look good to me. I am constantly worried about my Chokher Bali.' She sighed as she spoke and, putting down her embroidery, rose to leave the room.

'Bouthan, please stay awhile,' Bihari begged, agitated.

Opening all the doors and windows of the room and stoking the flame of the kerosene lamp, Binodini pulled the piece of embroidery towards herself and sat down at the far end of the bed. 'Thakurpo, I can't remain here forever, after all, but when I am gone, please keep an eye on my Chokher Bali. See that she is not unhappy.' With these words, Binodini turned her face away as if to control her emotions.

'Bouthan, you must stay,' exclaimed Bihari. 'You have no one of your own to look after; please accept the

burden of protecting this simple girl always, in times
of sorrow or of joy. If you abandon her, I see no other
means of safeguarding her.'

'Thakurpo, you know the ways of the world. How
can I remain here permanently? What will people say?'

'Let them say what they will; you must ignore them.
You are a goddess; you alone can protect this helpless
young girl from the harsh blows inflicted by the world.
Bouthan, I had not understood you at first; please forgive
me. Like narrow minded common people, I, too, had
harboured unjust assumptions about you. At one time I
had even felt that you were jealous of Asha's happiness,
as if...but it is sinful even to utter such thoughts. I have
come to recognize your divine nature since then; the
deep devotion I have developed for you impels me to
confess all my sins to you today.'

Binodini felt every pore of her body infused with a
secret rapture. Although she had been feigning sincerity,
she could not spurn, even in her heart, the gift of Bihari's
devotion. She had never received such an offering from
anybody. For an instant, she felt as if her nature was
indeed pure and elevated; brought on by an undefined
pity for Asha, tears began to flow from her eyes. This
stream of tears, which she did not hide from Bihari,
created in her mind the illusion that she was indeed
divine.

Seeing Binodini weep, Bihari somehow controlled
his own tears, and rising, he went out into Mahendra's

room. Why Mahendra had suddenly declared himself a villain, Bihari could not understand. Entering the room, he found that Mahendra was not there. He was told that Mahendra had gone for an outing. Previously, Mahendra had never left home without a reason. Except in familiar company or in homes that he was accustomed to, Mahendra found it extremely tiring and uncomfortable to venture outside the house. Thoughtfully and with a slow step, Bihari made his way home.

Bringing Asha into her own bedchamber, Binodini drew her to her bosom, and wept, 'My dear Chokher Bali, I am very unfortunate, a bringer of ill-fortune.'

Deeply moved, Asha embraced her and said, in a voice filled with tenderness, 'Why, my friend, why do you say such things?'

Sobbing like a child, Binodini rested her head on Asha's bosom and said, 'I bring bad luck wherever I go. Let me go, my friend. Please release me, let me go back to the wilderness where I belong.'

Taking Binodini by the chin and holding up her face, Asha coaxed, 'Don't say such things, now there's a dear. I can't live without you: what has made you think of abandoning me?'

Unable to find Mahendra, Bihari found a reason to return to Binodini's room, hoping for a clearer explanation of her anxieties about the tension between Mahendra and Asha.

He came to request Binodini to inform Mahendra

that he was invited to a meal at Bihari's home on the following day. 'Binod Bouthan,' he called out as he suddenly stepped into the bright light of the kerosene lamp, stopping short when he saw the two tearful women caught in an embrace. In a flash, it occurred to Asha that Bihari must have said something insulting to her Chokher Bali today, which explained why she had insistently spoken of her own departure. How wrong of Biharibabu! He had an ungracious attitude. Annoyed, Asha left the room. Bihari, too, departed quickly, his heart deeply moved, his respect for Binodini heightened.

That night, Mahendra told Asha, 'Chuni, I shall leave for Kashi by the passenger train tomorrow morning.'

Asha's heart missed a beat. 'Why?' she wanted to know.

'I have not seen Kakima in a long time.'

Hearing this, Asha felt ashamed. She should have thought of this earlier; engrossed in her own joys and sorrows, she had forgotten her loving mashima, while Mahendra had remembered this hermit in exile. She reproached herself for her own hard-heartedness.

'She has gone away, leaving in my charge her only treasured possession,' said Mahendra. 'Without seeing her once, I cannot rest in peace.'

As he spoke, his voice became choked with tears. With silent, affectionate blessings and unexpressed benediction, he stroked Asha's head with his right hand. Asha did not understand the full significance

---

of this sudden burst of affection, but her heart melted and she began to weep. She remembered all the things that Binodini had said to her that same evening in her unaccountable outburst of emotion. Whether these two things were somehow connected, she could not understand. But it seemed to her that this was the signal of some imminent change in her life. Whether it boded well or ill, who could tell?

Frightened, she clung to her husband. Mahendra sensed the force of her unaccountable fear. 'Chuni, the blessings of your pious Mashima are with you,' he assured her. 'Have no fear, none at all. She has renounced the world and gone away for your own good; no evil can ever befall you.'

Resolutely, Asha discarded all her fears. She accepted her husband's blessing like a talisman. In her mind, she repeatedly touched the sacred dust at her Mashima's feet, praying: 'Ma, may your blessings protect my husband always.'

The next day, Mahendra went away without saying goodbye to Binodini. 'Having done wrong himself, does he now make me the target of his anger?' Binodini asked herself. 'How sanctimonious! But such saintliness doesn't last long.'

23

When Annapurna, after her long period of seclusion, saw Mahendra arrive suddenly, she was overwhelmed with joy, but also filled with a sudden fear that perhaps Mahendra had had another confrontation with his mother regarding Asha. She thought he had probably come to her to air his grievances and receive consolation. Since childhood, Mahendra had run to his Kaki whenever there was any kind of trouble or distress. If he was angry, Annapurna would quell his rage; if he felt unhappy, she would advise him to bear it with ease. But after his marriage, his situation became so precarious that she had neither a solution, nor any comfort to offer. When she realized that any intervention on her part would double Mahendra's domestic trauma, she renounced the world. Like the distraught mother who goes away to another room when her sick child cries for water that the physician has forbidden, Annapurna had cast herself into exile. Living in a distant place of pilgrimage, performing the regular rituals of prayer, she had remained largely unmindful of worldly matters of late. Had Mahendra come to reopen her concealed wounds by reviving the subject of all those conflicts?

But Mahendra made no complaint about his mother's attitude towards Asha. Then, Annapurna's fears took a different turn. Previously, Mahendra could not even bear to part from Asha to go to college; why, then, had he travelled to Kashi in search of his kaki? Had Mahendra's attraction towards Asha slackened over time? With some anxiety, she asked Mahendra, 'Tell me, Mahin. By my word, tell me truly, how is Chuni?'

'She's quite well, Kakima.'

'What does she do nowadays, Mahin? Are the two of you as immature as ever, or have you turned your attention to household tasks and domestic matters?'

'No more childishness now. The root of all our troubles, the *Charupath* primer, has vanished and is nowhere to be found. Had you been there, you would have been pleased to see that Chuni is wholeheartedly performing the womanly duties she had neglected on account of her studies.'

'Mahin, what does Bihari do these days?'

'He's doing everything but his own work. His property is in the hands of attorneys and revenue-collectors; I don't know if they have an eye on the property. That has always been Bihari's situation.

Others mind his own affairs, while he attends to other people's business.'

'Won't he marry, Mahin?'

'Why, I see no eagerness on his part,' laughed Mahendra.

Annapurna felt a deep, hidden pain in her heart. She knew for certain that Bihari had been eager to marry after seeing her bonjhi, only to find his desire suddenly and unjustly crushed. 'Kakima, you must never urge me again to get married,' Bihari had said. Those words of reproach still rang in Annapurna's ears. Unable to offer him any consolation, she had left her beloved, devoted Bihari in a heartbroken state. Dismayed and fearful, Annapurna began to wonder, 'Is Bihari still in love with Asha?'

At times flippantly, at times seriously, Mahendra told her all the news about the latest developments in their household, but he made no mention of Binodini.

College being in session, Mahendra ought not to have remained in Kashi for many days. But staying here with Annapurna, Mahendra was enjoying a pleasure akin to that of convalescing in a healthy environment after a difficult illness. Days passed by, but he stayed on. The internal conflict that had threatened his mind disappeared very quickly. As he spent a few days in the constant presence of the devout and affectionate Annapurna, everyday duties began to seem so easy and enjoyable, that his earlier anxieties now struck

him as ridiculous. Binodini seemed to mean nothing
to him anymore. In fact, Mahendra could not even
remember her face very clearly. Ultimately, he declared
to himself: 'I can't think of anyone, anywhere, who
could dislodge Asha ever so slightly from her place in
my heart.''Kakima, I have been missing college,' he told
Annapurna. 'I must take my leave now. Although you
have renounced your worldly ties, please permit me to
visit you occasionally and touch the dust at your feet.'

Tears welled up in Asha's eyes when Mahendra
returned, carrying affectionate gifts from her mashi—a
sindoor container and a white stone jar with inlay
work. Recalling mashima's loving patience and the
various wrongs inflicted on her by the newly-weds and
Rajalakshmi, Asha's heart was wrenched. She informed
her husband, 'I have a great desire to visit Mashima once,
to obtain her forgiveness and pay her my respects. Can
it not be arranged in some way?'

Mahendra understood Asha's anguish, and even
agreed to her visiting her Mashima at Kashi for a few
days. But he was hesitant to miss college again in order
to escort Asha there.

'Jethaima, my paternal aunt, will be travelling
to Kashi shortly. Perhaps I could accompany her?'
suggested Asha.

'Ma, my wife wants to go and see Kakima in Kashi,'
Mahendra told Rajalakshmi.

'If your wife wishes it, then go she must,' said

Rajalakshmi sarcastically. 'Go, take her there.'

It displeased Rajalakshmi that Mahendra had again started visiting Annapurna. When Asha's visit was proposed, she was secretly even more annoyed.

Mahendra said, 'I must attend college, I cannot escort her there. She will go with her Jyathamoshai—her father's elder brother.'

'That is a good idea,' replied Rajalakshmi. 'Jyathamoshai belongs to an affluent family; he never comes anywhere near poor folk like us. It would be a matter of pride for her to travel with him.'

His mother's sarcastic remarks hardened Mahendra's heart into obstinacy. He left without offering any reply, determined to send Asha to Kashi.

When Bihari came to meet Rajalakshmi, she appealed to him: 'O Bihari, have you heard? Our Bouma wants to go to Kashi, it seems.'

'What's this, Ma, must Mahinda miss college again to visit Kashi?'

'No, no, why should Mahin go? How would that prove her queenliness? Mahin will remain here, and Bou will travel to Kashi with his lordship, her jyatha. We're all aspiring to be lords and ladies now.'

Bihari was inwardly agitated, but not at the thought of modern versions of lordliness. 'What is the matter?' he wondered. 'When Mahendra went to Kashi, Asha remained here; now, when Mahendra has returned, Asha wants to leave for Kashi. Something serious has happened between the two of them. How long can matters continue like this? As friends, can't we find some way to remedy the situation? Must we stand and watch from a distance?'

Extremely upset at his mother's behaviour, Mahendra was sulking in his bedchamber. In the adjoining room, Asha was trying to persuade Binodini, who had not met Mahendra since his return, to visit his room.

At this moment, Bihari came to Mahendra and asked, 'Has Asha Bouthan's visit to Kashi been arranged?'

'Why shouldn't it? What's to stop her?'

'Who said anything about stopping her? But how did the idea suddenly occur to the two of you?'

'The desire to visit one's mashi, a strong concern for relatives who are far away in exile—such feelings are not unknown to human nature.'

'Are you going with her?'

As soon as he heard the question, Mahendra thought, 'Bihari has come to argue that it is not appropriate for her to travel with her jyatha.' Lest his rage boil over if he tried to say too much, he answered curtly, 'No.'

Bihari knew Mahendra, and was not unaware of his growing fury. He also knew that, once possessed of a stubborn idea, Mahendra's resolve could not be shaken. Hence, he refrained from suggesting that Mahendra, too, should go on the trip. He thought to himself: 'If poor Asha is leaving with a heavy heart, it would console her to have Binodini for company.' So, he gently said,

'Couldn't Binod Bouthan accompany her?'

'Bihari, speak your mind clearly,' roared Mahendra. 'I see no reason for you to dissemble with me. I know you secretly suspect me of being in love with Binodini. That is a lie. I don't love her. There is no need for you to act as my bodyguard in order to protect me. Now, it is time for you to defend yourself. If you only had simple friendship in mind, you would have revealed your thoughts to me long ago and then removed yourself from the inner quarters of your friend's house. I say this to your face: you have fallen in love with Asha.'

Pale and speechless, Bihari got up from the chowki and rushed towards Mahendra, like an injured man blindly hitting out at the assailant who has wounded him in a tender spot. He stopped suddenly and, with great difficulty, said, 'May God forgive you! I shall take my leave.' With these words, he lurched out of the room.

From the next room, Binodini ran up to him and said, 'Bihari Thakurpo!'

Leaning against the wall and trying to summon up a small smile, Bihari asked, 'What is it, Binod Bouthan?'

'Thakurpo, I shall accompany Chokher Bali to Kashi.'

'No, no, Bouthan, that would not do, it simply would not do. I beg you, please do nothing at my bidding. I don't belong here; I have no wish to interfere in these matters, for no good would come of it. You are a devi, a goddess; do whatever you think is best. I shall take your leave.'

With these words, Bihari folded his hands in a respectful gesture of farewell, and left.

'I am no devi, Thakurpo,' Binodini called after him. 'Please hear me out before you leave. If you go away, it will not benefit anybody. Don't blame me for anything that happens after this.'

Bihari went away. Mahendra sat, stupefied. Darting at him a sharp sidelong glance like a flash of lightning, Binodini went into the adjoining room, where Asha was cringing in acute shame and embarrassment. Hearing Mahendra declare that Bihari was in love with her, she hung her head, unable to raise her face. But Binodini no longer felt any pity for her. If Asha had looked up at that moment, she would have felt frightened. It was as if Binodini was out to destroy the whole world.

Falsehood indeed! So, nobody loved Binodini! Everybody loved this shy little butter-doll, this delicate darling!

Ever since he had declared himself a villain, Mahendra, once his agitation subsided, had felt awkward about his sudden self-revelation to Bihari. He felt as if all his innermost thoughts had been exposed. He did not love Binodini, yet Bihari was certain that he did—this annoyed him greatly. Whenever they had met after that, Mahendra felt that Bihari was trying to ferret out some private secret. Today, at the slightest provocation, all the annoyance accumulated in Mahendra's mind had burst into the open.

But the way Binodini came anxiously rushing out of the next room, the anguished tones in which she tried to persuade Bihari to stay, her readiness to accompany Asha to Kashi at Bihari's bidding—Mahendra had never imagined all this possible. Witnessing this scene, he was overwhelmed, crushed as if by a powerful blow. He had declared that he did not love Binodini; but what he heard, and what he saw, left him no peace of mind, tormenting him in a myriad different ways. And constantly, with vain regret, he thought, 'Binodini heard me say that I do not love her.'

24

Mahendra began to fret. 'I said, "That's a lie, I don't love Binodini." But I said it very harshly. Even if it is untrue to say that I love her, to say that I don't would be too harsh. There is no woman who would not be hurt by such a statement. Where and when will I find the opportunity to deny it? I can't quite say that I love her, but that I don't love her is something I must communicate in a subtle, gentle way. It would be wrong to let such a cruel yet false impression persist in Binodini's mind.'

So saying, Mahendra extracted her three letters from his box, and read them again. He said to himself, 'There is no doubt that Binodini loves me. Then why did she fuss over Bihari like that, yesterday? That was only for my benefit. When I had stated clearly that I did not love her, what else could she do but find an opportunity to deny her love to me? After being rejected by me in this way, she might even fall in love with Bihari.'

Mahendra's agitation grew to such proportions that he was afraid at his own restlessness. So what if Binodini had heard that Mahendra did not love her—what was the harm in that? So what if, at his words, a reproachful Binodini had tried to wrest her heart away from him— what harm in that, either? Like the chain that tugs at the boat's anchor during a storm, Mahendra, in his anguish, seemed to cling to Asha with excessive desperation.

At night, he held Asha's face against his chest and said, 'Chuni, tell me truly, how much do you love me?'

'What kind of question is that?' wondered Asha. 'Has his terribly shameful accusation of Bihari created a shadow of suspicion on him?' Cringing with embarrassment, she pleaded, 'For shame, why do you ask this question today? I implore you, please tell me frankly, when and where have you found anything lacking in my love?'

Tormenting Asha to extract her sweetness, Mahendra demanded: 'Then why do you want to go to Kashi?'

'I don't want to go to Kashi, I shall not go anywhere.'

'But you did want to go.'

'You know why I wanted to go there,' Asha reminded him. She was extremely hurt.

'You would probably have been happier at your Mashi's place, away from me.'

'Never. I did not want to go there in search of happiness.'

'I tell you truly, Chuni, you could have been far happier if you had married someone else.'

Asha instantly moved away, and lay stiffly with her face hidden in the pillow; a moment later, she burst into uncontrollable sobs. Mahendra tried to draw her close in order to console her, but Asha would not let go of the pillow. His devoted wife's petulant reaction filled Mahendra with joy, pride and self-contempt.

The sudden direct articulation of all that had hitherto remained concealed, only hinted at, created a general confusion in everyone's mind. Binodini began to wonder why Bihari had made no attempt to counter such an open accusation. Even if he had attempted a false denial, she would have been somewhat pleased. Serve him right! Bihari deserved the blow that Mahendra had inflicted on him. Why should a noble man like Bihari fall in love with Asha? It was almost as if Binodini felt relieved that the blow had driven Bihari away.

But Bihari's pale, bloodless countenance, the face of one struck by a lethal arrow, seemed to follow Binodini everywhere as she went about her work. The nurturing feminine spirit in Binodini began to weep at the image of Bihari's anguished visage. Like the mother who paces up and down, rocking the sick child she clasps to her breast, Binodini began to dandle that agonized image in her heart. In her heart was born an impatient urge to see the image healed, to see that countenance enlivened again by the renewed flow of blood and the blossoming of a smile.

After remaining distracted and absent-minded in the midst of all her work for a few days, Binodini could bear it no more. She wrote a letter of consolation, in which she said:

Thakurpo, ever since I saw your unhappy face the other day, I have been praying with all my heart and soul that you should recover, and be as you were before. When will I see that easy smile again? When can I hear those words of wisdom again? Please write to me to let me know how you are.
  Your Binod Bouthan.

Binodini had the doorman deliver the letter to Bihari's address.

Bihari had not imagined in his wildest dreams that Mahendra could accuse him so rudely, and in such a contemptible way, of being in love with Asha. He himself had never allowed such a thought to lodge so clearly in his mind. At first, he was thunderstruck; then, struggling with anger and disgust, he fumed, 'This is unjust, inappropriate and baseless.'

But once the idea had been articulated, it could not be stifled completely. The few seeds of truth it contained soon took root and began to sprout. Again and again, he began to remember the evening when he had visited the house with the fragrant garden, to see his prospective bride. Thinking that she was to be his, he had observed

148

the shy young girl's charming face with a melting, tender heart. An unknown feeling clutched at his heart, and an acute agony wrung him from within, rising up to his throat. The long night was spent lying on the terrace, pacing up and down the path before his house, and what had remained suppressed in Bihari's mind now revealed itself completely. What had been restrained was now set free; what had remained unproven even to him, grew larger than life at Mahendra's words, engulfing Bihari's whole self, inside and out.

Now he understood himself to be guilty. He told himself, 'It doesn't behoove me to be angry; I must beg Mahendra's forgiveness and take my leave. That day, I had departed as if Mahendra was the offender, and I the judge; now, I shall go to him and acknowledge that I was wrong.'

Bihari was under the impression that Asha had left for Kashi. One evening, he slowly walked up to Mahendra's door. Seeing Sadhucharan, Rajalakshmi's distantly related uncle, he asked, 'Sadhuda, I have not been able to visit for a few days; I hope all is well here?' Sadhucharan assured him that everyone was well.

'When did Bouthan leave for Kashi?' asked Bihari.

'She did not go,' Sadhucharan informed him. 'She will not be going to Kashi.'

Hearing this, Bihari's felt an irresistible urge to go to the private quarters of the house. It maddened him to know that he could no longer joyfully climb the familiar staircase to the inner quarters like a member of the family, and engage in light hearted conversation with everyone there. Just once more, for the very last time, to go there again, to talk to Rajalakshmi like a son of the family, and to address the veiled Asha as Bouthan, to exchange a few pleasantries with her—became his supreme desire.

'Come inside, brother, why stand outside in the dark?' invited Sadhucharan.

Bihari took a few quick steps towards the interior of the house, then turned around and told Sadhu, 'I must go, I have some work.' He rushed away. That very night, Bihari travelled west.

The doorman, having failed to find Bihari, returned with Binodini's letter in his hand. Mahendra was strolling in the small garden in front of the porch. 'Whose letter is that?' he asked. The doorman told him all. Mahendra took the letter from him.

At first, he thought of returning the letter to Binodini: he would look upon the guilty Binodini's embarrassed face just once, without saying a word. Mahendra had no doubt that the contents of the letter would cause awkwardness for Binodini. He remembered a previous occasion when another letter had been dispatched, addressed to Bihari. Mahendra could not rest content, until he had acquainted himself with the contents of the letter. He convinced himself that Binodini was under his guardianship, and that he was responsible for her welfare. Hence, it was his duty to open and read such suspicious letters. He could not let Binodini take the wrong path.

Opening the short letter, Mahendra read it. Written in simple language, it clearly expressed the spontaneous feelings of the writer. Reading the letter over and over again and pondering over it, Mahendra could not determine the direction of Binodini's thoughts. He kept worrying, 'Because I insulted her by saying that I do not love her, in a fit of pique, Binodini is trying to divert her mind elsewhere. In anger, she has given up all hope of me.'

This thought made it impossible for Mahendra to sustain his patience. He could not rest in peace, considering the possibility that a moment's folly would cause him to lose all control over Binodini, who had been willing to surrender herself to him. Mahendra thought, 'It would be beneficial for Binodini to be secretly in love with me, for that would keep her from straying. I know my own mind; I would never do her harm. She can safely love me. I love Asha; Binodini has nothing to fear from me. But if she is attracted to anyone else, who knows what disaster might befall her.' Mahendra decided that, without surrendering himself, he had to find an opportunity to capture Binodini's heart once again.

As soon as he entered the inner quarters, Mahendra saw Binodini standing in the pathway as if awaiting someone anxiously. Instantly, jealousy flared in his mind. 'You are standing there in vain,' he told her, 'you will not get to see him. This letter of yours has come back.' He flung the letter at her.

'But why is it open?'

Mahendra went away without answering her question. Thinking that Bihari had opened and read the letter, and returned it unanswered, Binodini felt a throbbing in all the veins in her body. She sent for the doorman who had carried the letter for her; he was away on some other errand, and could not be found. Like the burning drops of oil that drip from the wick of the prayer lamp, the agony in Binodini' s heart began to flow in the form of teardrops from her glowing eyes as she lay in her closed bedchamber. Tearing her own letter to shreds brought her no consolation. Why was there no way of completely erasing, completely denying, both from the past and the present, those few lines etched in ink? An angry bee will sting any person that encounters it; similarly, Binodini, in her anger, was ready to set fire to the whole world around her. Were all her desires to be met with rebuffs? Would she be denied success in all she ever tried to accomplish? If happiness were denied her, then the supreme accomplishment of her frustrated life would lie in defeating and reducing to dust the people who obstructed all her happiness, who had diverted her from success and deprived her of all possible comfort.

25

That day, at the touch of the first spring breeze in the month of Phalgun, Asha had promptly occupied the mat spread out on the terrace in the early evening. In the dim light, she was reading with great attention a story serialized in a monthly periodical. Her heart was quaking in anxiety, for the hero of the narrative, on his way home for the Durga Puja vacation after a year-long absence, had fallen into the clutches of dacoits; meanwhile, at that very moment, the unfortunate heroine had awakened in tears from a nightmare. Asha could not hold back her tears. She was a very broad-minded critic of Bangla stories. Whatever she read struck her as wonderful. 'My dear Chokher Bali, I insist that you read this story,' she would say to Binodini. 'How beautiful it is! I couldn't stop my tears after reading it.' Critically assessing the story, Binodini would dampen Asha's effusive enthusiasm.

Just as Asha closed the magazine, having decided that she would make Mahendra read today's story, he arrived on the scene. At the sight of Mahendra's face, Asha grew agitated.

'Alone on the terrace, which fortunate man are you thinking of?' asked Mahendra with forced gaiety.

Utterly forgetting the hero and heroine of the story, Asha inquired, 'Are you not well today?'

'I am in good health.'

'Then there's something on your mind. Please tell me what it is.'

Taking a paan from the container in Asha's hand, Mahendra replied, 'I was thinking, it's been so long since your poor Mashima got to see you. If you were to suddenly arrive at her doorstep, how happy she would be!'

Speechless, Asha gazed at Mahendra's face. She could not understand why he would revive this idea.

Seeing that Asha was silent, Mahendra asked, 'Don't you feel like going there?' This was a difficult question to answer. She felt a desire to visit her mashi, yet was unwilling to leave Mahendra behind. 'During the college vacations, when you are free to go, I shall accompany you,' she replied.

'There is no possibility of my going even during the vacations; I must prepare for my examinations.'

'Then let it be, I may as well not go now.'

'But why let it be? You had wanted to go, so why not proceed?'

154

'No, I have no wish to go.'

'Just the other day, you were so keen, and now you suddenly have no wish to go!'

At this, Asha sat silently with lowered eyes. Mahendra was secretly impatient for an opportunity to make amends to Binodini. Asha's silence made him unaccountably angry. 'Do you harbour some secret suspicions about me?' he demanded. 'Is that why you want to keep a constant watchful eye on me?'

Asha's natural gentleness, modesty and patience suddenly seemed utterly unbearable to Mahendra. He told himself, 'If she wishes to visit her mashi, then she should just say, I must go, send me there by any means possible; instead, to say yes one moment, no the other, and to sometimes remain silent—what kind of behaviour is this!'

Seeing this sudden aggressiveness in Mahendra, Asha was surprised and frightened. Try as she might, she could not think of a suitable reply. Why Mahendra should be sometimes so loving and sometimes so cruel, she could not understand at all. The more inscrutable Mahendra appeared to her, the more Asha's quaking heart seemed to cling to him in fear and in love.

To suggest that Asha secretly suspected Mahendra and wished to keep him under constant vigil! Was this bitter sarcasm, or heartless suspicion? Was she to contradict him by swearing a solemn oath by her honour, or was this something to be laughed off lightly?

Impatient with Asha's stunned silence, Mahendra swiftly arose and left the spot. Forgotten was the hero of that story in the monthly periodical, forgotten the story's heroine. The glow of sunset faded into the darkness, the brief spring breeze of early evening gave way to the cold winter wind; but there Asha remained, lying prone on that same floor mat.

Late at night, entering her bedchamber, Asha saw that Mahendra had gone to sleep without calling her to him. Mahendra was contemptuous of her indifference towards her loving mashi, she concluded. Climbing onto the bed, Asha embraced Mahendra's feet and rested her head on them. Full of pity and consternation, Mahendra tried to draw her close. But Asha would not rise from her position. 'If I have committed any offence, please forgive me,' she begged.

Moved by compassion, Mahendra assured her, 'Chuni, you have committed no offence. I am an utter villain, that is why I have wronged you so unjustly.'

Drenching Mahendra's feet as if to consecrate them, Asha's tears began to flow. Sitting up, Mahendra forced her to rise, and holding her in his arms, lay her down beside him. When Asha's tears had abated, she said, 'Of course I long to visit my mashi. But I don't feel like leaving you behind. That is why I was reluctant to go; please don't be angry with me on that account.'

Slowly wiping the tears of anguish from Asha's cheek, Mahendra asked, 'Is this a matter for anger, Chuni?

Would I be angry because you don't feel like leaving me? There is no need for you to go anywhere.'

'No, I shall go to Kashi.'

'Why?'

'Now that you have accused me of refusing to go because I doubt you, I must go, even if it is only for a few days.'

'Must you do penance for some offence on my part?'

'That, I don't know. But I, too, must have done some wrong, or else such impossible ideas would never have arisen. Why must I have to listen to accusations about things that have never occurred to me, even in my dreams?'

'That is because the extent of my villainy is unknown to you even in your dreams.'

Agitated, Asha exclaimed, 'Again! Don't raise that subject again. But this time, I must go to Kashi.'

'Very well, you may go, but what if I go astray in your absence?' smiled Mahendra.

'There is no need for you to frighten me. Does it look as if I'm restless with suspicion?'

'But you should worry. If you are careless enough to let such a husband go astray, who would you blame afterwards?'

'I shall not blame you, don't worry.'

'Would you take the blame, then?'

'A thousand times, yes.'

'Very well, I shall go to your Jyathamoshai tomorrow

to settle matters.' With these words, Mahendra turned over on his side. 'It's very late.'

After a while, he turned back towards Asha and said, 'Chuni, it's best avoided; you had better not go, after all.'

Asha pleaded, 'Why do you forbid me, again? If I don't go now, I shall be forced forever to remember your rebuke. Send me for just a few days.'

'All right,' consented Mahendra. Then he turned over on his side, again.

The day before she left for Kashi, Asha embraced Binodini. 'My friend Bali, there's one thing you must solemnly promise me,' she said.

Pinching Asha's cheek, Binodini asked, 'What is it, my friend? Would I ever turn down a request from you?'

'Who knows, my friend, you have grown so strange nowadays. You seem so utterly reluctant to appear before my husband.'

'As if you don't know the reason for my reluctance, my friend. Didn't you hear, with your own ears, the words that Mahendrababu spoke to Biharibabu? Tell me, Bali, now that all these matters have arisen, would it be appropriate for me to appear before your husband?'

Asha was aware that it was not quite appropriate. How awkward such matters could be, she herself had recently understood. Still, she insisted, 'Such questions often arise, but if you can't put up with them, then what's love worth, my friend? You must forget the things that were said.'

'Very well, my friend, I shall forget them.'

'I'm off to Kashi tomorrow, but you must take special care to ensure that my husband suffers no inconvenience. It won't do for you to keep evading him as you have been doing of late.'

Binodini remained silent. Grasping her hand, Asha said, 'Upon my word, my friend Bali, you must promise me this one thing.'

'Very well,' promised Binodini.

26

As the moon declines in one direction, the sun rises in another. Asha went away, but Mahendra was still not fortunate enough to sight Binodini. He would wander about, sometimes appearing in his mother's chamber at odd hours, but Binodini continued to elude him, avoiding capture.

Seeing such a vacuum in Mahendra's life, Rajalakshmi thought, 'After his wife's departure, nothing in this house appeals to Mahin anymore.' It pierced her heart to think that, in comparison with Mahendra's wife, she herself had become utterly redundant to his joys and sorrows; but still, she was pained at seeing Mahendra in such a wretched, dejected state. She sent for Binodini. 'Ever since that bout of influenza, I have developed an asthma-like affliction,' she told her. 'I can't climb the stairs frequently, as I used to before. My child, you must personally supervise Mahendra's meals. It is his lifelong habit; Mahin can't manage unless someone looks after him. Don't you see how strange he has become ever since his wife's departure? I wonder, too, at Bou's behaviour—how could she go away like this?'

Slightly pursing her lips, Binodini started picking at the bed sheet 'What is it, Bahu, what are you thinking?' asked Rajalakshmi. 'There is nothing to worry about. Let people say what they will, you are no stranger to our family.'

'I'd rather not, Ma.'

'Very well, then, you had rather not. Let me see, I'll do what I can on my own.' She immediately made as if to ascend to the third floor to set Mahendra's room in order.

Flustered, Binodini said, 'You are physically infirm; please don't go. I'll go instead. Forgive me, Pishima, I shall do as you command.'

Rajalakshmi did not take public opinion seriously. Since her husband's death, nobody in the world, or in society, meant anything to her, except Mahendra. She was annoyed at Binodini's suggestion that some social stigma might be attached to Mahendra. She had known Mahendra all his life; where would one find such a good boy? If people dared cast aspersions on a person such as Mahin, may their tongues fall off! When it came to acting upon her own judgment and her own preferences, Rajalakshmi stubbornly ignored what all the people in the world might say.

When Mahendra returned from college, he was amazed to see his own bedchamber. As soon as he opened the door, he found the room redolent of sandalwood and incense. The mosquito net was festooned with pink silk tassels. A dazzling white bedspread covered the divan, and on it, in place of the old pillows used previously, were square English-style cushions, embroidered in silk and wool. The intricate designs were the product of Binodini's labour; she had spent days embroidering them. Asha would ask her, 'Who are these items meant for, my friend?' 'For my final bed, the cremation pyre,' Binodini would laugh. 'Death is my only beloved.'

Mahendra's framed photograph on the wall was embellished with expertly tied bows of coloured ribbon on all its corners. Below the picture, at the base of the wall, were bunches of flowers arranged in two vases placed on either side of a teapoy, as if Mahendra's image had received the prayer offerings of some unknown devotee. The room looked altogether different. The bed had been moved slightly from its place. The room had been divided in two; lengths of fabric had been hung on two clotheshorses placed before the bed to create a secluded space, separating the night-time bed from the divan on the floor. Within the glass almira in which Asha's favourite bric-a-brac and china dolls had been displayed, pleated red cotton was arranged; the contents of the cupboard were now invisible. The new décor, wrought by a different hand, had completely obscured all traces of the past history of the room.

Mahendra, reclining in fatigue on the white-covered divan, discerned a mild fragrance as soon as he placed his head on the new cushions; the cotton stuffing of the cushions was scented with the pollen of the nagkeshar flower, and some attar.

Mahendra's eyelids grew heavy, and he began to feel as if he could smell the fragrance of the delicate, jasmine-like fingers that had produced the artwork on the cushions with such an expert touch.

At this moment, the maidservant brought a silver platter of fruits and sweetmeats, and iced pineapple juice in a glass tumbler. All this was somewhat different from the previous routine, and presented with great care and neatness. The pervasive touch of novelty in all he tasted, smelt or saw, overwhelmed Mahendra's senses.

After he had eaten with relish, Binodini slowly entered the room, carrying paan and spices in a silver bata . 'Forgive me, Thakurpo, for I have not been able to attend to your meals in person these last few days,' she smiled. 'Whatever else you do, give me your solemn promise that you will not inform my Chokher Bali of the neglect that you have suffered. I am doing my best, but I can't help it, my friend, all the work of the household is upon my shoulders.'

Binodini pushed the casket of paan towards Mahendra. Even the paan had the special new fragrance of keyakhoyer, catechu with a floral flavour.

'All the better if there are occasional lapses of this sort,' observed Mahendra.

'Why is that, I'd like to know?'

'Afterwards, by delivering a few jibes, one can extract compensation with interest.'

'How much interest has accumulated, Mister Usurer?'

'You were not present at mealtime; now, having made up for your absence by attending upon me after lunch, you still owe me something more.'

'What a tough reckoner!' laughed Binodini. 'Once one has fallen into your clutches, there can be no rescue.'

'Whatever the reckoning, have I been able to extract anything from you?'

'What do I possess that you can extract from me? Yet you hold me captive.' As she spoke, she suddenly turned jest into seriousness, letting out a small sigh.

Mahendra, too, became a little grave. 'My friend Bali, is this a prison house, then?' he asked.

At this moment, the bearer brought in the lamp as usual, placed it on the teapoy, and left.

Shielding her eyes with her hand from the sudden glare of light, Binodini said with lowered gaze, 'How would I know, my friend! Who can match you in argument? Let me go now, I have work to do.'

Mahendra suddenly grasped her hand. 'Now that you have acknowledged your own bondage, where would you go?' he said.

'For shame, let me go; why confine a person who has nowhere to escape?' Snatching her hand away, Binodini left.

Mahendra remained on the bed, reclining on the scented pillow, the blood pounding in his chest. The hushed evening, the secluded room, the fresh spring breeze, the anticipation of Binodini's near-surrender— maddened by all this, he felt he would soon lose his grip on himself. He quickly turned off the light and secured the entrance to his room, then fastened the glass paned door, and, even before it was time to retire, lay down in his bed.

But this was not his old, familiar bed. With the addition of four or five light mattresses, the bed felt much softer than before. Again, a fragrance—whether it was aguru, the scented wood, or cuscus, the aromatic pearl-millet root, he couldn't tell for sure. Mahendra tossed and turned, as if in search of some trace of the past that he could cling to. But nothing came to hand.

At nine o'clock, there was a knock on the closed door. From outside the room, Binodini called, 'Thakurpo, here is your dinner, please open the door.'

Starting up, Mahendra at once reached for the bolt on the glass door to open it. But he refrained. Flinging himself to the ground, he cried, 'No, no, I am not hungry, I shall not eat.'

From outside the door came an anxious query: 'You

are not ill, are you? Shall I fetch some water? Is there anything you need?'

'I want nothing at all. There is no need for anything.'

'I insist, you must not pretend with me. If you are not ill, please open the door, just once.'

'No, I shan't open the door,' declared Mahendra. 'Never! Please go away.' Mahendra rose quickly to his feet and climbed into bed once again. He lay down, and in the dark, he began to grope within the empty bed and inside his restless mind for memories of the absent Asha.

When sleep refused to come, Mahendra turned on the lamp and sat down with pen and ink to write a letter to Asha: *Asha, don't leave me alone much longer. You are Lakshmi, my goddess of well-being and prosperity; in your absence, all my instincts break loose, dragging me I know not where. Where is the light for me to see my way? That light is to be found in the gaze of your trusting, tender, loving eyes. Come soon, my benefactor, my lodestar, my only one. Keep me steadfast, protect me, make me whole. Save me from the great sin of doing you the slightest wrong, the horror of forgetting you for a single moment.*

Thus, to force his mind to concentrate on Asha, Mahendra stayed up late, writing. In the distance, the clock towers of several churches rang out the chimes for three o'clock. On the streets of Kolkata, the sound of carriages had almost ceased; even the song of a prostitute, rendered in the ragini bihag and audible from the far end of the neighbourhood, had been drowned by an atmosphere of all-encompassing peace and somnolence. Fixing his mind on the memory of Asha, and expressing his mental agitation in diverse ways in his long letter, Mahendra felt greatly consoled, and he fell asleep as soon as he lay down on the bed.

When Mahendra awakened, it was late in the day and sunlight was pouring into the room. He sat up quickly; all the events of the previous night seemed to have faded in his mind. Getting off the bed, he saw, placed under the inkpot on the teapoy, the letter that he had written to Asha the previous night. Reading the letter again, he thought, 'What have I done! It reads like a novel. Thank goodness I did not dispatch it! If Asha had read it, what would she have thought? She wouldn't even have understood half the things I've said.' Mahendra was embarrassed at the excessive anguish he had suffered the previous night over a trifling reason; he tore the letter to shreds. In simple language, he wrote a brief missive to Asha: *How much longer will you stay away? If your Jyathamoshai has no plans of returning soon, let me know. I shall fetch you myself. I don't like being alone here.*

27

When Asha arrived in Kashi a few days after Mahendra's departure from there, Annapurna was alarmed. She began to ask Asha all sorts of questions: 'Tell, me, Chuni, do you truly feel that there is no woman in the world more talented than this Chokher Bali of yours?'

'Truly, Mashi, I am not exaggerating. She is as intelligent as she is beautiful, and equally adept at housework.'

'She is your friend and companion; of course you would regard her as blessed with every talent. But what do other members of your household say about her, I wonder?'

'Ma is all praise for her. Chokher Bali has only to speak of returning to her native place for Ma to grow agitated. Nobody can match her capacity for devoted service. Even when our servants and housemaids fall ill, she tends to them like a sister, or a mother.'

'What does Mahendra think of her?'

'You know him, Mashi, he simply does not like anyone except for close members of the family. Everyone loves my Bali, but she has not been able to get along with him, until now.'

'How is that?'

'Even if I make a great effort to bring them together, they barely speak to each other. You know what a cloistered life he likes to lead; people mistake it for arrogance, but that is not so, Mashi, he can't tolerate any but two or three people in his life.'

Having uttered the last statement, Asha was suddenly embarrassed; her cheeks flushed red. Pleased, Annapurna smiled to herself. 'That is so indeed,' she agreed. 'When he came here the other day, Mahin didn't even mention your Bali to me.'

'That is the trouble with him,' complained Asha. 'If he doesn't love someone, he acts as if they don't exist. He behaves as if he has never seen her, never made her acquaintance.'

'But then, if he loves someone, he acts as if she is the only one he has ever seen or known, all his life,' pointed out Annapurna, with a gentle smile. 'He has this other tendency, too. What do you say, Chuni?'

Without replying, Asha lowered her gaze and smiled. Annapurna asked, 'Chuni, tell me, what news of Bihari? Will he never marry?'

Instantly, Asha's countenance grew grave; she could not think of a suitable reply. Alarmed at Asha's silence, Annapurna exclaimed, 'Tell me the truth, Chuni: he has not fallen ill, has he?'

In this childless woman's affections, Bihari reigned supreme, an image of her ideal son. Ever since she had chosen exile, she was plagued daily by the knowledge that before leaving home, she had not seen Bihari settled in domestic life. She had attained a measure of fulfilment in all other areas of her circumscribed life; only the memory of Bihari's unmarried, uncared-for condition prevented her from detaching herself completely from worldly matters.

'Mashi, don't ask me about Bihari Thakurpo,' begged Asha.

'But why?' asked Annapurna in surprise.

'That I can't tell you.' With these words, Asha rose and left the room.

Sitting in silence, Annapurna began to think, 'Could a fine boy like Bihari have changed so much in such a short time that Chuni would leave the room at the mention of his name? This is a game of destiny. Why was Chuni proposed as a match for him, and why, then, did Mahendra snatch Chuni away from him?'

After many days, Annapurna's eyes again overflowed with tears. She told herself, 'Ah, if my poor Bihari has done something unworthy of him, then he must have acted under great provocation; such behaviour could not have come easily to him.' The thought of Bihari's pain tormented her.

In the evening, when Annapurna was at her prayers, a carriage came and stopped at her door, and the coachman began banging on the closed door, shouting to those within. From inside the prayer room, Annapurna called out, 'Oh dear, I had completely forgotten. Kunja's mother-in-law and her two bonjhis are supposed to arrive from Allahabad today. It must be them. Chuni, just take the lamp and open the door.'

Carrying the lantern, Asha opened the door to find Bihari standing there. Bihari exclaimed, 'What is this, Bouthan, I was told you would not be travelling to Kashi after all!'

The lantern fell from Asha's hand. As if she had seen a ghost, she ran breathlessly up to the first floor and cried out in an anguished voice, 'Mashima, I fall at your feet and beg of you, please ask him to leave immediately.'

Starting up from the prayer mat, Annapurna asked, 'Ask whom, Chuni? Who is it?'

'Bihari Thakurpo has followed me here as well.' With these words, she went into the adjoining room and shut the door.

From downstairs, Bihari heard all that was said. He prepared to rush away immediately, but when Annapurna abandoned her prayers and came downstairs, she found that Bihari, drained of all his strength, had collapsed to a sitting position on the ground, near the door.

Annapurna was not carrying a light. In the dark, she could not see Bihari's expression, nor could he see hers.

'Bihari!' cried Annapurna.

Alas, where was the honeyed, affectionate tone that she had always used in the past! Her voice resonated with the thunder of harsh condemnation. Mother Annapurna, against whom did you raise your scimitar! Tonight, the unfortunate Bihari had come to you in the darkness to lay his head at your sacred feet, seeking your benediction.

Bihari felt a shock run through his body, as if he had been struck by lightning. 'Kakima, no more, please, don't say another word. I take your leave.'

With these words, Bihari bowed and touched his forehead to the ground; he did not even touch Annapurna's feet. Like a mother who ritually drowns her offspring in the waters of the Gangasagar, Annapurna silently surrendered Bihari to the darkness of the night; she did not even call him back. In an instant, the carriage, with Bihari in it, had vanished.

The same night, Asha wrote to Mahendra: *Bihari Thakurpo arrived here suddenly this evening. It is uncertain when Jyathamoshai and the others will return to Kolkata; please come soon to take me away from here.*

28

After the sleeplessness and emotional turbulence of that night, Mahendra's mind and body felt a certain fatigue the next morning. It was mid-Phalgun, the beginning of hot weather. On other days, Mahendra would sit with his books at a table in the corner of his bedchamber. Today, he reclined on the cushions of the divan. The day grew long, but he did not have a bath. A hawker went down the road, calling out his wares. There was the ceaseless sound of office carriages on the road. The neighbours were building a new house; as they beat the roof to flatten it, the women labourers began singing together in a monotonous rhythm. In the slightly warm southerly breeze, Mahendra's troubled nerves had relaxed; on this languid, drifting morning in spring, no difficult decision, challenging effort or mental conflict seemed appropriate.

'Thakurpo, what's the matter with you today? Will

you not bathe? Your food is ready. What is this, my friend, why are you lying down? Are you ill? Do you have a headache?' With these words, Binodini came up to Mahendra and touched his forehead.

His eyes half-shut, Mahendra said indistinctly, 'I don't feel too well today; I shall not have a bath.'

'If you won't bathe, at least have something to eat.' Binodini coaxed Mahendra to go up to the dining area, and with anxious care, she persuaded him to eat.

After his meal, Mahendra again came to lie down on the divan; Binodini sat by his head, and gently massaged his forehead. Opening his eyes, Mahendra said, 'My friend Bali, you have not eaten yet; please go and have your meal.'

Binodini could not be persuaded to go. In the warm, languid afternoon breeze, the curtains of the room began to flutter, and the meaningless murmur of the swaying coconut trees near the boundary wall wafted into the room. Mahendra's heartbeat steadily increased, and in the same rhythm, Binodini's deep breaths began to ruffle the locks of hair on Mahendra's forehead. Neither uttered a word. Mahendra began to think, 'Drifting along in the endless stream of universal life, how does it matter where and when one's boat momentarily touches the shore? How long would it continue to matter, anyway?'

As she sat beside him stroking his forehead, Binodini's head bent lower and lower, bowed down by the weight of youthful ardour; ultimately, loose strands of her hair brushed Mahendra's cheek. Swayed by the breeze, the trembling, delicate touch of the tendrils made his entire body shiver; suddenly, he felt that he was about to choke, as if his breath was trapped in his chest. Starting up, Mahendra said, 'No, I must go to college. Let me go.' He rose to his feet without looking at Binodini.

'Don't rush, let me fetch your clothes.' Binodini brought Mahendra his outfit.

Mahendra left for college quickly, but once there, he simply could not remain calm. After a long and futile struggle to concentrate on his studies, he came home early.

Entering his room, he found Binodini lying prone on the divan, reading a book, her bosom resting on a pillow, her dark, open tresses spilling over her back. Perhaps she had not heard Mahendra's footsteps. Mahendra slowly tiptoed up to her. He heard Binodini sigh deeply as she read.

'Oh my tender-hearted one, don't waste your emotions on some imaginary man,' said Mahendra. 'What is it you are reading?'

Flustered, Binodini sat up and quickly hid the book in her aanchal. Mahendra tried to snatch it from her to see what it was. After much grappling and wrestling, he pulled the book from the defeated Binodini's aanchal, and saw that it was *Bishabriksha*. Panting, Binodini sat in silence, her face turned away in rage.

Mahendra's heart was in turmoil. With great effort, he smiled. 'For shame, you have cheated me. I had thought it would be something of a very secret nature. After all this wrestling, to discover that it was *Bishabriksha*!'

'What secrets would I have, I wonder!'

In a flash, Mahendra blurted out, 'Well, what if there was a letter from Bihari?'

At once, Binodini's eyes flashed like lightning. All this while, the love god's floral arrow had been idling in a corner of the room, but now it was reduced to ashes for a second time as it were. Like a suddenly ignited flame, Binodini rose to her feet. Clasping her hand, Mahendra said, 'Forgive me! Please forgive my jest.'

Wrenching her hand away, Binodini said, 'Who are you jesting about? If you had been worthy of his friendship, I would have tolerated your mockery of him. You have a narrow mind, no strength to sustain a friendship, and yet you indulge in mockery!'

As Binodini prepared to leave, Mahendra embraced her feet with both his arms in an attempt to stop her.

At this moment, a shadow fell across them. Releasing Binodini's feet, Mahendra raised his startled face to see that it was Bihari.

Scorching both of them with his steady gaze, Bihari said, in a calm, patient voice, 'I have arrived at a very inopportune moment, but I shall not stay long. I have come to say one thing. I had gone to Kashi, not knowing that Bouthakrun was there. Unwittingly, I appeared guilty in her eyes; I have no chance of begging her forgiveness, so I have come to beg yours. If any sinful thoughts have ever crossed my mind at any time, with or without my knowledge, may she never suffer on that account: this is my humble request.'

The thought that his weakness had been exposed to Bihari inflamed Mahendra. This was no time for large-heartedness on his part. Smiling a little, he said, 'I see you are like the child who denies having eaten the bananas offered to the deity in the prayer room, even though no one has accused him of the deed. I have not asked you to acknowledge or to deny your guilt; why have you come here to sanctimoniously seek forgiveness?'

For a while, Bihari stood stiffly, like a wooden puppet. Then, when his lips began to tremble as if desperately trying to speak, Binodini exclaimed, 'Bihari Thakurpo, don't reply. Don't say anything. The words that man has uttered have tainted his own tongue; that taint has not touched you at all.'

It was doubtful whether Bihari heard Binodini's words; like a sleepwalker, he turned away from the entrance to Mahendra's room, and started descending the stairs. Running after him, Binodini pleaded, 'Bihari Thakurpo, do you have nothing to say to me? If I deserve a reprimand, please rebuke me.'

When Bihari walked on without answering, Binodini stepped in front of him to obstruct his path, and clasped his right hand in both of hers. With boundless contempt,

Bihari flung her off and went away. He didn't even notice that Binodini was thrown to the ground by this violent gesture.

Hearing her fall, Mahendra rushed to the spot. He saw blood pouring from a cut on Binodini's elbow.

'Oh, this is a deep cut!' Mahendra immediately tugged at his flimsy tunic, tore off a piece, and prepared to bandage the wound.

'No, no, leave it alone, let the blood flow,' said Binodini, quickly moving her arm away.

'Let me bandage it and administer some medicine. You will feel no more pain then: it will heal soon.'

'I don't want to cure the pain. Let the wound remain,' Binodini insisted, moving away.

'Today, in my impatience, I have exposed you to public humiliation. Can you forgive me?'

'Forgive you for what? It was well done of you. Am I afraid of other people? I don't care about anybody. Those who hurt me, abandon me and go away, are they my only recourse? And those who clasp my feet to keep me from leaving, do they mean nothing to me?'

Driven to a frenzy, Mahendra asked tremulously, 'Binodini, then you will not spurn my love?'

'I shall cherish your love, bearing it on my head like a crown. Since I was born, I have never received such a surfeit of love that I could reject it as something unwanted.'

At this, Mahendra grasped Binodini's hands in his

own. 'Then come into my room. Today, we have hurt each other, and until that is erased completely, I can have no happiness, neither in food nor in sleep.'

'Not today, please let me go. If I have hurt you, please forgive me.'

'You must forgive me, too, or I will not be able to sleep at night.'

'I forgive you.'

Mahendra grew desperate to receive from Binodini some instant sign of her forgiveness and her love. But seeing her face, he stopped short. Binodini walked down the stairs; Mahendra slowly climbed the stairs, and began to pace on the terrace. The thought that he had been caught red-handed by Bihari gave rise in his mind to a certain joy at his own liberation. The sense of shame that accompanied the game of hide-and-seek he had been playing was considerably reduced at having been discovered. Mahendra told himself, 'I no longer want to pretend that I am a virtuous person. I am in love! I am in love: that is not pretence.' Pride in his own love increased his daring to such an extent, that, in his own mind, he began to boast arrogantly of his own sinfulness. In the silence of the evening, disdainful of the endless universe stretching out beneath the quiet radiance of the sky, he declared to himself, 'However sinful people might consider me, I am in love.' With these words, Mahendra allowed Binodini's image to overshadow the whole sky, the whole world, and all sense of duty. It was as if, by suddenly arriving on the scene, Bihari had overturned the tightly corked inkpot of Mahendra's life and smashed it; in an instant, Binodini's dark eyes and dark hair seemed to spread out, smear and obliterate the black and white of all that had been inscribed there before.

29

The next day, as soon as he awoke, Mahendra's heart was flooded with a delicious sweetness. It was as if the early morning sun had tinted his thoughts and desires with gold. How beautiful was the world, how nectar-sweet the sky, his mind adrift like flower pollen in the breeze!

In the morning, the Vaishnav mendicants had started singing to the accompaniment of the khol and kartal, their musical instruments. When the doorman tried to send them away, Mahendra scolded him and immediately gave the singers a rupee. The bearer accidentally smashed the kerosene lamp when he came to fetch it away; he glanced fearfully at Mahendra's face. Without rebuking him at all, Mahendra cheerfully ordered: 'You there, sweep that area properly; make sure the shards of glass don't pierce anyone's feet.' Today, no loss or damage affected him.

The love that had been hiding offstage all these days had now raised the curtain to reveal itself. The screen that covered the whole world had been rolled back. All the triviality of the everyday world had vanished. Trees, animals and birds, the crowds on the street, the babble of the city—today, everything appeared exquisite. Where had such all-pervading freshness been hiding all along?

Mahendra began to feel as if his encounter with Binodini on this day would not follow the usual pattern. Today, it would be more appropriate to speak in verse and express oneself in music. Mahendra wanted to fill this day with luxury and beauty, to transform it into something beyond the everyday world, beyond mundane societal norms, to make it resemble an extraordinary day straight out of some Arabian novel. It would be real, yet a fantasy—shorn of all worldly rules and customs, all responsibility, all factual truth.

From the start of the day, Mahendra wandered restlessly, unable to go to college. After all, the almanac could not predict when the auspicious moment of union might suddenly arrive.

As Binodini went about her household work, her voice reached Mahendra's ears, sometimes from the storeroom, sometimes from the kitchen. This did not please Mahendra: today, in his mind, he had placed Binodini far away from worldly matters.

Time hung heavy on his hands. Mahendra had his bath and his meal. As all domestic work came to a halt, the afternoon grew silent. But still, there was no sign of Binodini. In grief and in joy, in impatience and in hope, Mahendra's mind began to vibrate like the strings of a metal instrument.

On the divan lay the copy of *Bishabriksha* that they had wrestled over the previous night. Seeing it, Mahendra felt a thrill at the memory of their struggle. Drawing towards him the pillow upon which Binodini had lain, Mahendra placed his head on it, and, picking up the copy of *Bishabriksha*, he began turning over the pages. Gradually, he became absorbed in reading; he did not realize when it had crossed five in the evening.

At this moment, carrying a patterned Moradabadi tray bearing fruits and sandesh on a large dish and a smaller metal plate of iced, sugared, fragrant watermelon pulp, Binodini entered the room. Placing the tray before Mahendra she asked, 'What are you doing, Thakurpo? What's the matter with you? It's past five o'clock, and you haven't washed and changed your clothes yet?'

Mahendra's heart reeled as if from a blow. Why ask what the matter was with him? Was Binodini unaware of what had happened? Was today like all other days? For fear of receiving a rebuff that would dispel his pleasurable expectations, Mahendra could not make any claims based on memories of the previous night.

He sat down to eat. Binodini carried in Mahendra's clothes from the terrace where they had been spread out in the sun, and folding them deftly, she began to put the garments away in the almira.

'Wait a bit,' said Mahendra. 'I shall help you after I finish eating.'

With folded hands, Binodini pleaded, 'I beg of you, do whatever else you like, but please don't try to help me.'

'Indeed!' said Mahendra, arising from his meal. 'So you have declared me useless! Very well, let today be a test of my ability.' With these words, he began trying in vain to fold the clothes properly.

Snatching the clothes from Mahendra, Binodini exclaimed, 'Oh sir, please let it be, don't add to my work.'

'In that case, please continue with your work, while I watch you and learn from your example.' He came closer to Binodini and sat cross-legged on the floor in front of the cupboard. On the pretext of shaking out the garments, Binodini swatted Mahendra on the back with them, then neatly folded them and put them away in the cupboard.

Thus began their encounter on this day. There was no trace of the exquisiteness that Mahendra had been anticipating since dawn. A union of this sort did not merit the composition of verse, the singing of songs or the writing of novels. All the same, Mahendra did not feel sad; in fact, he was rather relieved. He had been uncertain how to sustain his imagined ideal, what sort of ambience to arrange, what words to speak, what feelings to express, how to keep all ordinariness at bay. In this shaking out and folding of clothes, amidst all the laughter and joking, he seemed to have escaped the clutches of an impossible, unattainable, self-created ideal.

At this moment, Rajalakshmi entered the room. 'Mahin, why are you sitting there while Bahu puts away the clothes?'

'Just look at him, Pishima, he is needlessly delaying me in my work,' complained Binodini.

'How extraordinary! I was only helping her,' protested Mahendra.

'Upon my word!' said Rajalakshmi. 'What help could you offer! Do you know, Bahu, Mahin has always been like this. Pampered by his mother and aunt all his life, it would be a marvel if he could accomplish any task on his own.'

With these words, Rajalakshmi cast a doting glance at the inept Mahendra. How to provide every sort of comfort to this useless, extremely mother-dependent, grown-up son—this was Rajalakshmi's only subject of discussion with Binodini. Relying upon Binodini to look after her son devotedly, she was utterly content, extremely happy. Rajalakshmi also noted with joy that Mahendra, of late, had grown to appreciate Binodini's worth and that he now took pains to ensure that she would stay on. For Mahendra's benefit, she remarked, 'Bahu, today you have sunned Mahin's woollens and put them away, now tomorrow you must embroider his initials on his new handkerchiefs. Ever since I brought you here, I have not been able to look after you properly, my child; I have only worked you to death.'

'Pishima, if you say such things, I shall think you are treating me formally, like a stranger.'

'Ah, my girl, where will I find someone closer to my own heart?' said Rajalakshmi affectionately.

When Binodini finished arranging the clothes, Rajalakshmi asked, 'Shall I put the sugar syrup on the fire now, or do you have some other work to do?'

'No, Pishima, I have no other work. Come, let's go and prepare those sweets.'

'But Ma, you were just regretting the fact that you have worked her to death, and now you are immediately dragging her off to work?' said Mahendra.

Tapping Binodini's chin, Rajalakshmi replied, 'This angelic girl likes to work, after all.'

'This evening I have nothing to do; I had thought I would read a book with Bali,' complained Mahendra.

'Pishima, that's a good idea; this evening both of us will come here to listen to Thakurpo read aloud from his book. What do you say?'

Rajalakshmi thought, 'My Mahin is extremely lonely, now all of us must keep him entertained.' She answered, 'Very well, when we finish preparing Mahin's food this evening, we shall come and listen to him read. What do you say, Mahin?'

Binodini cast a sidelong glance at Mahendra's face.

'Very well,' he agreed. But he had no enthusiasm left. Binodini left the room with Rajalakshmi.

Angrily, Mahendra thought, 'I, too, shall go out today, and come back late.' He immediately dressed as if to go out. But his resolve did not translate into action. Mahendra paced the terrace for a long time, glanced at the stairway many times, and in the end, he came into the room and sat down. Bitterly, he decided, 'Today, I shall leave the sweets untouched, and inform my mother that the syrup loses its sweetness if overcooked.'

At mealtime, Binodini brought Rajalakshmi along with her. Rajalakshmi usually avoided climbing the stairs for fear of an asthma attack, but had come tonight at Binodini's insistence. With an extremely glum face, Mahendra sat down to eat.

'What is this, Thakurpo, why are you not eating properly today!' inquired Binodini.

'You are not ill, are you?' asked Rajalakshmi anxiously.

'I made the sweets with so much effort, you must taste some,' persisted Binodini. 'Are they not to your liking? Then let them be. No, no, there is no point forcing yourself to eat at other people's request. No, no, you had best not have them.'

'You have placed me in an awkward position. It's the sweets that really look tempting, and they taste good, too; though you are trying to stop me, why should I listen?' laughed Mahendra. He ate two whole sweets, wasting not a crumb.

After the meal, the three of them came and sat in Mahendra's bedchamber. Mahendra did not revive the earlier proposal of reading to them.

'That book you mentioned, why don't you start reading it?' prompted Rajalakshmi.

'But it says nothing about gods and goddesses; you won't enjoy listening to it.'

Not enjoy it! Whatever it took, Ralalakshmi was determined to enjoy the reading. Even if Mahendra read aloud in Turkish, she must enjoy it. Poor dear Mahin, all alone, his wife away in Kashi—whatever he enjoyed, his mother would, too.

'I have a suggestion, Thakurpo,' Binodini intervened. 'There is a copy of the Bengali *Shanti Shatak* in Pishima's room; why don't you read that aloud tonight, putting aside your other books? Pishima would find it to her taste, and the evening would pass pleasurably.'

Mahendra cast a piteous glance at Binodini's face. At this moment, the housemaid came to announce, 'Ma, Kayet Thakrun is here. She is waiting in your room.'

Kayet Thakrun was Rajalakshmi's intimate friend. It was hard for Rajalakshmi to resist the temptation of gossiping with her in the evening. All the same, she told the housemaid, 'Tell Kayet Thakrun that I have some work in Mahin's room tonight, but she must positively, positively come tomorrow.'

Mahendra quickly suggested, 'But why, Ma, why don't you go and meet her?'

'There is no need for you to bother, Pishima. You stay here; I'll go and sit with Kayet Thakrun instead,' offered Binodini.

Unable to resist temptation, Rajalakshmi told her, 'Bahu, you remain here; in the meantime, let me see if I can get rid of Kayet Thakrun. Start reading, don't wait for me.'

Once Rajalakshmi had left the room, Mahendra could contain himself no longer. He exclaimed, 'Why do you deliberately torment me like this?'

As if extremely surprised, Binodini asked, 'What do you mean, my friend! When have I tormented you? Have I done wrong, then, in visiting your room? Better not, let me go.' She made as if to rise, her face dejected.

Mahendra grasped her hand. 'This is how you torture me with hell fire.'

'Oh, I had no idea I had such fire in me; your heart is tough, too, to withstand so much. It is impossible to tell from your appearance that you have been scorched and roasted to such an extent.'

'What could you tell from appearances?' With these words, Mahendra caught Binodini's hand and pressed it to his heart.

Binodini cried out in pain. Mahendra quickly released her hand. 'Did I hurt you?' he asked.

He found that the wound on Binodini's arm, where she had hurt herself the previous day, was bleeding again. Full of remorse, Mahendra said, 'I had forgotten—it was very wrong of me. I shall apply some medicine right away, and bandage the area; I shan't let you escape on any account, today.'

'No, it is nothing. I shall not apply any medicine.'

'Why not?'

'Why not, indeed! There is no need for you to play the doctor; let the wound remain as it is.'

Instantly, Mahendra became grave. 'It is impossible to understand a woman's mind!' he said to himself.

Binodini arose. Without stopping her, Mahendra asked petulantly, 'Where are you going?'

'I have work to do.' She walked away, slowly.

After a minute, Mahendra quickly got to his feet and ran after Binodini to bring her back, but at the top of the stairs, he turned back, and began to pace the terrace alone.

Binodini drew him to her every hour of the day, yet would not let him near her for a single moment. Mahendra had recently relinquished his proud claim that he was invincible, but must he also relinquish his claim that he could conquer others at the slightest effort? Today, he had conceded defeat, but was unable to inflict defeat in return. In matters of the heart, Mahendra rated himself very highly; he did not recognize anyone as his equal, but today, in that very arena, his head rolled in the dust. In return for the loss of his supremacy, he had not gained anything, either. He felt like a beggar who must stand empty-handed before a closed door in the darkness of the evening.

In the spring, during the months of Phalgun and Chaitra, Bihari received mustard-honey from his estates. As always, he sent some to Rajalakshmi this year as well.

Binodini carried the jar of honey to Rajalakshmi. 'Pishima, Bihari Thakurpo has sent some honey.'

Rajalakshmi instructed her to put it away in the store. Having stored away the honey, Binodini came to sit beside Rajalakshmi. 'Bihari Thakurpo never fails to enquire after you,' she observed. 'Poor man, has he no mother of his own, that he should regard you as his own mother?'

Accustomed to regarding Bihari as Mahendra's shadow, Rajalakshmi had never given much thought to his situation; he was beholden to them, a person of no worth, requiring no special care. When Binodini described Rajalakshmi as a mother-substitute for the motherless Bihari, Rajalakshmi's maternal heart was unexpectedly touched. All of a sudden, she thought, 'True indeed, Bihari has no mother of his own; it is me he regards as his own mother.' She remembered how, in times of sickness, difficulty and danger, Bihari had always served her with silent devotion, unasked, and without any outward display of ceremony. Rajalakshmi had accepted this as naturally as breathing; it had never occurred to her to feel grateful to anybody for this. But who had ever cared to ask news of Bihari's well-being? When Annapurna was there, she had asked after him. 'To keep Bihari under her thumb, Annapurna makes a great show of her affection for him,' Rajalakshmi had believed then.

Today, she sighed, 'Indeed, Bihari is like a son to me.'

Immediately, it occurred to her that Bihari did a great deal more for her than her own son; and without ever receiving much in return he remained steady in his devotion to them. The thought caused her to heave a heartfelt sigh.

'Bihari Thakurpo loves to eat food prepared by you,' Binodini reminded her.

With indulgent pride, Rajalakshmi acknowledged, 'He does not relish fish curry made by anyone else?' Even as she spoke, she remembered that it had been a long time since Bihari had visited them. 'Tell me, Bahu, why don't we get to see Bihari these days?' she said.

'That's just what I was wondering myself, Pishima. Well, ever since your son got married, he has been so preoccupied with his wife; why would his friends visit, after all?'

Rajalakshmi found this statement extremely apt. Taken up with his wife, Mahendra had kept all their well-wishers at a distance. Bihari had every right to be offended; why should he visit them? Discovering that Bihari was on her side, Rajalakshmi's sympathy for him increased greatly. She began to describe to Binodini how, from his very childhood, Bihari had unselfishly helped Mahendra, how much he had suffered on his friend's account on so many occasions. Through her description of Bihari, she began to substantiate her own complaints against her son. If the brief spell of joy with his newly wedded wife had caused Mahendra to neglect his lifelong friend, what was the future of justice or duty in this world?

'Tomorrow is Sunday; it will make Bihari Thakurpo happy if you invite him to a meal.'

'You are quite right, Bahu. Let me send for Mahendra; he can send an invitation to Bihari.'

'No, Pishima, please invite him yourself.'

'I can't read and write like all of you.'

'So what, let me write on your behalf.'

Binodini wrote and dispatched a letter of invitation in Rajalakshmi's name.

That Sunday was a day Mahendra awaited very eagerly. From the previous night itself, his imagination ran wild, although, until now, nothing had happened as he had imagined. All the same, the light of dawn on Sunday rained nectar on his eyes. The babble of the awakening city was exquisite music to his ears.

But what was the matter? Did his mother have a special fasting ritual to observe? She was not resting as on other days, leaving Binodini in charge of all the housework. Today, she was bustling about.

In this state of confusion, it turned ten o'clock, but Mahendra had not found a moment alone with Binodini on any pretext. He tried to read a book, but his mind refused to concentrate; for fifteen minutes, his gaze remained fixed on a useless advertisement in the newspaper. Then he could contain himself no longer. Going downstairs, he found his mother cooking at a portable stove placed in the veranda outside her room, and Binodini busy attending to her needs, her aanchal tucked firmly into her waist.

'What's the matter with both of you today?' Mahendra wanted to know. 'Why such hustle and bustle?'

'Did Bahu not tell you? We have asked Bihari over today.'

Asked Bihari over! Mahendra's entire body seemed instantly aflame. 'But Ma, I'm afraid I can't stay,' he said at once.

'Why?'

'I have to go out, that's why.'

'Go after your meal, it won't take long.'

'But I have been invited out to a meal.'

Casting a swift sidelong glance at Mahendra, Binodini observed, 'If he has been invited, then why not let him go, Pishima? Bihari Thakurpo may as well eat by himself today.'

But how could Rajalakshmi bear to forgo the pleasure of feeding Mahendra the dishes she had lovingly cooked? The more she pestered him, the more obstinate Mahendra became. 'It's a very urgent invitation. I can't turn it down on any account. You should have consulted me before inviting Bihari.'

Through his anger, Mahendra saw to it that his mother was punished in this way. Rajalakshmi lost all her enthusiasm. She felt like throwing away all the food and leaving the place.

'Pishima, don't worry. Thakurpo is speaking brashly, but he won't be eating out today,' Binodini assured her.

Rajalakshmi shook her head. 'No, my child, you don't know Mahin. Once he decides on something, it's impossible to change his mind.'

But Binodini understood Mahendra's nature better than Rajalakshmi, as events were to prove. Mahendra had surmised that it was Binodini who had invited Bihari. The more this assumption tormented him, the harder he found it to leave the scene. He had to observe Bihari's behaviour and Binodini's. The sight would scorch his heart, but it was necessary to watch them, all the same.

Today, after many days, Bihari entered the private quarters of Mahendra's house as an invited member of the family. Approaching the door of the room so familiar to him since childhood—the room he used to enter freely to play in mischievously like a son of the house—he stopped short for a moment. At once, a wave of tears welled up in his heart, struggling to break forth. Controlling himself, he entered the room with a smiling countenance and touched the feet of the freshly bathed Rajalakshmi. Earlier, when Bihari had been a regular visitor to the house, this was not their customary form of greeting. Today, it was as if he had returned home after a long exile. When he arose from his obeisance, Rajalakshmi affectionately touched his head.

Today, out of a deep sympathy, Rajalakshmi expressed far greater love and affection towards Bihari than before. 'Oh Bihari, why didn't you visit us all these days? Every day, I would think: today, surely, Bihari will come. But there was no sign of you.'

'If I came every day you would not spare a thought for your own Bihari, Ma,' smiled Bihari. 'Where is Mahinda?'

'Mahin was invited out somewhere today,' Rajalakshmi informed him sadly. 'It was not possible for him to stay home.'

Hearing this, Bihari lost heart. For an old childhood friendship to end in this way? Sighing deeply to blow away the vapours of dejection from his mind, Bihari asked, 'So, what have you cooked today?' He began to ask about his favourite dishes. Earlier, on days when Rajalakshmi cooked the food, Bihari would make a great show of being tempted; by displaying his love of food, Bihari would steal the heart of the motherly Rajalakshmi. Today, too, seeing Bihari's excessive curiosity about her own cooking, Rajalakshmi smilingly reassured her greedy guest.

At this moment, Mahendra arrived on the scene. In a dry, formal tone, he inquired, 'So, Bihari, how are you?'

'Why, Mahin, did you not attend your lunch engagement?' asked Rajalakshmi.

'No, I have managed to wriggle out of it,' replied Mahendra, trying to cover his embarrassment.

When Binodini appeared after her bath, Bihari was at first rendered speechless. Etched on his mind was the scene he had witnessed between Binodini and Mahendra.

Coming close to Bihari, Binodini asked in a low voice, 'Why, Thakurpo, don't you recognize me?'

'Is it possible to recognize everybody?'

'It is indeed possible, if one is a person of judgment,' asserted Binodini. 'Pishima, the food is ready.'

Mahendra and Bihari sat down to eat; Rajalakshmi watched over them from her place near at hand, and Binodini began to serve. Mahendra paid no attention to the food, watching only for signs of partiality in the way their meal was being served. It seemed to Mahendra that Binodini was getting special pleasure out of serving Bihari. There was an excellent reason why special helpings of fish head and cream of curd were offered to Bihari: Mahendra was of the host family, Bihari an invited guest. But because there was no good reason to expressly complain, Mahendra's heartburn grew more acute. For the occasion, after much searching, out-of-season tapshi fish had been obtained of which one was with roe; when Binodini tried to offer it to Bihari, he exclaimed, 'No, no, give it to Mahinda, he is very fond of it.' His pride bitterly wounded, Mahendra protested, 'No, no, I don't want it.' Without even offering it to him a second time, Binodini tossed the fish onto Bihari's plate.

After the meal, when the two friends arose and came out of the room, Binodini quickly came up to them and said, 'Bihari Thakurpo, don't leave immediately, come and sit upstairs for a little while.'

'Won't you eat?' asked Bihari.

'No, today is Ekadashi, the eleventh lunar day, a day for fasting.'

The subtle hint of a cruel, mocking smile appeared at the corner of Bihari's lips, implying his sarcasm at Binodini's observance of a ritual such as Ekadashi. There were no lapses where rituals were concerned.

That hint of a smile did not elude Binodini's gaze, but she bore it as she had borne the wound on her arm. In a tone of abject supplication, she pleaded, 'I insist, you must come upstairs and sit for a while.'

In a sudden outburst of agitation, Mahendra exclaimed, 'You people have no sense! So what if there's work to be done, duties to be performed? Whether he wants to or not, he must be importuned to stay. I don't understand the meaning of such excessive pampering.'

Binodini laughed out loud. 'Bihari Thakurpo, just listen to this! Listen to what your Mahinda is saying. Pampering means pampering, the dictionary offers no other word for it.'

'Whatever you may say, Thakurpo, nobody can match your experience of excessive pampering, ever since you were a child.'

Bihari said, 'Mahinda, there is something I must

discuss with you; please come aside.' Without bidding Binodini farewell, Bihari led Mahendra outside. Binodini remained standing silently on the veranda, holding the railing and gazing at the emptiness of the vacant courtyard.

Once outside, Bihari demanded, 'Mahinda, I want to know, is this the end of our friendship?'

At this time, Mahendra's heart was on fire; Binodini's mocking laughter seared his mind like a flash of lightning. He said, 'A reconciliation might be especially advantageous to you, but to me, it does not seem desirable. I don't want to let outsiders into my domestic life; I want my private quarters to remain private.'

Without a word, Bihari left.

Pierced with envy, Mahendra vowed he would not meet Binodini. Then, in the hope of meeting Binodini, he wandered restlessly in and out, upstairs and down.

30

One day, Asha asked Annapurna, 'Tell me, Mashima, do you remember Meshomoshai, your husband?'

'I was widowed at eleven; my husband's image has grown shadowy in my mind.'

'Mashi, who do you think about, then?'

'I think of God, in whom my husband now resides,' replied Annapurna, with a faint smile.

'Does that bring you happiness?'

Affectionately stroking Asha's head, Annapurna said, 'My child, how would you understand my state of mind? That is something known to my heart, and to Him I meditate upon.'

Asha thought to herself, 'The person I meditate upon night and day, does he not know my state of mind? Because I can't write letters properly, should he stop writing to me?'

Asha had not heard from Mahendra for several days.

'If Chokher Bali had been close at hand, she could have inscribed my thoughts accurately in writing,' she sighed to herself.

Thinking that a poorly written, paltry letter would not win her husband's respect, Asha was reluctant to write to him. The harder she tried, the worse her handwriting became. The more she tried to arrange her thoughts, the more impossible it became for her to somehow complete a sentence. If a single term of address, followed by her signature, could have sufficed for Mahendra to have read her thoughts correctly, as if he was an all-knowing deity, then alone would Asha's letter writing have proved successful. Destiny had endowed her with such capacity for love, but could she not have been granted a little felicity with language?

Returning home after the evening aarti, the lamp-ritual at the temple, Asha sat at Annapurna's feet, gently stroking her feet. After a long silence, she ventured, 'Mashi, you say it is a wife's sacred duty to serve her husband devotedly as if he were a deity; but a wife who is illiterate, who has no intelligence, who does not know how to serve her husband, what is she to do?'

Annapurna gazed at Asha's face for a while. 'My child, I am illiterate, too,' she answered, suppressing a sigh, 'but I still serve God.'

'But He knows your mind, so He is pleased. But suppose a husband is not pleased at the devotion offered by an illiterate woman?'

'Everyone doesn't have the power to please everyone, my child. If a wife serves her husband and performs her household duties with heartfelt devotion, care and respect, then, even if the husband spurns her offering, God Himself would stoop to accept it.'

Asha remained silent. She tried to derive consolation from her aunt's words, but her mind refused to believe that God could value someone who had been rejected by her own husband as unworthy. Her face bent low, she sat stroking her mashi's feet.

Annapurna grasped Asha's hand and drew her even closer; she kissed her head, and, struggling to free her choking voice, she said, 'Chuni, just listening to wisdom will not grant you the knowledge that is learnt through the direct experience of pain and hardship. Once upon a time, even this mashi of yours had tried to bargain with the world, just like you. Then, just like you, I used to ask why the person I served should not feel satisfied. If I prayed to a deity, why would I not be entitled to receive his prasad, food consecrated by his blessing? If I strove for someone's well-being, why would he not appreciate the value of my effort? At every step, I found that this was not to be. Ultimately, unable to tolerate this, I felt one day that all my efforts in this world had been futile. That very day I renounced the world and came here. Today, I realize that none of my efforts were fruitless. O my child, He with whom I have a real bargain to strike, He who is the main source of wealth in this world's market, had been receiving all I had to offer, and today, having taken his place within my heart, He has acknowledged it. If only I had known this, at the time! If I had performed my worldly duties knowing them to be my duties to Him, if I had surrendered my heart to the world as an offering meant for Him, could anybody have hurt me?'

Lying in bed, Asha stayed up very late, pondering upon many issues, but she still could not grasp anything clearly. But having boundless respect for her virtuous mashi, she took her aunt's words to heart, even without completely understanding them. Sitting up in bed, she bent in a posture of obeisance towards the deity who reigned supreme above all worldly things, according to her mashi. 'I am a young girl,' she prayed. 'I do not know You, I only know my husband, but please do not blame me on that account. O Lord, please ask my husband to accept the prayers that I offer him. If he spurns them, I shall die. I am not a virtuous woman like my Mashima; I cannot save myself by making You my refuge.' With these words, Asha bowed in obeisance again and again, upon the bed.

It was time for Asha's jyathamoshai to return home. On the eve of their departure, Annapurna drew Asha onto her lap. 'Chuni, my little girl, I don't have the power to protect you always from all the sorrow, unhappiness and ill fortune of this world. This is my advice to you: whatever the nature and source of your suffering, be steady in your faith and devotion; may your adherence to dharma, your sacred duty, remain unshaken.'

'Give me your blessings, Mashima, that it may be so,' beseeched Asha, touching her feet.

31

When Asha came back home, Binodini was extremely petulant: 'You were away for so long! Shouldn't you have written to me at least once?'

'You didn't write either, my dear Bali.'

'Why should I be the first to write? You were supposed to write to me.'

Embracing Binodini, Asha acknowledged that she had been at fault. 'You know I can't write properly, my friend. I feel especially ashamed of writing to a learned person like you.'

In no time at all, the two women forgot their quarrel, and love blossomed between them.

'You have spoiled your husband by giving him constant company, day and night,' Binodini told Asha. 'Now he can't live without a companion.'

'That's why I had given you that responsibility. You are better than me at the art of companionship.'

'In the daytime, I could relax after somehow sending him off to college, but in the evening, there was no respite—there must be conversation, books must be read aloud, there was no end to his whims.'

'So you were caught in your own trap. When you know how to beguile people's minds, why should people let you off lightly?'

'Be careful, my friend. Sometimes Thakurpo behaves so outrageously, I begin to suspect that I may know the art of witchcraft.'

'Who but you would know such things?' laughed Asha. 'If I could acquire but a little of your skill, it would save my life.'

'Why, who is the person you wish to destroy? Take care of the one you have at home, don't try to beguile those who are not your own, my dear Bali. It leads to a lot of trouble.'

Asha pushed Binodini away. 'Oh, what nonsensical things you say!'

The first time they met after her return from Kashi, Mahendra observed: 'I can see you kept good health there; you've come back looking quite plump.'

Asha felt very embarrassed. She should not have kept such good health, on any account, but with foolish Asha, nothing was ever as it should be. While her mind was so disturbed, her wretched body had blossomed; it was bad enough that she did not have words to express her inner thoughts, but to top it all, even her body conveyed the wrong impression.

'How have you been?' Asha inquired in a low voice.

In the past, Mahendra would have responded, half seriously, half in jest, 'I was all but dead.' Now he was unable to treat it as a joke; his throat felt constricted. 'I was quite well, not too bad,' he answered.

Asha noticed that Mahendra seemed thinner than before. His face was pale, and there was a sharp glitter in his eyes, as if he was consumed from within by the flames of some deep inner hunger. Secretly pained, Asha thought, 'Ah, my husband did not keep well. Why did I abandon him to go away to Kashi?' Her husband had lost weight, yet she had grown plump; Asha felt ashamed of her own good health.

Wondering what else to talk about, Mahendra asked, after a pause: 'I hope Kakima is well?'

Having been assured of kakima's well-being, he could not think of any other topic of conversation. An old, torn newspaper lay nearby; pulling it towards him, Mahendra began to read it in an absent-minded manner. Her head bent, Asha began to think, 'Having met after so many days, why did he not speak to me properly, or even look me in the face? Is he angry because I could not write to him these last three or four days? Is he annoyed that I stayed too long in Kashi at Mashi's request?' With a deeply troubled mind, she began to search within herself, to discover where she had gone wrong.

Mahendra returned from college. When he took his

evening snack, Rajalakshmi was present; Asha was also standing not far away, her head covered, leaning against the door, but there was nobody else.

Anxiously, Rajalakshmi asked, 'Are you unwell today, Mahin?'

'No, Ma, why would I be unwell?' responded Mahendra irritably.

'But then, why aren't you eating properly?'

'Of course I'm eating properly, can't you see?' Mahendra sounded very annoyed.

On that summer evening, he wore a light wrap around his shoulders and began to walk up and down on the terrace. He was hoping in his heart that their regular reading session would not be ruled out today. They had almost completed *Anandamath*, with only two or three chapters remaining; however heartless Binodini might be, she would surely come and read those few chapters to him today. But the evening passed, and the time for reading was over. His heart weighed down in despair, Mahendra took himself off to bed.

Dressed for the occasion, looking very bashful, Asha slowly entered the bedchamber. She saw Mahendra lying in bed. She paused hesitantly. After a period of separation comes a new, short-lived shyness; mutual greetings must be exchanged before returning to the same footing as before. Tonight, how was Asha to enter uninvited the familiar bed on which she had earlier enjoyed such bliss? She stood at the door for a long time, but there was no sound from Mahendra. Very slowly, step by step, she began to advance. If, in her carelessness, one of her ornaments produced the slightest sound, she cringed with embarrassment. With quaking heart, Asha came up to the mosquito net and sensed that Mahendra was asleep. It seemed to her then that her own dress and ornaments were mocking her, constricting her entire body. She wished she could leave the room at lightning speed, to go and sleep somewhere else.

As noiselessly as possible, Asha cautiously climbed onto the bed. Even then, there was enough sound and movement to awaken Mahendra, had he been really asleep. But tonight, he did not open his eyes, because he was not asleep. Mahendra was lying on his side at the opposite end of the bed, so Asha lay down facing his back. Even with his back turned to her, Mahendra could sense quite clearly that Asha was shedding silent tears. His own cruelty wounded his heart, which felt as if it was being ground in a mill. But Mahendra simply could not imagine what to say to her, or how to express his fondness for her; he struggled with himself, but though this created agony for him, it afforded him no solution. He thought, 'At dawn, I can no longer pretend sleep; when we are face to face, what shall I say to Asha?'

Asha herself solved Mahendra's problem. Very early in the morning, she left the bed with all her spurned adornments; she, too, was unable to face Mahendra.

32

'Why did this happen? What have I done?' Asha began to wonder. She did not recognize where the real source of danger lay. The possibility that Mahendra might fall in love with Binodini had never occurred to her. She had no experience of the world. Besides, she had never imagined that Mahendra could be any different from the image of him that she had formed in her mind shortly after their marriage.

That day, Mahendra left for college early. When it was time for him to leave, Asha would always come and stand at the window, and Mahendra would raise his head once to glance up at her from his carriage: such was their regular daily routine. Accordingly, as soon as she heard the carriage, Asha appeared mechanically at the window. By force of habit, Mahendra, too, flashed a quick glance upwards; he saw Asha standing there, unbathed, wearing faded clothes, her hair undone, her face dejected, and he instantly lowered his gaze and began to scrutinize the books on his lap. Where had it gone, that silent signal, that meaningful smile at parting?

The carriage rolled away; Asha collapsed to the ground on that very spot. The whole world had lost its appeal. It was half past ten, the peak hour for the office-going crowds of Kolkata; there was a ceaseless flow of carriages, tram after tram raced down the road, and close to the hustle and bustle of the workaday world, this depressed heart, stupefied with pain, seemed extremely out of place.

All at once, a thought occurred to Asha. 'Now I understand. He is angry at the news of Thakurpo having gone to Kashi. Apart from that no other unpleasant event has occurred during this time, after all. But how was I to blame for that?'

For one moment, as she took in this idea, Asha's heart missed a beat. Suddenly, she was afraid that Mahendra might suspect that she had been involved in Bihari's visit to Kashi. That the two of them had planned it together. For shame! To harbour such a suspicion! What an embarrassment! She had already invited contempt when her name had been linked with Bihari's, but if Mahendra suspected her, how would she survive? But if there was any reason for suspicion, if she had committed some offence, then why did Mahendra not say so clearly, why did he not judge her and punish her appropriately?

Instead of articulating anything, Mahendra seemed to

be constantly avoiding Asha, making her think that he harboured some suspicion which he himself knew to be false, which he was ashamed even to admit to her. Else, why would he appear so guilty? An angry judge is not supposed to seem so constrained, after all.

All day, Mahendra could not erase from his mind the image of Asha's woebegone countenance as he departed in his carriage. In the midst of college lectures, sitting among rows of students in class, he was haunted by the image of Asha with her unwashed, rough hair, her stale attire, and her unhappy, desperate gaze.

After college, he wandered on the banks of the Goldighi. Gradually, evening descended, but still he could not determine how he ought to behave towards Asha. Would kind deception be appropriate or direct cruelty? The question of relinquishing Binodini did not arise in his mind at all. How would Mahendra satisfy the dual claims of kindness and of love?

Mahendra then convinced himself that very few wives were fortunate enough to receive the amount of love he still felt for Asha. Offered this affection, this love, why should Asha not remain content? His heart was large enough to accommodate both Binodini and Asha. The pure love that Mahendra shared with Binodini would in no way disrupt his conjugal life.

Mahendra thus persuaded himself to shed the heavy burden that was weighing down his mind. His heart became cheerful at the thought that, without giving up either Binodini or Asha, he would be able to spend the rest of his life in this manner, like a planet with two satellites. He hurried home, determined that tonight he would go to bed early, and through tender care and gentle conversation wipe away all the pain from Asha's mind.

Asha was not present at dinner, but expecting her to join him sooner or later, Mahendra went to bed. But in the silent room, lying in the empty bed, what was the memory that enveloped Mahendra's heart? Was it the daily amorous play of newly wedded bliss that he had enjoyed with Asha? No. As moonlight pales in the presence of sunshine, those memories had now faded; the brightly shining image of a young woman had taken radiant shape, overshadowing the simple girl's gentle, modest image. He began to remember his struggle with Binodini over the copy of *Bishabriksha*. After dark, as Binodini read aloud from *Kapalkundala*, evening would fade into night, and the people in the house would fall asleep. In the silent isolation of that lonely chamber, Binodini's voice would grow sweeter with the force of emotion, until she almost choked. Suddenly restraining herself, she would fling away the book and get up. 'Let me see you down the stairs,' Mahendra would insist. Remembering all this over and over again, he felt a rapture that spread to all parts of his body. The night drew on; Mahendra began to feel a little anxious, expecting Asha to appear at any moment, but she did not come. Mahendra thought, 'I was prepared to do my duty, but if Asha stays away out of vain peevishness, what can I do?' He immersed himself deeper in his meditation on Binodini.

When it struck one, Mahendra could bear it no longer; pulling at the mosquito net, he stepped out of bed. Emerging onto the terrace, he saw that the moonlit summer night had a very romantic aspect. The enormous silence and somnolence of Kolkata seemed almost tangible, like the still waters of the ocean. Above row upon row of palatial houses, deepening the slumber of the great city, blew a soft, light breeze.

Mahendra's desire, long suppressed, could be controlled no longer. Ever since Asha had returned from Kashi, Binodini had not appeared before him. The moonlit solitude of the night enchanted Mahendra, driving him inexorably towards Binodini. Mahendra descended the stairs. Arriving at the veranda in front of Binodini's room, he found that the room had not been locked. Entering the room, he found the bed made, but not slept in.

Hearing footsteps, Binodini called out from the open veranda to the south of the room: 'Who is it?'

'Binod, it is me,' said Mahendra, in a bemused, agonized voice. He went straight to the veranda.

In the summer night, on a floor mat, Rajalakshmi lay with Binodini. 'Mahin, what are you doing here, so late at night?' she exclaimed.

From beneath her dark, black eyebrows, Binodini's eyes flashed fire and lightning at Mahendra. Without replying, Mahendra departed as quickly as possible.

33

The next morning was overcast. After a spell of unbearable heat, soft dark clouds filled the scorching sky. Mahendra had left for college early. His discarded clothes lay on the floor. Asha was handing Mahendra's garments to the dhobi, checking them off on a list.

Mahendra was an absent-minded, forgetful person by nature; hence, he had asked Asha to search his pockets before sending his clothes to the laundry. In one of the pockets, Asha's found a letter.

Had that letter turned into a poisonous snake and instantly bitten Asha's fingers, it would have been better. For if a deadly poison enters the body, it can produce lethal results within five minutes, but if the poison enters the mind, it brings death throes but no death.

Extracting the open letter, she saw at once that it bore Binodini's signature. Asha's face instantly turned pale. Carrying the letter into the next room, she read:

After the outrage you committed last night, are you still not satisfied? Why have you sent me a secret letter again by Khemi's hand? For shame! What must she have thought? Would you disgrace me before the whole world?

What do you want from me? Love? Why such a beggarly attitude? From the day you were born, love is all you've ever received, yet, there is no end to your craving for it.

In this world, I have no right to love or be loved. So, I play games to compensate for the lack of love in my life. When you had the opportunity, you, too, participated in that false game. But is there no end to your playtime? Domestic life calls you; why do you still peep into the playroom? Now shake off the dust and go home. As I have no home, I shall play by myself, in my mind, but I shall not call you.

You write that you love me. Such statements are admissible during play, but to tell you the truth, I don't believe your words. Once you thought that you loved Asha, but that was false; now you think you love me, but this, too, is a falsehood. You love only yourself.

The thirst for love has parched my heart and my breast, but I have seen, only too clearly, that you do not have the power to quench that thirst. I implore you again and again, please let me go; don't follow me around, don't shame me by your shamelessness. I have lost my taste for games; now, even if you call, I shall not answer. In your letter, you call me cruel: that might be true. But I have some pity, too; hence, today, out of pity, I let you go. If you answer this letter, I shall know that unless I run away from you, there will be no release for me.

Reading this letter, Asha felt as if all support had collapsed around her, all her nerves and sinews paralysed, no air left for her to breathe, all light snatched from her eyes by the sun. Clutching at the wall for support, then at the almira, and finally the chowki, Asha fell to the floor. Recovering consciousness after some time, she tried to read the letter again, but could make no sense of it. The black characters seemed to dance before her eyes. What was this? What had happened? How did it happen? Was this the end of everything? What she should do, whom she should call upon, where she should go, she could not determine. Like a beached fish gasping for water, her heart began to writhe in agony. Like a drowning man frantically stretching his arms towards the sky for help, Asha desperately sought some support to which her heart could cling. Ultimately, clasping her breast, she cried out, panting, 'Mashima!'

As soon as she had uttered that beloved name, tears began to pour forth from her eyes. Sinking to the ground, she sobbed and sobbed. When her tears subsided, she began to wonder, 'What am I to do with this letter?' If her husband learnt that this letter had fallen into Asha's hands, how terribly humiliated he would feel! The thought made Asha cringe. She decided to replace the letter in the pocket of the same garment, which she would leave on the clotheshorse instead of sending to the laundry.

With this plan in mind, she carried the letter to the bedchamber. Meanwhile, the dhobi had gone to sleep, leaning against the bundle of washing. Picking up Mahendra's garment, Asha was about to put the letter into the pocket, when she heard a voice call: 'My friend Bali!'

Quickly dropping the letter and the garment on the bed, she sat down on them. Entering the room, Binodini said, 'The dhobi has been mixing up all the clothes. Let me take away the garments that have no mark on them.'

Asha could not bear to look at Binodini's face. Lest her expression reveal everything, she turned her face to the window and gazed at the sky; she pressed her lips together for fear that her eyes might shed tears.

Stopping short, Binodini looked closely at Asha once, and told herself, 'Oh, I see. So you know what happened last night, and all your anger is directed at me! As if I am the culprit!'

Binodini made no attempt to speak to Asha. Choosing a few garments, she quickly left the room.

The simple friendship that Asha had hitherto enjoyed with Binodini created a sense of constraint even in the midst of her bitter suffering. She wanted to try once more to match the cruel letter with the ideal image of her friend that she had cherished in her heart.

As she opened the letter and started reading it, Mahendra rushed into the room. Some sudden thought had prompted him to leave college in the middle of a lecture and hurry back home.

Asha hid the letter in her aanchal. Mahendra, too, stopped short when he saw Asha in the room. Then he began to look about the room in agitation. Asha knew what Mahendra was looking for, but did not know how to replace the letter unnoticed before escaping the scene.

Mahendra began to examine the washing, one item at a time. Observing Mahendra's fruitless efforts, Asha could bear it no more. Flinging the letter and the garment on the floor, she grasped the bedpost with her right hand and covered her face with her arm. Quick as lightning, Mahendra picked up the letter. For an instant, he gazed at Asha in silence. After that, Asha heard the sound of Mahendra's swift footsteps receding down the stairs. At that moment, the dhobi was calling, 'Ma thakrun, how much longer will it take for you to give me the washing? It's getting late. I don't live close by, after all.'

34

That day, since morning, Rajalakshmi had not sent for Binodini. Going to the storeroom as usual, Binodini found that Rajalakshmi would not look her in the eye.

Although she had noticed this, she inquired, 'Pishima, are you ill? It's hardly surprising. The way Thakurpo behaved last night! Coming upon us like a madman. I couldn't sleep afterwards.'

Rajalakshmi remained grave, offering no reply, affirmative or negative.

'He must have had some trifling quarrel with Chokher Bali,' continued Binodini. 'For then there would be no stopping him: he must instantly drag me into the matter, either to hear his complaint or to sort things out for him. He wouldn't have the patience to wait the night out. Whatever you might say, Pishima, forgive me for pointing this out: your son may have a thousand virtues, but he doesn't have the slightest patience. We have many quarrels on that account.'

'Bou, you speak to no purpose; today, nothing you say is to my liking.'

'Pishima, nothing is to my liking, either. For fear of hurting your feelings, I have been trying to cover up your son's guilt by uttering such falsehoods. But things have come to such a pass, that it can be concealed no more.'

'I know my son's virtues and weaknesses, but I did not know that you were such a sorceress.'

Binodini checked the retort that rose to her lips. 'You are right, Pishima,' she observed. 'Nobody really knows anybody else. Do we even know our own minds? Out of jealousy of your daughter-in-law, have you never wished to use this sorceress to beguile your son's mind? Think about it and see if it is true.'

'You wretched woman!' cried Rajalakshmi, blazing with fury. 'Can you so malign a mother's feelings for her own son? May your tongue fall off!'

'Pishima, we belong to the tribe of witches,' retorted Binodini, unperturbed. 'I was not aware of my own powers of seduction, but you recognized them; you, too, were not quite aware of your own artfulness, but I saw it. There must have been some magic; the art of illusion must have been called into play, or else this could never have happened. I cast my spell, part knowingly, part unbeknownst to myself. You, too, laid your trap part deliberately, part unconsciously. Such is the customary behaviour of our tribe, for we are witches.'

Rage choked Rajalakshmi's voice. She rushed out of the room.

For some time, Binodini remained standing in the empty room. A fire blazed in her eyes.

After completing her domestic chores for the morning, Rajalakshmi sent for Mahendra. He realized that there would be a discussion of what had occurred the previous night. At that moment, Binodini's reply to his letter had overwhelmed his mind. That blow had driven all his passions towards Binodini, in waves of turbulence. It was impossible for him to argue with his mother when his emotions were in such turmoil. Mahendra knew that if his mother rebuked him about Binodini, he would instantly rebel and blurt out his innermost thoughts, and this would immediately lead to a domestic war. Hence, at this moment, it was best for him to escape from home and clearly think things through.

'Tell Ma that I have some special work at college,' Mahendra instructed the servant. 'I must go now. I'll see her when I return.' He rushed out of the house like a truant child, without dressing or eating his food. He had been carrying Binodini's terrible letter in his pocket, reading it over and over again; now, in his extreme haste, he left the letter behind in the pocket of his kurta, and went away.

After a shower of heavy rain, the sky remained overcast. Binodini was in a highly irritable frame of mind. When perturbed, she increased her household activities. Hence, today, she had collected all the clothes she could find, and was putting laundry marks on them. When she went to Asha to collect some garments, the expression on the young girl's face only added to her annoyance. If Binodini must live in this world as a sinner, why should she have to suffer all the disgrace of sinfulness, while being denied all its joys?

The rain came down heavily with splashing sounds. Binodini sat on the floor of her room, a heap of clothes before her. Khemi, the maid, was handing her the garments, one at a time, and Binodini was inscribing initials on them with marking ink. Without knocking, Mahendra opened the door and came straight into the room. Dropping her work, Khemi covered her head and ran from the room.

Quick as lightning, Binodini flung aside the clothes on her lap and rose to her feet. 'Go away!' she ordered. 'Leave my room and go away.'

'Why, what have I done?'

'What have you done, indeed! You unmanly coward! What are you capable of doing, anyway? You neither know how to love, nor how to do your duty. In the process, why must you ruin me in the eyes of other people?'

'How can you say I don't love you?'

'That is precisely what I am saying. Always playing hide and seek, covering up everything, now swaying this way, now that! Having seen your underhand ways, I feel only contempt for you. I don't enjoy this anymore. Please go away.'

Utterly deflated, Mahendra asked, 'Do you despise me, Binod?'

'I despise you.'

'There is still time to make amends, Binod. If I vacillate no more, if I forsake everything and leave, are you prepared to come with me?' With these words, Mahendra caught Binodini's hands in a powerful grip and drew her to him.

'Let go, you are hurting me,' protested Binodini.

'So, let it hurt. Say, will you go with me?'

'No, I shall not. Never!'

'Why not? It was you who dragged me to my own ruin; you cannot abandon me now. You must come with me.'

Mahendra clasped Binodini to his heart in a hard embrace, and declared, 'Even your contempt will not break my resolve. I shall take you away with me, and somehow, you must love me.'

Binodini wrenched herself free.

'You have set a great fire blazing, all around us,' said Mahendra. 'You can neither quench the flames nor escape them.' As he spoke, Mahendra's voice rose. 'Why did you play such games, Binod?' he shouted. 'You cannot escape now by pretending it's a game. You and I must die the same death.'

Rajalakshmi came into the room. 'Mahin, what are you doing?' she demanded.

For just an instant, Mahendra's wild gaze turned to rest upon his mother's face; then, confronting Binodini once again, he said, 'I am going away, sacrificing everything; say you will go with me.'

Binodini glanced once at the distraught Rajalakshmi's face. Then, advancing towards Mahendra, she calmly took his hand and announced, 'I will go.'

'Then wait for just this one day,' Mahendra told her. 'I take your leave now. From tomorrow, there will be no one but you in my life.'

With these words, Mahendra went away.

Just then, the dhobi came to Binodini and complained, 'Ma thakrun, I can't wait any longer. If you people have no time today, I'll come tomorrow to collect the washing.'

Khemi came and reported, 'Bou thakrun, the groom says he has run out of grain for the horses.' Binodini would weigh out a week's rations of grain for the stable. Standing at the window, she would personally supervise the feeding of the horses.

The servant Gopal came to inform her, 'Bou thakrun, Jharu, our kitchen hand, has quarrelled with Dadamoshai Sadhucharan today. He says, once his kerosene account has been settled, he will claim his salary from the steward and quit his job.'

On the domestic front, it was work as usual.

35

All these days, Bihari had been studying at the medical college. Just before the examinations, he quit. If anyone expressed surprise, he would say, 'I'll attend to other people's health later; I must take care of my own health first.'

Actually, Bihari had boundless energy and could never remain idle, but he had no thirst for fame, no greed for wealth, or any need to earn a livelihood. After obtaining his college degree, he had at first gone to Shivpur to learn engineering. Having acquired knowledge enough to satisfy his curiosity and as much manual skill as he considered necessary, he switched to medical college. Mahendra had joined the medical college a year earlier, having obtained his degree. To the Bengali students at the college, the two of them were known for their mutual friendship. They were jokingly called the Siamese twins from the land of darkness, Shyam. Since

Mahendra had failed his examinations the previous year, the two friends were now classmates. Why the pair broke up at such a juncture was something the other students could not understand.

Bihari could not bear to continue frequenting a place where he was bound to meet Mahendra daily, but on altered terms. Everyone expected Bihari to win honours and awards for his performance in the examinations; but he did not even sit for them.

In a hut beside Bihari's house lived a poor Brahmin named Rajendra Chakrabarti. He earned his livelihood working in a printing press as a compositor for a salary of twelve rupees. 'Let your son stay with me,' Bihari proposed to him. 'I shall personally teach him to read and write.'

The Brahmin was relieved at this life-saving opportunity. Happily, he surrendered his eight-year-old son Basanta to Bihari's care.

Bihari began to teach him according to his own methods. 'I shall not make him read books before the age of ten,' he declared. 'I'll teach him everything orally.' He began spending his days playing with the boy, wandering with him in Garer Maath, the museum, the Alipore zoo, the Shivpur gardens. Bihari's day was spent in teaching the boy spoken English, narrating history to him as if it were a story, testing the boy's ability in a variety of ways and improving his performance; he did not spare a moment for himself.

That evening, it was impossible to go out. After a dry spell in the afternoon, it had been raining since early evening. Sitting in his room on the first floor, having lit the lamp, Bihari was engaging Basanta in games devised according to his own system of learning.

'Basanta, tell me quickly how many beams there are in this room. No, no counting.'

'Twenty.'

'You lose—the answer is eighteen.'

Suddenly whipping the blinds open, he asked, 'How many shutters do these blinds have?' He closed the blinds.

'Six,' said Basanta.

'You win. What would be the length of this bench? How much does this book weigh?' In this way, Bihari was refining Basanta's senses. At this juncture, the bearer came and said, in Hindi, 'Babuji, ektho aurat . . . Babuji, there's a woman . . .'

Before he could finish speaking, Binodini entered the room.

'Bouthan! How extraordinary!' Bihari exclaimed in amazement.

'Aren't any of your female relatives here?' demanded Binodini.

'Neither relatives, nor strangers. My Pishi lives in the house in our native village.'

'Then take me to the house in your native village.'

'How would I introduce you there?'

'As your dasi, a housemaid. I shall do housework there.'

'Pishi will be a little surprised; she has not told me that she needs a maid. First tell me what gave rise to this resolve. Basanta, go to bed.'

Basanta went away.

Binodini said, 'From an account of external happenings, you will not understand the inside story.'

'So what if I don't understand, or even misunderstand? What harm in that?'

'Very well, then, misunderstand if you will. Mahendra loves me.'

'That's not new, and it's not the kind of news one wants to hear repeated.'

'I have no wish to repeat it. That is why I have come to you. Please give me refuge.'

'You have no wish to repeat it? Who caused this disaster? Who led Mahendra astray?'

'It was my doing. I shall not conceal it from you: all this is my doing. I may be evil, or whatever else you please, but put yourself in my place for once, and try to understand me. With the flame that burnt in my heart, I kindled the fire that has destroyed Mahendra's domestic life. I once thought I loved Mahendra, but I was wrong.'

'Would love lead anyone to ignite such a blaze of destruction?'

'Thakurpo, these are words from your scriptures. I

have still not developed an inclination for such talk. Thakurpo, put aside your punthis, those scriptural texts, and look into my heart as a deity might do. Today I want to reveal to you all that is good and bad about myself.'

'Is it for nothing that I keep my scriptural texts open, Bouthan? Leave it to God's omniscience to interpret the language of the heart; but if we ordinary mortals don't follow what the scriptures decree, how would we keep our balance?'

'Listen, Thakurpo, I say without shame that you could have turned me away. Mahendra might love me, but he is completely blind, and does not understand me at all. I had once felt that you understood me, that you had once respected me; tell me if that was true. Don't try to suppress that truth, today.'

'I tell you truly, I had respected you.'

'You were not mistaken, Thakurpo. But if you did understand and respect me, why did you stop at that? What prevented you from loving me? Today, I have come to you shamelessly, and I ask you without shame, why did you not love me? It was my misfortune that you, too, fell deeply in love with Asha. No, you must not be angry. Sit down, Thakurpo. I shall speak frankly, hiding nothing. Even when you were unaware of your own love for Asha, I was aware of it. But what all of you see in Asha, I simply do not understand. Good or bad, what notable qualities does she possess? Has destiny not granted insight to men, along with their masculine gaze? You men are beguiled by what you see, and by seeing so little! Fools! You are blind!'

Rising to his feet, Bihari declared, 'I shall listen to whatever you have to say, but I beg you not to utter that which should not be spoken.'

'Thakurpo, I know where it hurts. But for me to have relinquished all fear and shame tonight, to rush to the person whose respect I had once received, and whose love would have made my life worthwhile—think of the enormous agony that has driven me to it, and be patient awhile! I tell you truly, if you had not loved Asha, I would not have thus become the instrument of Asha's ruin.'

Bihari turned pale. 'What has happened to Asha? What have you done to her?'

'Abandoning his entire household, Mahendra is ready to go away with me tomorrow.'

'This cannot be allowed to happen!' roared Bihari suddenly. 'Never!'

'Never? Who can stop Mahendra now?'

'You can.'

After a short silence, Binodini fixed her gaze on Bihari. 'Stop him for whose sake?' she asked. 'For your Asha? Have I no joys and sorrows of my own? Must I give up all claims to life in this world for Asha's benefit, for the benefit of Mahendra's household? I am not so virtuous, nor am I so well versed in what the religious scriptures say. What will I get in return for what I am to relinquish?'

Bihari's expression hardened into extreme severity. 'You have tried to speak frankly,' he said. 'Now let me also be honest. The outrage you have committed today, and the words you spoke, are largely derived from the literature that you read. Seventy per cent of it belongs to fiction and drama.'

'Fiction! Drama!'

'Yes, fiction and drama. And that, too, of not a very high calibre. You imagine these to be your own sentiments, but that is not so. All these are echoes of the printing press. If you had been an utterly foolish, illiterate, simple young girl, even then you would not have been denied love in this world. But the heroine of a play belongs on stage, it would not do to take her home.'

Where had they vanished—Binodini's brilliant radiance, her daring arrogance? Like a snake under a charmer's spell, she remained motionless, with bowed head. After a long pause, she asked, in a calm, polite voice, 'What would you advise me to do?' She did not look at Bihari's face.

'Don't try to do anything extraordinary. Act according to the common sense of an ordinary woman. Go back to your native place.'

'How would I go there?'

'I could put you into the ladies' carriage and escort you up to your station.'

'Let me stay the night here, then.'

'No, I don't trust myself thus far,' said Bihari.

Hearing this, Binodini instantly rose from the chowki and flung herself to the ground. With all her might, she clutched Bihari's feet to her bosom and pleaded: 'Please retain that little weakness, Thakurpo. Don't be rigid and pure like a stone god. Loving an evil one, allow yourself to become a little evil.'

With these words, Binodini kissed Bihari's feet again and again. For a moment, her sudden, unexpected behaviour seemed to shake Bihari's self-control. Like knots being loosened, all the joints in his body and mind seemed to grow slack. Sensing Bihari's overwhelmed silence, Binodini released his feet. Raising herself to a kneeling position, she wrapped her arms around Bihari's neck as he sat on the chowki. She begged, 'My life, I know you are not mine forever, but today, love me for just one moment. After that, I shall go away to the wilderness where I belong; I shall never again ask anything of anybody. Give me something that I can remember to my dying day.' Binodini closed her eyes and raised her lips to Bihari's.

For an instant, the two of them remained motionless and the entire room was silent. Then, sighing, Bihari slowly disengaged himself from Binodini's arms and went to sit on another chowki. Clearing his choked voice, he said, 'There is a passenger train at one o'clock tonight.'

After a short silence, Binodini said in an indistinct voice, 'I'll take that train.'

At this moment, barefoot and bare chested, Basanta came and stood beside Bihari's chowki, his body well-built, fair and handsome. Solemnly, he studied Binodini. 'Why haven't you gone to bed?' asked Bihari. Without replying, Basanta stood in grave silence.

Binodini stretched out her arms towards him. Hesitating at first, Basanta slowly went up to her. Clasping him to her bosom, Binodini broke down in a flood of tears.

36

Even the impossible becomes possible, the intolerable comes to be tolerated, or else Mahendra's household could not have lived through that night. Having asked Binodini to be ready, Mahendra wrote a letter that very night. In the morning, the letter arrived at Mahendra's house by post.

Asha was then in bed. Carrying the letter in, the bearer said in Hindi, 'Ma-ji, chitthi. Here's a letter, Madam.'

The blood pounded in Asha's heart. In an instant, a thousand hopes and fears resounded together in her bosom. Quickly raising her head, she took the letter. Binodini's name was inscribed on it in Mahendra's hand. Immediately, her head fell back on the pillow. Without a word, Asha returned the letter to the bearer. The bearer asked, 'To whom should I deliver this letter?'

'I don't know,' said Asha.

It was about eight in the evening when Mahendra
rushed up to Binodini's room to find it in complete
darkness. Taking a matchbox out of his pocket, he lit
a match; the room was empty. Binodini was gone, and
so were all her belongings. He went to the southern
veranda and saw that it was vacant. 'Binod!' he called,
but there was no reply.

'A fool! I am a fool. I should have taken her with
me then and there. Ma must have upbraided Binodini,
making it impossible for her to remain in the house.'

As soon as this possibility occurred to him, he
believed it to be true. In restless impatience, Mahendra
immediately went to his mother's room. This room
was also in darkness, but even in the dark, he saw that
Rajalakshmi was lying on the bed.

'Ma, what have all of you been saying to Binodini?'
demanded Mahendra, in a tone of outrage.

'We have said nothing.'

'Then where has she gone?'

'How would I know?'

'You don't know?' Mahendra asked in disbelief. 'Very
well, I am going in search of her. Wherever she may be,
I shall surely find her.'

With these words, he walked away. Swiftly rising
from her bed, Rajalakshmi followed him, saying,
'Mahin, please don't go Mahin, come back, listen to me.'

Without pausing for breath, Mahendra ran out of
the house. A moment later, he came back to ask the

237

doorman, 'Where has Bouthakurani gone?'

'She did not tell us where she was going; we don't know anything.'

'You don't know!' roared Mahendra.

'No, sir, I don't know,' replied the doorman, his hands folded in supplication.

'Ma has instructed them to say this,' Mahendra thought to himself. 'Very well, so be it,' he said aloud.

On the main street of the great city, in the dimness of evening illuminated by gas lamps, the ice seller was hawking ice and the fishmonger was calling out to advertise his topshi fish. Entering the noise and bustle of the crowd, Mahendra vanished from sight.

37

*B*ihari never sat down to meditate upon himself in the darkness of the night. He had never considered himself a subject for self-analysis. He would remain busy with his studies, work, friends and other people. He lived happily, giving more importance to the world around him than to himself. But one day, a sudden shock shattered his world—in the darkness of the apocalypse, he was forced to stand alone with himself, on the mountain peak of an agony that rent the sky. Ever since then, he had begun to fear being alone with himself; taking on an enormous burden of work, he avoided all chances of being alone in his own company.

But tonight, Bihari could not fend off this other self that lived inside him. Ever since he had escorted Binodini to her native place the previous day, engaged though he might be at work or in company, his reclusive, agonized heart kept drawing him ceaselessly in the direction of his own deep solitariness.

Tonight, fatigue and dejection got the better of him. It was about nine o'clock; on the south-facing terrace before Bihari's house, the romantic evening summer breeze stirred restlessly. In the moonless dark, Bihari sat in an armchair placed on the terrace.

This evening, he had not tutored the child Basanta—he had let the boy off early. Tonight, yearning for consolation, for companionship, for the life full of affection and sweetness to which he had been accustomed, his heart, like an infant abandoned by its mother, seemed to stretch out its arms, searching for someone in the darkness. Tonight, the dam of his harsh, rigid self-control had broken. His whole heart strained towards those he had resolved not to think of, and he had not the slightest power to stop it.

In his mind, Bihari spread out the map that charted the entire narrative of his love for Mahendra, from its beginnings in childhood, to the time when it had ended—a long story, illuminated in many colours, a rolled-up mental map that featured land, water, mountains and rivers. He tried to determine the point where the tiny world in which his life was rooted had collided with some evil planet. At first, someone had entered from outside. Glowing in the rosy radiance of sunset, Asha's shy young countenance took shape in the darkness, to the accompaniment of the sound of conch shells announcing a sacred festival. This auspicious planet, approaching from some unknown corner of the sky of destiny, came to a halt between the two friends. It seemed to cause a degree of separation, bringing with it a deep pain that could neither be expressed in words, nor cherished in the mind. But still, this separation—this pain—remained suffused with affection, filled with the glow of sweetness.

After this, the malignant planet had appeared on the horizon, shattering all bonds of friendship, conjugal love, domestic peace and purity—Binodini, whom Bihari, in extreme contempt, tried with all his might to spurn. But how extraordinary! The blows he struck looked very feeble, seeming not to touch her at all. The exquisitely beautiful, enigmatic figure, with her deep, dark, mysterious, steady gaze, came and stood motionless before Bihari. The gusty summer breeze touched Bihari's body like her own heavy breath. Gradually, the burning radiance of those unwavering eyes began to fade; the dry, thirsting, piercing gaze, moistened and softened by tears, was rapidly flooded with deep emotion. In an instant, the figure fell at Bihari's feet and clasped his thighs to her breast with all her might. After that, like an exquisite magic vine, she twined herself around Bihari, reaching upwards to present a kissable countenance like a freshly blooming, fragrant cluster of flowers close to Bihari's lips. Bihari shut his eyes, trying to banish this imagined shape from his memory, but his hands seemed incapable of striking her a blow; an unfinished kiss remained suspended agonizingly close to his face, filling him with rapture.

Bihari could no longer remain in the darkness of the lonely terrace. To divert his mind, he quickly entered the lamp-lit room.

In the corner, on the teapoy, was a framed photograph covered in silk. Removing the cover, Bihari carried the picture to the centre of the room, where he could study it in the lamplight. Placing it on his lap, he began to examine the photograph.

The picture was of Mahendra and Asha, taken shortly after their marriage. Behind the picture, Mahendra had inscribed 'Mahinda' in his own handwriting, and Asha had written just her name—'Asha'—in her own hand. In the picture, the sweetness of new love had not faded. Mahendra sat on the chowki, his face bearing the youthful, fresh emotion of a newly married man. Beside him stood Asha; the photographer had not allowed her to cover her head, but he had not been able to remove the bashfulness from her face. Today, Mahendra was ready to move far away, abandoning his companion Asha to tears of lamentation. Yet the inanimate picture had preserved every line of fresh love on Mahendra's countenance; permitting no change, it blindly, foolishly, perpetuated the irony of fate.

Holding this picture on his lap, Bihari tried to summon up a feeling of contempt, to banish Binodini to some far-off place. But her lovelorn, youthful, tender arms continued to clasp Bihari's thighs. In his mind, Bihari accused her: 'You broke up such a beautiful, loving home!' But Binodini's countenance, tilted upwards with its offer of a kiss, answered him wordlessly, 'I love you. In the whole world, you are the one I have chosen.'

What sort of reply was this? Could this declaration alone override the terrible anguished cries of a broken home? The she-devil!

She-devil! Did Bihari use the term in utter condemnation, or was there also an overtone of fondness in it? At a moment when Bihari, having been denied all claims to love and friendship, had taken to the streets like a beggar, was it possible for him to wholeheartedly reject the gift of such unsolicited, unlimited love? What had Bihari ever received that could bear comparison with this? Until now, in return for dedicating his whole life, he had only begged for leftover crumbs of affection from the storehouse of love. But now that the beneficent goddess of plenty had sent him a feast on a golden platter meant exclusively for him, why should the wretched man be hesitant enough to deny himself such a feast?

Having fallen into a reverie with the picture on his lap, he started at a sound near him, and saw that it was Mahendra. As soon as he started to his feet, the picture slipped onto the floor, but Bihari did not notice it.

'Where is Binodini?' demanded Mahendra, without any preamble.

Advancing towards Mahendra, Bihari grasped his

hand. 'Mahinda, please wait, we can discuss everything.'

'I don't have the time to wait or to discuss anything. Tell me, where is Binodini?'

'Your question cannot be answered in a single word. You must be patient and wait awhile.'

'Would you offer me advice? I have read those words of advice since I was a child.'

'No, I have neither the right nor the ability to offer advice.'

'Would you rebuke me? I know I am a villain, the meanest of beings, and whatever you wish to call me. But the fact of the matter is that you don't know where Binodini is.'

'I do.'

'Will you tell me or not?'

'No.'

'You have to tell me. You have abducted her and hidden her away. She is mine, return her to me.'

'She is not yours,' said Bihari firmly, after a short silence. 'I have not abducted her; she surrendered herself to me of her own accord.'

'That is false!' roared Mahendra. He started banging on the closed door of the adjoining room, calling out loudly, 'Binod, Binod!'

Hearing the sound of weeping inside the room, he cried out, 'Have no fear, Binod. This is Mahendra, come to rescue you. Nobody can keep you locked up.'

With these words, Mahendra gave a powerful shove, and the door opened instantly. Rushing inside, he found the room in darkness. He saw a shadowy figure crouching on the bed, stiff with fear, clutching at the pillow with an inarticulate sound. Quickly entering the room, Bihari lifted Basanta off the bed and into his arms, consoling him: 'Don't be afraid, Basanta, there is nothing to be afraid of. Nothing at all.'

Rushing out of the room, Mahendra checked all the other rooms in the house. When he came back, Basanta was still sobbing in bouts of fear. Having turned on the lamp, Bihari had placed him on the bed and was stroking him gently, trying to put him to sleep.

Mahendra came to him and demanded: 'Where have you put Binodini?'

'Mahinda, don't create a commotion. You have needlessly frightened this boy so much that he might fall sick. I tell you, there is no need for you to enquire after Binodini.'

'O saint! O great-hearted one! Don't speak of any religious ideals. Holding my wife's picture in your lap at night, what deity were you meditating upon, and with what words of prayer? You hypocrite!'

With these words, Mahendra flung the picture to the ground, and trampled the glass to smithereens. Tearing the photograph to shreds, he flung the pieces at Bihari.

Seeing his mad behaviour, Basanta again cried out in fear. Bihari's voice was close to choking. 'Get out!' he cried, pointing at the door.

Mahendra stormed out of the room.

38

As she gazed out of the window of the vacant ladies' compartment of the train, and saw ploughed fields and tree-shaded villages, Binodini felt drawn to the prospect of a gentle, secluded life in a rural setting. She began to feel that, within the enclosing shade of trees, in the nest of her imagination, with her favourite books, she might find a temporary respite from all the anger, bitterness and pain of urban life. Watching the sun set in the dusty, uncultivated summer fields that extended up to the horizon, Binodini began to believe that she wanted nothing more. As if her mind had no other need except to close its eyes and lose itself in this golden, silent expanse of peace; to steer the boat of her life away from the turbulent sea of joy and sorrow, to touch the shore and tie the boat to an immobile banyan tree in the silence of the evening. As the train journeyed on, the fragrance of mango blossom wafted occasionally into the compartment; she was deeply enchanted by the gentle peace of the countryside. She told herself, 'It's just as well. I can't drag myself about anymore. Now, I shall forget everything, and go to sleep. I'll become a country girl once more, living in peace and comfort, performing my duties at home and in the village.'

Cherishing such hopes in her thirsting heart, Binodini entered her hut. But alas, where was peace to be found? There was only emptiness and poverty. All around her, everything was worn out, unclean, unkempt and faded. The steamy odour of the damp, closed room seemed to stifle her. The few items of furniture in the room had been almost destroyed; they were moth-eaten, chewed by rats and full of dust. Binodini had arrived there in the evening; the hut was joyless and dark. When she managed to light the lamp with mustard oil, the meagreness of the room became even more apparent in the dim, smoky light. What had never bothered her before, now seemed intolerable. 'I can't stay here a single moment,' her rebellious heart protested. A few books and magazines lay, covered in dust, in a recess in the wall, but she did not want to touch them. Outside, in the airless mango grove, the buzzing of mosquitoes and crickets began to resound in the darkness.

Binodini's elderly guardian had locked up the hut and gone to visit her daughter at her son-in-law's house far away. Binodini went across to her neighbours. They seemed startled to see her. Look at this! Binodini's complexion has grown fairer, and she's smartly turned out, like a memsahib! They exchanged meaningful glances as they observed Binodini. As if the signs they detected confirmed what hearsay had suggested.

At every step, Binodini began to feel that she had alienated herself from her own village in every possible way. She was an exile in her own home. Nowhere could she feel relaxed for a single moment.

The old postman had known Binodini since she was a child. The next day, while preparing to bathe at the ghat, the paved area at the edge of the pond, she saw the postman walking along the road, carrying his postbag. Unable to control herself any longer, she dropped her gamchha, quickly ascended to the path, and called out to him: 'Panchudada, is there any mail for me?'

'No,' replied the old man.

'There might be,' insisted Binodini anxiously. 'Let me see.'

She picked up a few letters, turned them over and saw that none were addressed to her. When she returned to the waterside with a dejected countenance, one of her female companions cast a mocking sidelong glance at her and asked, 'What's the matter, Bindi, why such desperation for a letter?'

'Well, well!' remarked another saucy woman. 'After all, how many people are fortunate enough to receive letters in the mail? My husband, brother-in-law and brother work abroad, but the postman never takes pity on me.'

Their taunts grew more explicit and their sidelong glances sharper. Before her departure, Binodini had requested Bihari to write a few lines to her at least twice a week, if not every day. It was highly unlikely that she would hear from Bihari so soon, but so keen was her desire, that Binodini could not relinquish even such a remote possibility. It seemed a long time since she had left Kolkata.

Thanks to her enemies and friends, the fact that shameful rumours linking Mahendra's name with Binodini's had spread all over the village was something she could not ignore. Where was peace to be found? She tried to remain aloof from all the people of the village. That incensed her neighbours all the more. They did not want to be denied the pleasure of condemning and tormenting a fallen woman in their midst.

It was futile to try avoiding people in a tiny locality. Here, there was no dark, private corner where she might have the chance to nurse her broken heart. From all directions, sharp, inquisitive eyes would gaze upon her wounds. The more Binodini's inner self thrashed about like a captured fish in the fisherman's basket, the more she hurt herself within the narrow confines of her environment. Here, there was no space even to fully savour her pain.

On the second day, when the time for mail delivery was past, Binodini shut her door and sat down to write:

Thakurpo, don't be afraid, I do not intend to write you a love letter. You are my judge; I bow before you in obeisance. You have punished me harshly for my sins; at your command, I have taken that punishment upon my head with great deference. Sadly, you could not witness the harshness of the punishment you have inflicted. I have been deprived even of the pity you would have felt, had you seen or known it. Remembering you, mentally bowing down to you, I shall bear even this. But my lord, does a captive in prison not even receive any nourishment? Not a feast, to be sure, but surely, she is entitled to the minimum rations required for her to stay alive? A two-line letter from you would be such sustenance for me in exile; if I don't receive it, you would have condemned me not only to exile, but to death. Don't test me thus far, my judge. There were no limits to the arrogance of my sinful heart; I had not imagined, even in my dreams, that I would ever have to bow my head thus before anyone else. Victory is yours, my lord; I shall not rebel. But have pity on me: let me live. Offer me sustenance, in meagre portions, during my stay in this wilderness. Nobody and nothing then can shake my faith in your authority. I disclose to you only this small part of my suffering. I have vowed not to let you know all the other things that are in my mind, which my heart yearns to tell you. I hereby keep my vow.

Yours
Binod Bouthan.

Binodini posted her letter. Her neighbours cried shame. To remain at home behind closed doors, writing letters, accosting the postman in the hope of receiving a letter! Even if one had fallen upon hard times in Kolkata, should one be so disgracefully brazen about it?

Even the next day, there was no letter. All day, Binodini remained still and silent; her face hardened. Hurt and humiliated, tormented from within and without, a cruel, destructive power took shape deep within the dark recesses of her heart, and struggled to burst forth. In fearful anticipation, Binodini locked her door.

She had nothing of Bihari's with her—no picture, not even a one-line letter, nothing. She seemed to be groping for something in empty space, some token of Bihari's self to clasp to her breast and to bring tears into her dry eyes. She wanted to melt all the hardness of her heart in a flood of tears, to quench the flames of rebellion, and to enshrine Bihari's harsh decree in the tenderness of her love. But her heart blazed like the noontime sky during a drought, with no sign of tears anywhere on the horizon.

Binodini had heard that a person invoked in prayer during intense meditation cannot but appear. Hands folded in supplication, eyes shut, she began to call Bihari: 'My life is empty, my heart is empty; emptiness is all around me. Into this emptiness, please come just once, come for just one moment, you have to come, I shall not give you up.'

Repeating these words with heartfelt fervour, Binodini

felt herself grow stronger. It seemed to her that the force of her love, the power of her invocation would not be in vain. Merely wallowing in nostalgia, watering the plant of despair with the heart's blood, makes the heart dejected. But through intense meditation, exerting the full force of one's desire, one feels empowered. As acute desire single-mindedly seeks to attract its target, the desired one seems to draw closer, slowly and surely, moment by moment.

When her deep meditation on Bihari had permeated the dark, unlit room in the evening, when world and society, village and neighbourhood, the universe itself, had faded away from her consciousness, drowned in the flood of her love, Binodini suddenly heard a knock on the door. Swiftly arising from the floor, she rushed to open the door, calling out in complete certainty: 'My lord, have you come?' She was firmly convinced that at this moment, nobody else in the world could have come to her door.

'I have come, Binod!' announced Mahendra.

With boundless indifference and tremendous contempt, Binodini exclaimed, 'Go, go! Go away from here. Go at once.'

Mahendra was stunned.

An elderly neighbour came up to Binodini's door. 'Hello, Bindi, if your Didishashuri, your mother-in-law's aunt, were to arrive tomorrow . . .' Then she exclaimed, 'Oh, my goodness!' and covering her face and head with her aanchal, she ran off at great speed.

39

The matter created a stir in the neighbourhood. The village elders gathered at the chandimandap, the shrine meant for the annual Durga Puja. 'This cannot be tolerated!' they declared. 'We could ignore what was happening in Kolkata, but the brazenness of writing letter after letter to Mahendra, to drag him here, right into our neighbourhood! We cannot permit such a fallen woman to remain in the village.'

Binodini was certain of receiving Bihari's reply to her letter by the next morning, but no reply arrived. She began to ask herself, 'What claim does Bihari have upon me? Why did I accept his decree? Why did I let him believe that I would bow to his will? Beyond the need to protect his beloved Asha, does he have no further interest in me? Have I no claims of my own, no demands, not even for a paltry two-line letter? Am I so worthless, so contemptible?' At this, Binodini's bosom swelled with the poison of envy. 'One may suffer all this pain for anyone else, but surely not for Asha! To bear this poverty, this exile in the wilderness, this public opprobrium, this negligence, this frustration in every area of my life just for Asha's sake! Why did I allow myself to be cheated so! Why did I not carry out my vow of revenge and destruction before I came away? What a fool I am! Why did I fall in love with Bihari?'

As Binodini sat stiffly in her room like a wooden statue, her didishashuri, back from her son-in-law's house, accused her: 'You wretched woman, what's all this I hear?'

'What you hear is entirely true.'

'Then what was the need for you to bring such disgrace into this neighbourhood? Why did you come here?'

Suppressing her rage, Binodini remained silent. 'My child,' her didishashuri informed her, 'you cannot remain here. I was unfortunate enough to survive the loss of all who were near and dear to me, but I cannot tolerate matters of this nature. For shame! You have disgraced us. Please leave at once.'

'I shall leave at once.'

Right then, Mahendra suddenly arrived on the scene, unwashed, unfed, his hair uncombed. His eyes were bloodshot from a sleepless night, and his face was wan. He had decided to come early in the morning, while it was still dark, to make a second attempt at taking Binodini away. But smarting from Binodini's unprecedented display of contempt on the previous day, many doubts arose in his mind. Gradually, as the day rolled on, and the hour of the train's departure drew close, he emerged from the waiting room at the station, and sweeping aside all doubt and hesitation, mounted his carriage and drove straight to Binodini's door. Spurred by the arrogant power that accompanies a defiant, daring deed, Mahendra experienced a wild joy. All his lethargy and hesitation evaporated. To his frenzied eyes, the curious villagers seemed like lifeless clay dolls. Without glancing in any direction, Mahendra came straight up to Binodini. 'Binod,' he declared, 'I am not coward enough to leave you here in the face of public ignominy. I must take you away from here somehow. After that, if you wish to abandon me, you may do so; I shall not stop you. I swear it will be exactly as you wish: if you take pity on me, I shall live; if you do not, I shall remove myself from your life. I have committed many faithless deeds in my life, but do not mistrust me today. We are facing a deluge; this is no time for deception.'

With an unperturbed air, in a very natural tone, Binodini replied, 'Take me with you. Do you have a carriage?'

'I do.'

Emerging from the hut, Binodini's didishashuri intervened: 'Mahendra, you don't know me, but we are no strangers. Your mother Rajalakshmi belongs to our village; as a fellow-villager, I am like her mami, her maternal aunt. I ask you, what sort of behaviour is this? To wander about in this shameless, wild fashion, leaving your wife and mother at home! How will you show your face in civilized society after this?'

Though lost in a realm of lunacy, Mahendra was jolted by her words. He had a mother, a wife, and a place in what was known as civilized society. This simple fact resurfaced in his mind with renewed urgency. Once, he could never have imagined that he would have to listen to such words at the door of an unfamiliar house in some unknown, far-off rural locality. In broad daylight, in front of the entire village, for him to coax a young, respectable, widowed lady out of her home and into the street was indeed a strange episode in the story of Mahendra's life. But still, he had a mother, a wife, and a place in civilized society.

When Mahendra stood silent without offering any reply, the old woman ordered: 'If you must leave, go at once, right now. Don't remain standing in the veranda outside my hut, don't delay a moment longer.'

With these words, she entered the hut and locked the door from within. Unwashed, dressed in stale clothes, and on an empty stomach, Binodini entered the carriage empty-handed. When Mahendra tried to climb into the carriage, Binodini stopped him. 'No. The station is not far away; you must walk.'

'But all the village folk will see me.'

'Do you still have any shame?' With these words, Binodini closed the carriage door. 'Take me to the station,' she ordered the coachman.

'Won't Babu go with us?' the coachman inquired.

After some hesitation, Mahendra's courage failed him. The carriage drove away. Leaving the village street, Mahendra took the winding path through the fields, and walked towards the station with his head bent low.

At that time, the village women had completed their bath and their morning meal. Just a few industrious elderly matrons, who were free only at this late hour, were walking with their gamchhas and bowls of oil towards the secluded edge of the pond, a shaded area redolent with mango blossom.

40

In her anxiety over Mahendra's disappearance, Rajalakshmi could neither eat nor sleep. Sadhucharan was searching for him in all sorts of places, probable and improbable, when Mahendra returned to Kolkata with Binodini. Establishing her in a rented flat at Potoldanga, Mahendra returned to his own home at night.

Entering his mother's room, Mahendra found it in almost complete darkness, except for the dim glow of the shaded kerosene lantern. Like a patient, Rajalakshmi lay on the bed, and sitting at her feet, Asha was gently massaging her legs. At long last, the bride of the house had found her rightful place at her mother-in-law's feet.

As soon as Mahendra appeared, Asha gave a start and left the room. Shedding all hesitation, Mahendra declared, 'Ma, it is not convenient for me to study at home; I have taken an apartment near the college; that is where I shall stay.'

Pointing to the end of the bed, Rajalakshmi said, 'Mahin, wait awhile.'

Self-consciously, Mahendra sat on the bed.

'Mahin, stay wherever you please, but don't torment my Bouma,' said Rajalakshmi.

Mahendra remained silent. Rajalakshmi continued, 'It is my misfortune that I failed to perceive the angelic nature of my daughter-in-law.' As she spoke, her voice choked with emotion. 'But having known her so long, loved her so much, how could you ultimately inflict such suffering upon her?' Unable to control herself, Rajalakshmi burst into tears.

Mahendra longed to get up and escape somehow, but he found himself suddenly unable to rise. In the dark, he sat on the edge of his mother's bed, motionless.

'You will stay here tonight, won't you?' inquired Rajalakshmi, after a long silence.

'No.'

'When will you leave?'

'Right away.'

'Right away?' exclaimed Rajalakshmi, sitting up with difficulty. 'Will you not even meet Bouma once?'

Mahendra did not reply.

'Have you any idea how Bouma has spent these last few days? You shameless boy, I am heartbroken at your cruelty.' With these words, Rajalakshmi collapsed like a branch severed from a tree.

Leaving his mother's bed, Mahendra went out.

Noiselessly, with a gentle tread, he crept up the stairs to his bedchamber. He wanted to avoid Asha.

When he arrived upstairs, Mahendra found Asha lying on the floor of the covered terrace in front of their bedchamber. She had not heard Mahendra's footsteps. Suddenly seeing him before her, she sat up quickly, straightening the folds of her sari. At that moment, if Mahendra had called out, 'Chuni,' she would have instantly taken all the blame upon her own head, and cried her heart out, clasping Mahendra's feet like a forgiven sinner. But Mahendra was unable to utter that term of endearment. Try as he might, much as he wanted to, much as he suffered, he could not forget that any amorous gesture towards Asha tonight would in truth be empty mockery. What was the use of offering her verbal consolation, when Mahendra himself had closed the door on any possibility of his giving up Binodini?

Asha was frozen with embarrassment. She felt too shy to stand up, or to go away, or to make any movement at all. Without speaking a word, Mahendra began to slowly pace on the terrace. The moon in its dark quarter had not yet risen. In a corner of the terrace, two flowers bloomed on separate stems of the tuberose planted in a small flowerpot. From above, the stars in the dark sky gazed down at them in silence—the same constellations, the Great Bear and the Orion, which on many previous evenings had been silent witnesses to many private acts of love.

Mahendra began to wish for the brief tale of his recent rebellion to be wiped out by the darkness that stretched across the sky, so that he could spread a mat on this open terrace and take his permanent place beside Asha, just like before! No questions, no answerability, just the same trust, the same love, the same simple joy as before! But alas, in this world, there remained no way for them to return to that tiny space, their shared past. That corner of the mat, on this terrace, by Asha's side, was lost to Mahendra forever. All these days, Mahendra had enjoyed a free and flexible relationship with Binodini. There was the wild pleasure of love, without its unbreakable bonds. Now that he had severed all her links with society, there was no other place where Binodini could be kept, or to which she could be returned. Mahendra was her sole refuge. Now, whether or not he wanted to, he had to bear full responsibility for Binodini. Mahendra was inwardly tormented at the thought. Suddenly, their domestic nest on this terrace, this peaceful atmosphere, the nights of free conjugal intimacy in complete seclusion seemed a great luxury. But this easy comfort, to which he alone had a right, was now beyond Mahendra's reach. Having taken a lifelong burden upon his shoulders, not for an instant could Mahendra put it down to seek some relief.

With a sigh, Mahendra glanced at Asha. She still sat motionless, her heart full of silent tears. Like a mother's aanchal, the darkness of the night covered her embarrassment and her pain. Mahendra stopped his pacing to suddenly come and stand beside her as if he wanted to say something. All the blood in her body rushed to Asha's head and began pounding in her ears. She closed her eyes. Mahendra forgot what he had been about to say. What was there to say, indeed! But he could not turn back without saying something. 'Where is the bunch of keys?' he asked.

The bunch of keys lay beneath the mattress on the bed. Asha got up and went into the room. Mahendra followed her. Extracting the keys from beneath the mattress, Asha placed them on the bed. Taking the bunch of keys, Mahendra began trying them, one by one, on the lock of his almira. Asha could bear it no longer. In a low voice, she said, 'I did not keep the keys to that almira.'

Asha could not bring herself to utter the name of the person who kept the keys, but Mahendra understood. She quickly left the room for fear that she might burst into tears in Mahendra's presence. Her face averted, she stood in a corner of the terrace, and began to weep, trying with all her might to restrain her overflowing tears.

But there was not much time to cry. She remembered suddenly that it was time for Mahendra's meal. Asha raced down the stairs.

'Where is Mahin, Bouma?' Rajalakshmi asked her.

'Upstairs.'

'Then why did you come down?'

'His dinner . . .' faltered Asha, with lowered head.

'I shall arrange for his dinner, Bouma; you go and freshen up a little. Quickly, put on that new Dhakai sari, and come to me. I'll do your hair.'

Asha could not ignore her mother-in-law's affection, but cringed with embarrassment at her suggestion that she should dress up. Just as Bhishma, wishing for death, had silently endured the shower of arrows, Asha, too, bore with supreme patience the ordeal of submitting her body to the adornments chosen by Rajalakshmi.

Her toilette complete, Asha climbed the stairs unhurriedly, with a silent tread. She glanced at the terrace but found that Mahendra was not there. Slowly approaching the door, she saw that Mahendra was not in his room, either; his food lay untouched.

Lacking the key, Mahendra had forced open the almira, taken a few essential garments and medical textbooks with him, and left the house.

The next day was Ekadashi, the eleventh day of the lunar quarter. Ailing and in pain, Rajalakshmi lay on the bed. Outside, storm clouds were gathering. Slowly, Asha entered the room. Gently placing herself on Rajalakshmi's bed, she touched her feet. 'I have brought milk and fruits for you, Ma; please come and eat.'

Seeing her unhappy daughter-in-law's unaccustomed attempt to care for her, Rajalakshmi's eyes brimmed with tears. Sitting up, she drew Asha onto her lap and kissed her tear-wet cheeks. She asked, 'What is Mahin doing now, Bouma?'

Asha was terribly ashamed. 'He has gone away,' she whispered, in a low voice.

'When did he go away? I didn't even get to know!'

'He left last night,' replied Asha, her head bent low.

As soon as she heard this, Rajalakshmi's tenderness seemed to evaporate. When she caressed her daughter-in-law, there remained no trace of affection in her touch. Sensing a silent rebuke, Asha hung her head and slowly left the room.

41

The first night, when Mahendra went home for his clothes and books, leaving Binodini in the Potoldanga flat, she sat alone amidst the ceaseless hubbub of the Kolkata crowds, thinking about herself. The world had always afforded her very limited refuge, but at least if things grew uncomfortable in one place, there had been space enough for her to turn elsewhere; today, her shelter had become extremely constricted. If the boat on which she rode the current were to tip ever so slightly to the right or left, she would be thrown into the water. Hence, it was important to hold the punting rod steady; there was no room for the smallest mistake or the slightest restless movement. No woman's heart could fail to be shaken, in such a situation. In these narrow confines, where was the space required for that little bit of playfulness, that little bit of seclusion so essential to hold another's heart captive? She had to prepare herself to spend the rest of her life constantly face-to-face with Mahendra. The only difference was that Mahendra had the means to clamber ashore, and Binodini did not.

The more clearly Binodini understood her own helpless condition, the harder she tried to summon up courage in her heart. She must find a way out: she could not continue like this.

From the day Binodini had offered her love to Bihari, the dam of her patience had been breached. Day and night, like a prayer offering, she carried about with her the proffered kiss which, once withdrawn from Bihari's face, could not be planted anywhere else in the world. Binodini's heart did not know how to completely give up hope under any circumstances; she did not acknowledge the possibility of despair. Day and night, her heart declared, with fierce insistence, 'Bihari must accept my offering of devotion.'

Added to this tremendous love was Binodini's acute need for self-protection. She had no recourse but Bihari. Binodini had come to understand Mahendra very well: if one tried to depend on him, he could not bear the burden. He could be captured only when set free, but if one clung to him, he longed to run away. Only Bihari could provide the calm, reliable, stable support so essential for a woman. Binodini could not afford to relinquish Bihari.

The day she left the village, Binodini had sent a special message through Mahendra, requesting the post office adjoining the station to forward all her mail to the new address. Binodini refused to accept that Bihari would ignore her letters altogether. She told herself, 'I shall await a reply patiently for seven days, and then we shall see.'

With these words, Binodini opened the window of her dark chamber, and gazed abstractedly at the gas-lit city of Kolkata. That evening, Bihari was somewhere in that same city—crossing a few streets and lanes, one could reach his door right away—and afterwards, that small courtyard with the water tap, those stairs, that well decorated, neat, brightly lit, secluded room—Bihari sitting there in peaceful silence—with him, perhaps, that Brahmin boy, with his fair, beautiful, cherubic, simple, wide-eyed look, absorbed in turning the pages of a picture book. Imagining the entire scene down to the last detail, Binodini's whole body was filled with rapture. She could go there at once if she wished; Binodini began to play with the desire in her heart. In earlier days, she might have acted to fulfil her wish, but now, many things had to be considered. Now, she must not only satisfy her desire, but also accomplish her purpose. 'Let me first see what sort of reply I receive from Bihari, then I shall decide upon my course of action,' Binodini told herself. She did not dare disturb Bihari without understanding the situation.

She remained absorbed in these thoughts until it was almost nine or ten o'clock at night, when Mahendra arrived, moving with a slow gait. He had spent the past few days in a sleepless, irregular, highly excited state; having attained his goal of bringing Binodini back, he was now overwhelmed with fatigue. Tonight, he seemed to have no strength left to fight the world or his own situation. It was as if all the tiredness of his burdensome future existence had prematurely overpowered him.

Standing in front of the closed door, Mahendra felt too embarrassed to knock. Where was it, the wild exuberance with which he had defied the whole world? Why did he cringe before the gaze of total strangers in the street?

The newly appointed servant had gone to sleep inside; it took a lot of trouble getting him to open the door. Entering the darkness of the unfamiliar apartment, Mahendra's heart grew dispirited. Pampered by his mother, he had always been accustomed to items of luxury—punkahs and expensive chowkis and sofas; in the new household, the absence of these things became sharply apparent in the darkness of evening. It was up to Mahendra to provide all these necessities, for he was solely responsible for all such arrangements in the flat. Mahendra had never concerned himself with his own comfort or anyone else's, but from today, he had to attend to all the small details of a new, partially set up household. On the stairs, a kerosene lamp glimmered within a tin, producing an excessive amount of smoke; he must buy a proper lamp to replace it. The route through the veranda to the stairs was damp with the overflow of tap water; it was necessary to send for masons to repair the area with imported clay. He must quarrel with the landlord about the two street-facing rooms that had not yet been vacated by the tenants, owners of a shoe shop. As it dawned on him in a flash that he alone must perform all these tasks, an added burden weighed him down, aggravating his sense of exhaustion.

Standing near the stairs for a while, Mahendra pulled himself together, trying to arouse his love for Binodini. He persuaded himself that tonight was a night of joy, for the object of his desire, for whom he had defied the whole world, was now his; tonight, there was no obstacle between them. But the absence of obstacles was the greatest obstacle of all: tonight, Mahendra was a hindrance to himself.

Seeing Mahendra approach from the street, Binodini roused herself from her posture of meditation and turned on the lamp. Picking up a piece of embroidery, she bent her head over it in complete absorption. This item of embroidery was like a screen behind which Binodini could take refuge.

Entering the room, Mahendra remarked, 'Binod, you must find it very inconvenient here.'

'Not at all,' replied Binodini, busy with her sewing.

'I shall organize all the furniture and household items in two or three days; you'll have to bear with the inconvenience for a few days.'

'No, I won't allow it. Don't bring any more furniture; what we have here is more than sufficient for my needs.'

'Is an unfortunate fellow like me to be counted among the more-than-sufficient?'

'One should not place too high a value upon oneself; a little modesty is a good thing.'

The sight of Binodini's busy, self-absorbed image in the lonely lamplight instantly kindled something of the old magic in Mahendra's heart.

If they had been in his own home, he would have flung himself at Binodini's feet, but this was not home, hence Mahendra could not behave in such a manner. Tonight, Binodini was helpless, entirely at Mahendra's mercy; it would be extremely cowardly of him to act without restraint.

'Why did you bring your books and clothes here?' Binodini asked him.

'I count them among my necessities. They don't belong to the "more-than-sufficient" category.'

'I know, but why bring all those things here?'

'True, mundane necessities are out of place here. Binodini, fling all my books and other things out into the street, I shall not object at all; just don't throw me out as well.'

As he spoke, Mahendra moved a little closer and tossed the cloth-bound bundle at Binodini's feet.

Gravely, Binodini continued sewing. Without raising

her head, she declared, 'Thakurpo, it would not do for you to remain here.'

Driven to desperation by this rebuttal of his newly aroused desire, Mahendra asked, in a choking voice, 'Why, Binod, why do you want to keep me at arm's length? Is this what I receive, after sacrificing everything for your sake?'

'I shall not let you sacrifice everything for my sake.'

'That is no longer in your hands,' cried Mahendra. 'The world has fallen away from all around me; for me, you alone remain, Binod. Binod . . . Binod . . .'

As he spoke, Mahendra flung himself to the ground, utterly overwhelmed, and clasped Binodini's feet in a strong grip, kissing her delicate feet, soft as leaves, again and again.

Extricating her feet from his grasp, Binodini drew herself up. 'Mahendra, don't you remember your vow?' she reminded him.

'I remember,' answered Mahendra, controlling himself with a supreme effort. 'I had promised to act exactly as you wished; I would never do otherwise. I shall keep my vow. Tell me what I must do.'

'You must go and live in your own home.'

'Am I your only unwanted possession, Binod? If that is so, why did you drag me here? Why hunt down someone who is of no use to you? Tell me truly, was it I who deliberately surrendered myself to you, or you who deliberately took me captive? Must I also tolerate being treated as a plaything? All the same, I shall keep my vow. I shall go and live in the same house where I have trampled my own position to dust.'

Binodini resumed her position on the floor and started sewing again, without offering any reply.

After gazing fixedly at her face for a while, Mahendra exclaimed, 'Cruel, Binod, you are very cruel! It is my utter misfortune that I have loved you.'

Having made an error in her sewing, Binodini held it up to the light and began to carefully unpick the stitches. Mahendra wished he could crush her stony heart in his fist, breaking it to pieces. He felt like using physical force to brutally attack and demolish this silent cruelty and callous indifference.

Mahendra left the room and came back again. 'If I don't stay here, who will protect you when you are alone?' he wanted to know.

'Have no fears on that account. Pishima has dismissed Khemi, and today, she has taken up service here. We women will lock the door and be quite comfortable, the two of us together.'

The angrier he became, the more strongly Mahendra was attracted to Binodini. He wanted to clasp that unrelenting figure to his breast with all his might, to hurt and crush her. To escape the violence of that terrible desire, Mahendra rushed out of the house.

Wandering the streets, Mahendra swore to himself that he would answer Binodini's indifference with indifference. For her to spurn him with such silent contempt, so fearlessly and with such directness, even though he was her only support in the whole world—what greater humiliation could any man suffer? Though shattered, Mahendra's pride refused to die; it only felt tormented and trampled upon. 'Am I indeed so worthless?' he asked himself. 'How dare she behave so arrogantly with me! Apart from me, is there anyone else she can turn to?'

As he pondered upon these things, he suddenly thought of Bihari. For one instant, the blood seemed to freeze in his heart. 'It is Bihari upon whom Binodini has placed all her faith; for her, I am merely an instrument, a stepping stone or footrest, to be kicked around at every step. That is why she dares to show such indifference towards me.' He suspected that Binodini had been corresponding with Bihari, and had received some assurance from him.

Mahendra headed for Bihari's house. When he knocked on Bihari's door, the night was almost over. After a lot of knocking, the attendant opened the door. 'Babuji is not at home,' he said.

Mahendra was startled. He thought, 'While I have been running about the streets like a fool, Bihari has gone to Binodini. That is why Binodini insulted me so cruelly tonight, and I, too, ran away like a driven ass.'

'Bhoju, when did Babu go out?' Mahendra asked the old, familiar attendant.

'That would be about four or five days ago. He has gone west, on vacation.'

Mahendra was relieved to hear that. He thought, 'Now I may as well lie down and sleep in comfort for a while; I can't wander about all night, anymore.' He went upstairs, stretched out on the couch in Bihari's room and instantly fell asleep.

The very morning after Mahendra had entered his room at night and created a scene, Bihari had travelled west, unsure where to go. He felt that if he remained in Kolkata, this conflict with his former friend would someday assume hideous proportions, becoming a lifelong cause for regret.

The next morning, it was eleven o'clock when Mahendra awoke. Immediately, his eye fell on the teapoy before him. He saw a letter, addressed to Bihari in Binodini's hand, lying under a stone paperweight. Snatching it up, he saw that it was unopened. It awaited Bihari's return from distant parts. With shaking hands, Mahendra quickly opened the missive and began to read it. This was the unanswered letter that Binodini had written to Bihari from her own village.

Every character inscribed in the note began to eat into Mahendra's mind. Since their childhood, Bihari had always remained in Mahendra's shadow. When it came to matters of the heart, only Mahendra's stale, cast-off garlands came his way. But today, Binodini had spurned Mahendra's advances to welcome the

dry, colourless Bihari, even though he was unwilling.
Mahendra, too, had received a few letters from Binodini,
but in comparison with her letter to Bihari, they seemed
utterly fake, mere tricks to deceive a fool.

Recalling the eagerness with which Binodini had sent
him to inform the village post office of her new address,
Mahendra now understood the reason for it. With all
her heart and soul, Binodini was awaiting Bihari's reply
to her letter.

In his customary manner, Bhoju the attendant served
Mahendra tea and snacks from the market, although
his master was not at home. Mahendra forgot his
bath. Like a traveller running light-footed on hot
sand, Mahendra ran his eyes quickly over Binodini's
inflammatory letter, again and again. He swore never
to see Binodini again. But, he thought, if she did not
receive a reply to her letter in a day or two, Binodini
would come to Bihari's house, and learning all the
facts, she would be reassured. The possibility seemed
intolerable to him.

Carrying the letter in his pocket, Mahendra arrived
at the Potoldanga flat shortly before dusk. Binodini
took pity on his woebegone appearance. She realized
that Mahendra had probably spent the previous night
wandering sleeplessly about the streets.

'Didn't you go home last night?' she asked.

'No.'

Agitated, Binodini exclaimed, 'Have you not eaten

all day?' With these words, Binodini, ever devoted to serving others, at once got up to arrange a meal.

'Let it be, let it be, I have eaten.'

'Where?'

'At Bihari's house.'

For an instant, Binodini's face grew pale. After a momentary silence, she pulled herself together and asked, 'Bihari Thakurpo is well, I hope?'

'He's quite well. Bihari has gone west.' Mahendra spoke as if Bihari had set out that very day.

Binodini's face grew pale once more. Composing herself yet again, she observed, 'I have never met anyone so restless. Has he heard all about us? Is Thakurpo very angry?'

'Else, would any man fancy travelling west in this intolerable heat?'

'Did he say anything about me?'

'What is there to say? Here is Bihari's letter.'

Mahendra handed the letter to Binodini and fixed his piercing gaze upon her face.

Eagerly taking the letter, Binodini found that it was open. On the envelope was Bihari's name, inscribed in her own hand. Extracting the letter from the envelope, she saw that it was the letter she had written to Bihari. Turning it over and over, she could not find Bihari's reply anywhere.

After a short silence, she asked Mahendra, 'Have you read the letter?'

Binodini's expression frightened Mahendra. 'No,' he lied hastily.

Tearing the letter to little pieces, and then shredding it further, Binodini threw the pieces out of the window.

'I am going home,' Mahendra announced. Binodini offered no reply.

'I shall act according to your express wishes,' Mahendra persisted. 'I shall stay in my own home for seven days. On my way to college, I shall come by once a day, to make all the arrangements for this place, and leave Khemi in charge of everything. I shall not disturb you.'

It was impossible to tell whether Binodini heard a word of what Mahendra said, but she remained silent, merely gazing at the dark sky outside the open window.

Collecting his belongings, Mahendra went away. For a long time, Binodini sat frozen and motionless inside the empty flat. Finally, as if forcing herself back to consciousness, she tore the clothing off her breast and began raining cruel blows upon herself.

Frightened by the noise, Khemi rushed in. 'Bou thakrun, what are you doing?'

'Get out!' thundered Binodini, pushing Khemi out of the room. Then, slamming the door shut, her fists clenched, she flung herself to the ground and began to cry in pain like an animal mortally wounded by an arrow. Battering herself thus, tiring herself out, Binodini remained lying beneath the open window all night like one who had lost consciousness.

When daylight dawned, she suddenly felt suspicious: what if Bihari had not gone away, what if Mahendra had been lying to mislead her? Immediately sending for Khemi, she ordered, 'Khemi, go at once to Bihari Thakurpo's house and find out if all is well.'

Returning after about an hour, Khemi informed her, 'All the doors and windows of Bihari babu's house are closed. When I knocked on the door, the attendant said from within, 'Babu is not at home, he has gone west for a vacation.'

Binodini had no further cause for suspicion.

42

*U*pon hearing that Mahendra had left his bed at night, Rajalakshmi was very angry with her daughter-in-law. Convinced that Mahendra had been driven away by Asha's reproaches, she asked, 'Why did Mahendra go away last night?'

'I don't know, Ma,' replied Asha, lowering her head.

Rajalakshmi took this, too, as a reproach. 'Who knows, if you don't? Did you say anything to him?' she demanded angrily.

'No.'

Rajalakshmi did not believe her. Could this be possible? 'When did Mahin leave last night?' she asked.

'I don't know,' replied Asha, awkwardly.

Highly incensed, Rajalakshmi exclaimed, 'You don't know anything at all! You're an innocent little girl, aren't you? I know your clever tricks!'

In a sharp voice, Rajalakshmi declared that it was

due to Asha's behaviour and her shortcomings that
Mahendra had left home. Listening to the tirade with
bowed head, Asha went to her own room and began to
weep. She thought to herself, 'Why my husband loved
me once, I don't know, nor do I know how to win
back his love.' To please a man in love is easy, for the
heart is one's guide, but the art of winning the heart of
a man not in love was unknown to Asha. How could
she be shameless enough to seek the affection of a man
who loved another?

In the evening, they were visited by Daivajna Thakur,
the family astrologer, and his sister Acharya Thakrun,
a lady with spiritual powers. Rajalakshmi had sent for
them to ensure domestic peace for her son. Rajalakshmi
requested the astrologer to examine Bouma's horoscope
and her palm, and brought Asha to him for this purpose.
Extremely diffident at the prospect of discussing her
own misfortunes with other people, Asha had just taken
her place and extended her hand, when Rajalakshmi
heard a light footstep in the unlit veranda beside her
room. Somebody was trying to creep away in secret.
'Who is it?' she called.

At first, there was no answer. Then she called again,
'Who goes there!' Without answering, Mahendra
entered the room.

Far from being overjoyed, Asha was acutely
embarrassed at the sight of Mahendra's discomfiture. He
now had to creep into his own house like a thief. She

not imagine any relationship with Binodini that would be worthy of the beautiful state into which she had initiated him. When a lotus is uprooted, slime rises to the surface. What could he say, where could he find a place for her to ensure that the beautiful did not transform into the hideous? Besides, if it caused a tussle with Mahendra, the whole affair would take an unthinkably ugly turn. Having enthroned the goddess of his imagination in the solitude of the Ganga shore, surrounded by celestial music, Bihari burned his heart like incense at the shrine of love. Lest he receive news that might dispel this web of pleasing illusion, he did not write to enquire after Binodini.

One cloudy dawn, Bihari lay silently beneath the fruit-laden blackberry tree at the southern end of his garden, idly watching the pinnace plying to and fro from the cottages; gradually, it grew quite late. The servant came to ask if he wanted his meal. 'Not now,' Bihari replied. The chief mason came to call him, to inspect the work and offer his advice. 'After a while,' he said.

Suddenly, Bihari was startled to see Annapurna standing before him. Flustered, he rose to his feet, and clasping her feet in both his hands, he touched his head to the ground in obeisance. With deep affection, Annapurna touched Bihari's head and body with her right hand. In a tear-choked voice, she inquired: 'Bihari, why have you grown so thin?'

'Kakima, it was to regain your affection.'

At these words, tears gushed forth from Annapurna's eyes.

'Kakima, haven't you eaten yet?' asked Bihari anxiously.

'No, I haven't had the time.'

'Come, I shall make arrangements for you to cook,' said Bihari. 'Today, after a long time, I shall draw new sustenance from food cooked by you, and prasad—food blessed by your touch—from your plate.'

Bihari made no mention of Mahendra and Asha. Annapurna herself had once slammed the door on that possibility. With wounded pride, he obeyed that stern admonition.

At the end of the meal, Annapurna proposed: 'The boat is ready at the ghat, Bihari; please come with me to Kolkata.'

'What is the need for me to visit Kolkata?'

'Didi is very ill; she has asked to see you.'

Bihari was startled to hear this. 'Where is Mahinda?' he asked.

'He is not in Kolkata; he has gone west.'

At these words, Bihari's face instantly grew pale. He remained silent.

'Don't you know everything?' Annapurna asked him.

'I know some of it, but I don't have the latest deatils.'

Then Annapurna told him that Mahendra had travelled west with Binodini. Instantly, earth, water and sky changed colour for Bihari, and the nectar collected in his imagination turned bitter. 'Did the sorceress Binodini play games with me that evening, then? Her surrender to love was a deceitful trick! Leaving her village, she has shamelessly gone west with Mahendra! Shame upon her; and shame on me, that I was foolish enough to trust her for a single moment.'

Alas, it had vanished, the magic of the overcast monsoon evening and the full moon night after a shower of rain!

49

*B*ihari wondered how he would face the desolate Asha. When he entered the portico, he was instantly enveloped in the deep gloom of the house that had been abandoned by its master. Glancing at the faces of the watchman and the servants, Bihari bowed his head in shame for Mahendra, who had vanished in such a frenzied state. He could not greet these familiar attendants with affectionate queries, as before. When it came to entering the private quarters, his feet refused to carry him further. Bihari did not have the heart to see the cringing, wounded Asha subjected to public humiliation, the terrible humiliation that Mahendra had inflicted on her before the eyes of the entire world, the humiliation that takes away the last vestige of a woman's privacy, forcing her to stand exposed to the inquisitive, pitying gaze of the whole world.

But there was not much opportunity for such worry

or hesitation. As soon as he entered the private quarters, Asha hurried up to Bihari. 'Thakurpo, please come quickly,' she begged. 'Ma's condition has become acute.'

This was Bihari's first direct conversation with Asha. In times of sorrow and hardship, a single small jolt can fling aside all obstructions; in a sudden flood, those who live apart are flung together when cast up on a narrow strip of land.

Bihari was hurt by Asha's unreserved expression of anxiety. This minor instance demonstrated even more clearly what Mahendra had done to his household. Under the pressure of difficult times, just as the décor and beauty of the house was neglected, so, too, had the bride of the house lost all chance of preserving at least the semblance of modesty. Asha no longer had the time to pay any heed to the niceties of deportment such as covering her head or maintaining discretion in her social behaviour.

Bihari entered Rajalakshmi's room. Rajalakshmi had grown pale from a sudden, brief bout of breathlessness, from which she had partially recovered.

As Bihari offered his respects by touching her feet, Rajalakshmi signalled to him to sit by her side, and, pronouncing the words very slowly, asked: 'How are you, Bihari? It's been so long since I last saw you!'

'Ma, why didn't you send word to me earlier? Had I known of your illness, would I have delayed an instant?'

'Don't I know that, my child?' said Rajalakshmi in

a low voice. 'I did not bear you in my womb, but who in this world is more my own than you?' Tears began to roll down her cheeks.

Quickly rising to his feet, Bihari tried to pull himself together, pretending to examine the bottles and boxes of medicine placed in the niche in the wall. Returning to her, when he tried to examine Rajalakshmi's pulse, she resisted. 'Let my pulse be; tell me, why have you grown so thin, Bihari?' Rajalakshmi raised her thin hand to stroke Bihari's collarbone.

'These bones of mine can never be fleshed over unless I eat fish curry cooked by you. Get well quickly, Ma; meanwhile, let me make arrangements for you to cook.'

'Make arrangements quickly, my boy—but not for cooking!' Rajalakshmi smiled wanly. She grasped Bihari's hand. 'Bihari, bring home a bride, there's nobody to look after you. O Mejobou, get Bihari married now—just see what has happened to the poor boy's appearance!'

'You get well, Didi. This is your task; you must accomplish it, and we shall join in the fun, all of us,' Annapurna assured her.

'I shall not have the time anymore, Mejobou; you must take responsibility for Bihari. Make him happy. I could not repay my debt to him, but may God bless him.' She stroked Bihari's head with her right hand.

Asha could remain in the room no longer. She went

out to weep. Through her tears, Annapurna cast an affectionate glance at Bihari.

Rajalakshmi suddenly thought of something. 'Bouma, O Bouma!' she called.

As soon as Asha entered the room, she asked, 'You have made proper arrangements for Bihari's meal, haven't you?'

'Ma, everyone is well acquainted with this greedy son of yours,' Bihari informed her. 'The moment I entered the portico, I saw Bami rushing towards the inner quarters, carrying a basket full of large koi fish with roe. I realized that in this house my reputation had not vanished.' Bihari smiled, glancing once at Asha's face.

Today, Asha no longer felt shy. She accepted Bihari's joke with an affectionate smile. Before this, Asha had not fully realized the importance of Bihari's role in this household. She had often ignored him as an unwanted visitor; often, she had treated him with hostility. Full of remorse and self-condemnation, she now felt a strong urge to express her respect and sympathy for Bihari.

'Mejobou,' said Rajalakshmi, 'this is beyond the capacity of bamunthakur, our cook; you must personally supervise the cooking. This bangal son of ours from East Bengal can't dine unless the food is loaded with chillies.'

'Your mother was from Bikrampur, and you call a civilized Nadia boy a bangal? This is not to be borne,' joked Bihari.

There was much laughing and joking about this issue; after a long time the pall of gloom over Mahendra's house seemed to have lifted.

But in the course of all this conversation, nobody uttered Mahendra's name. Earlier, Mahendra had been the sole topic of conversation between Bihari and Rajalakshmi. Mahendra would joke with his mother about this. Today, Bihari was secretly astonished to find that Rajalakshmi did not take Mahendra's name even once.

When Rajalakshmi showed signs of drowsiness, Bihari came out and remarked to Annapurna: 'Ma's illness is not a simple one.'

'That is obvious.' Annapurna sat down by the window. After a long silence, she suggested: 'Won't you go and fetch Mahendra here, Bihari? It is not wise to wait any longer.'

'I shall do as you decree,' replied Bihari, after a short silence. 'Does anyone know his address?'

'Nobody knows exactly; it will have to be found. Bihari, let me say one more thing. Take a look at Asha's face. If you cannot rescue Mahendra from Binodini's clutches, Asha will not survive. If you observe her expression, you will realize that she has been struck by the arrow of death.'

Smiling bitterly to himself, Bihari thought, 'I am supposed to come to the rescue of other people, but Lord, who will come to my rescue?' He protested:

'Kakima, can I summon up a magic spell that would permanently protect Mahendra from Binodini's attraction? He may act with restraint for a few days, on account of his mother's illness, but how can I predict that he will never return to his old ways again?' At this moment, Asha came to sit at her mashima's feet, wearing faded clothes, her head partially covered. Knowing that Bihari and Annapurna were discussing Rajalakshmi's illness, she had come anxiously to listen. Seeing the quiet grace of silent sorrow on the countenance of Asha, the devoted wife, Bihari felt an extraordinary respect for her. Anointed with the scalding, sacred water of sorrow, this young woman had achieved the calm dignity of an ancient goddess. She was an ordinary woman no more; in her terrible grief, she seemed to have attained the maturity of the female ascetics described in the Puranas.

Having discussed Rajalakshmi's diet and medicine with Asha, Bihari saw her off. With a sigh, he promised Annapurna: 'I shall rescue Mahendra.'

Bihari visited Mahendra's bank, where he was told that Mahendra had recently begun conducting transactions with their Allahabad branch.

50

Arriving at the station, Binodini immediately entered the ladies' coach in the intermediate class and took a seat there.

'What are you doing?' exclaimed Mahendra. 'I'll buy you a second-class ticket.'

'What need for that? I shall be fine here.'

Mahendra was amazed. Binodini was a person of refined tastes. Before this, she had shown extreme distaste for anything that smacked of poverty; she used to be ashamed of her impoverished circumstances. Mahendra knew that the abundant flow of money in his house, the items of luxury available there, and their prestigious position as a rich family among ordinary people had once appealed to Binodini. She had been very excited at the prospect of becoming the mistress of all this wealth, all this comfort and social eminence. Today, when the time came for her to assume dominance over Mahendra, when she could enjoy all his wealth and possessions without having to ask, why did she so arrogantly embrace this painful, degraded state of poverty, spurning him with such unbearable indifference? She wanted to keep her dependence on Mahendra as limited as possible. In his state of frenzy, Mahendra had forced her to discard her respectability forever; Binodini now wanted nothing from him that could be construed as the price to be paid for her degradation. All these days, while Binodini lived in Mahendra's house, she had not adhered rigidly to the code of widowhood; but now, she denied herself all pleasure in life. Now she ate one meal a day and wore coarse fabric. Her endless flow of laughing banter had also disappeared . Now she was so still, so deeply veiled, so remote, so terrifying, that Mahendra did not dare to insist on anything. Angry, impatient and surprised, he wondered, 'Having managed with such extreme effort to pluck me from the treetop like a rare fruit, why does Binodini now fling the fruit to the dust without so much as sniffing its aroma?'

'What destination shall I buy tickets for?' he inquired.

'Let's go west, to any place you like. We'll get off at any station, wherever the train stops tomorrow morning.'

This manner of travel did not appeal to Mahendra. He found it hard to bear any hindrance to his comforts. If they did not find some proper accommodation in a big city, it would be very difficult for him. By nature, he was not resourceful enough to explore and improvise ways and means to get things done. Hence, he boarded the train in an extremely irritable, exasperated frame of mind. Meanwhile, he was haunted by the constant fear that Binodini might alight somewhere and give him the slip.

In their wanderings, Binodini seemed to spin like the planet Saturn, throwing Mahendra into a spin as well; she gave him no respite. Binodini could easily strike up a relationship with people; in a very short time, she would make friends with her co-passengers on the train. She would find out all about the place she wished to visit. She would take shelter in traveller's inns, and wherever she went, she would explore all the places of interest, getting about with the help of her friends. Feeling that Binodini had no need for him, Mahendra daily suffered a sense of humiliation. He had no task save purchasing tickets; the rest of the time, he fought his own desires. For the first few days, he wandered the streets with Binodini, but soon, he found it intolerable. Thereafter, Mahendra would try to catch a nap after meals, while Binodini roamed about all day. Nobody could have imagined that Mahendra, so lovingly pampered by his mother, could traverse the outside world in this fashion.

One day, at the Allahabad station, the two of them were waiting for a train which, for some reason, had been unexpectedly delayed. Meanwhile, other trains came and went, and Binodini carefully inspected all the passengers. Travelling around in the western region, looking at everything around her, she seemed to be searching for someone she desperately hoped to find. At least there was some peace to be found in this daily hunt, this hustle and bustle of the open road, rather than daily suffocating oneself, frozen immobile in a desolate flat in a blind alley.

When Binodini's gaze fell on a glass box at the station, she gave a sudden start. In this box, the post office had displayed letters addressed to people who were untraceable. Inscribed on one of the letters in the box, Binodini saw Bihari's name. The name Biharilal was not uncommon; there was no reason to imagine that the addressee of the letter was the Bihari Binodini sought. All the same, upon seeing Bihari's full name there, she had no doubt it was her one and only Bihari and no other. She memorized the address written on the letter. Approaching Mahendra, who sat on a bench looking very unhappy, she proposed: 'Let's stay in Allahabad for a few days.'

Mahendra's masculine pride was injured, and his spirit rebellious at the fact that Binodini manipulated him as she pleased, while still denying succour to his hungry, frustrated heart. He would be extremely relieved to stay on in Allahabad and get some rest. But even if this corresponded with his wishes, his mind was suddenly averse to the prospect of consenting to every whim of Binodini's. Angrily, he insisted, 'Now that we have set out, we must go on. We cannot turn back.'

'I shall not go.'

'Then you can stay here alone; I am going.'

'That's better.' Saying no more, she beckoned a porter and left the station.

Mahendra remained sitting on the bench, his face black as thunder, nursing his male pride. As long as Binodini was within sight, he remained still. When she had walked out without a backward glance, he quickly loaded his luggage on a porter's head and began to follow her. Emerging from the station, he saw Binodini enter a carriage that she had engaged. Without saying anything, Mahendra loaded his luggage onto the top of the carriage, and mounted the coachbox. He did not have the courage to throw his pride to the winds and sit facing Binodini inside the carriage.

But the carriage drove on and on. More than an hour had passed; having crossed the city, they were now travelling through ploughed fields. Mahendra felt ashamed to question the coachman, because this might give the impression that the woman inside the carriage was the decision maker, who had not even consulted this redundant male about their destination. Mahendra sat silently on the coachbox, angry, reproachful thoughts churning in his mind.

The carriage came to a stop inside a lovingly tended garden on the secluded banks of the Yamuna. Mahendra was amazed. Whose garden was this, and how did Binodini know its location?

The house was locked. After much calling and shouting, an old caretaker came out. 'The owner is a rich man,' he informed them. 'He lives not far away. If you obtain his permission, I can let you stay in this house.'

Binodini glanced at Mahendra's face. He was tempted at the sight of this beautiful house. He cheered up at the prospect of leading a stable existence for a few days, at long last. 'Then let's go to this rich man's house,' he suggested to Binodini. 'You will wait in the carriage while I go inside and fix the rent.'

'I can't travel around anymore. You go; I'll stay here and rest in the meanwhile. I see no reason to be afraid.'

Mahendra went away in the carriage. Calling the old Brahmin, Binodini asked about his children: who were they, where did they work, who had his daughters married? Hearing of his wife's death, she remarked sorrowfully: 'Ah, you must have a very hard life. To be left alone at this age! Is there nobody to look after you?'

After that, in the course of conversation, Binodini asked, 'Biharibabu was here, wasn't he?'

'Yes, he was indeed here for a few days,' replied the old man. 'Does Ma ji know him?'

'He is related to us.'

From the account of Bihari that Binodini received from the old man, there remained no doubt in her mind. Getting him to unlock the rooms, she found out which room Bihari had slept in, which room he had used as a sitting room, and other such information. Since the rooms had remained locked after his departure, it seemed that the presence of the invisible Bihari still lingered, filling the rooms, as if the breeze had failed to blow it away. Breathing it in, Binodini filled her heart with it, letting it caress her entire body in the stillness of the atmosphere; but of Bihari's whereabouts, there was no information. He might even return, but there was no clear indication. The old man assured Binodini that he would go and ask his master and then let her know.

Having paid advance rent and obtained permission to stay, Mahendra returned.

51

The snow on the Himalayan peaks eternally feeds the waters of the river Yamuna. Eternal, too, is the flow of romantic verse poured into the Yamuna by poets through the ages. What varied rhythms resound in the babbling of the waters, what age-old raptures of emotion well up in the play of waves!

When Mahendra came to sit on the bank of the Yamuna at dusk, the aura of heavy romance produced a deep sense of enchantment, permeating his gaze, his breath, his veins, his bones. In the sky, the rays of the setting sun resembled a golden veena, vibrating with exquisite melodies of agony, music for celestial ears.

On the desolate expanse of sand, in many-hued radiance, the daylight waned gradually. Lost in the realm of poetry, eyes half-closed, Mahendra could hear in his imagination the lowing of Brindaban cows as they returned to the fold at this twilight hour, their hooves kicking up a haze of dust.

The sky became overcast with rain clouds. The darkness of an unfamiliar place is not merely a black cloak, but also full of strange mystery. The faint glow and the dim shapes visible through such darkness speak an unknown, unuttered language. The indistinct paleness of the sand on the opposite shore, the ink-black darkness of the waveless waters, the heavy stillness of the dense foliage of the enormous neem tree in the garden, the curving line of the treeless, dusty shore—all this, combined with the blurred, indistinct shapes of that rainy Ashadh evening, enveloped Mahendra.

He remembered the descriptions in traditional Padavali verse of the heroine setting out for a romantic assignation in the rain. The heroine goes forth. At the far end of that Yamuna shore, she stands alone. How will she cross over? 'Ferry me across, O boatman, please ferry me across!' The call reached the inner recesses of Mahendra's heart: 'O ferry me across!'

The heroine stood far away, in the darkness of the other shore, but Mahendra saw her clearly. She was timeless and ageless, forever a Gopika, beloved of Krishna, but still, Mahendra recognized her: she was Binodini. With all her pangs of separation, all her agony, all her voluptuous youth, she had set out on her romantic rendezvous in those ancient times, and travelled through so many songs, so many rhythms, to arrive at the shores of the present time. Tonight, it was her voice that was heard, echoing in the sky above this desolate Yamuna shore—'O boatman, please ferry me across!' For how many ages must she remain standing alone on the shore, waiting in the dark for the ferry boat—'O ferry me across!'

The clouds parted at one end, to reveal the moon on the third night of its dark quarter. In the magic of the moonlight, river and riverbank, sky and horizon, were transported beyond the earthly realm, breaking free of worldly ties. The thread of time was broken, all history erased, all future consequences rendered invisible. Only this silver-flooded moment remained, an eternal present beyond the laws of earthly life, containing within it Mahendra and Binodini, this river and this riverbank.

Mahendra was intoxicated. That Binodini could spurn him, refusing to assume the role of Lakshmi to fulfil the promise of this secluded piece of heaven on this moonlit night, was impossible for him to imagine. Rising to his feet at once, he went towards the house in search of her.

Entering the bedchamber, he found the room redolent of flowers. Through the open windows and doors, the moonlight streamed in, to fall upon the white bed. Weaving garlands of flowers plucked from the garden, Binodini had placed them in her hair, around her neck, and around her waist. Adorned with flowers, she lay on the moonlit bed like a vine laden with the weight of its blossoms.

Mahendra's enchantment intensified. In a choked

voice, he said, 'Binod, I was waiting on the shore of the Yamuna; the moon brought me tidings that you awaited me here, so here I am!'

With these words, Mahendra advanced towards the bed.

Starting, Binodini quickly extended her right arm and said, 'Go away! Don't sit on this bed!'

Mahendra stood in stunned disbelief, like a boat in full sail when it strikes a sandbank. He remained speechless for a long time. Fearing that Mahendra might not accept her admonition, Binodini left the bed and rose to her feet.

'Who have you adorned yourself for, then? For whom are you waiting?' demanded Mahendra.

'He is inside my heart, the person for whom I have adorned myself,' answered Binodini, clutching her bosom.

'Who is he? Is it Bihari?'

'Don't bring his name to your lips.'

'Is it for him that you have been wandering in the west?'

'For him alone.'

'Is it for him alone that you are waiting here?'

'For him alone.'

'Have you found out his address?'

'I haven't, but I shall find it out, somehow.'

'I shall not let you find out under any circumstances.'

'If you don't let me find out, then you will never be able to oust him from my heart.'

With these words, Binodini closed her eyes and felt Bihari's presence in her heart. Simultaneously attracted and repelled by this image of the flower-bedecked Binodini racked by the pangs of separation, Mahendra suddenly grew violently angry.

Clenching his fists, he vowed, 'I shall carve him out of your heart with a knife.'

'Your knife will enter my heart more readily than your love,' rejoined Binodini, unperturbed.

'Why are you not afraid of me? Who is here to protect you?'

'You are here to protect me. You will protect me from yourself.'

'Do you still have that little bit of respect, that little bit of trust left in you?'

'Else, I would have killed myself. I would never have ventured forth with you.'

'Why didn't you kill yourself? Why do you drag me from place to place, with the noose of that little bit of trust cast round my neck as if to kill me? Think how beneficial your death would have been!'

'I know, but as long as there is hope of Bihari, I cannot die.'

'Until you die, my hopes will not die, either—there will be no release for me. From today, I shall pray for your death with all my heart. Don't be mine, and don't be Bihari's either. Go! Let me go, too. My mother weeps for me, my wife weeps for me—their tears scald me from afar. Until you die, until you are beyond hope for me and for everyone else on earth, I shall not have leave to wipe away their tears.'

With these words, Mahendra rushed out of the room. He had destroyed the web of enchantment that Binodini had woven around herself in solitude. Standing in silence, she gazed at the scene outside. All the nectar in her heart had evaporated, emptying the sky of moonlight. She saw the garden with its flowerbeds; beyond it the sandy riverside; beyond that the black waters of the river; and beyond that the indistinctness of the opposite shore. The entire scene seemed like a mere pencil sketch on white paper, utterly lifeless and futile.

Today, realizing how forcefully she had attracted Mahendra, how she had uprooted him like a tree in a tremendous storm, her heart grew even more turbulent. If she had such power, why did Bihari not come before her and break upon her shore like a swollen sea wave on a full moon night? Why, every day, was her mental peace disturbed by the onslaught of an unwanted love that broke her meditation with its lamentation?

Why, again and again, did an anguished cry intrude upon her heart from outside, not giving her inner tears a chance to spend themselves? What would she do all her life with this great turbulence that she had set in motion? How could she quieten it?

She tore off the floral garlands with which she had bedecked herself, knowing that Mahendra's enraptured gaze had fallen upon them tonight. All her powers, all her efforts, her entire life was futile; this garden, this moonlight, this Yamuna shore, this exquisitely beautiful world—everything was pointless.

Such frustration, yet her situation remained exactly the same as before; in the outer world, nothing had changed. The sun would rise tomorrow as usual, the world would not forget its smallest routine task, and Bihari would remain unperturbed and distant as he was, practicing a new lesson with his Brahmin boy.

Binodini burst into tears. It seemed she had been using all her strength, all her desire in trying to move a rock. Her heart bled, but her destiny did not alter in the slightest.

52

Mahendra could not sleep all night; towards dawn, worn out and tired, he dozed off. Waking up at eight or nine in the morning, he sat up abruptly. Some undercurrents of pain, persisting after the events of last night, seemed to have flowed through him in his sleep. As soon as he awakened, Mahendra began to feel the agony. After a little while, the events of the night came back to him clearly. In the clear light of day, in the fatigue of insufficient sleep, the whole world, his whole life, seemed utterly devoid of interest. Why should he have to bear the burden of disgrace for having abandoned his household, remorse for having forsworn his religion, and emotional distress for the wild existence that he led? In the early morning sunlight, shorn of all enchantment, Mahendra felt that he did not love Binodini. Glancing at the street, he saw that the whole world was awake, busily rushing to work. Mahendra now realized clearly the folly of flinging all his self-respect into the mire to enslave his life at the feet of a woman who was averse to him. After the exuberance of a violent emotion, there is a sense of exhaustion; the tired heart then wants to temporarily distance itself from the subject of its emotion. During this emotional ebb tide, all the concealed mire of the riverbed lies exposed; what had earlier seemed enchanting now appears distasteful. Today, Mahendra was unable to understand why he had degraded himself in this fashion. He told himself: 'I am superior to Binodini in every way, but still, accepting all forms of abject humiliation, I run after her day and night like a contemptible beggar. What devil has possessed me that I should give in to such strange lunacy!' Today, to Mahendra, Binodini was just another woman, nothing more. She had attracted a radiant aura all around her, drawn from all the beauty in the world, all the poems and tales ever composed. But today, the aura had vanished like a mirage, and only an ordinary woman remained with nothing unique about her.

Mahendra now became eager to sever himself from this condemnable spell of enchantment, so that he could return home. The peace, love and affection that had once been his now appeared to be, like the rarest nectar, beyond easy reach. Bihari's unwavering friendship, dating back to their childhood, now seemed invaluable to him. Mahendra remarked to himself: 'We fail to understand the value of that which is truly deep and stable, because we can immerse ourselves in it without any effort or hindrance. That which is merely a fleeting illusion, which brings no trace of happiness even in its fulfilment, impels us to give chase breathlessly as in a race; hence, we take it for coveted treasure.'

'I shall return home this very day,' Mahendra decided. 'I'll arrange for Binodini to stay wherever she wishes. Then I will be free.' *I will be free*—as soon as he had declared this resolve in words, his heart felt a sudden thrill, and the oppressive burden of hesitation that he had borne for so long was lightened. All these days, from moment to moment, he had vacillated between repulsion and submission; he was unable to say yes or no with any conviction; he would suppress the dictates of his conscience to take the path of transgression. Now, as soon as he declared, 'I will be free,' his tormented heart felt immediate relief and greeted his resolve with joy.

Leaving his bed at once, Mahendra washed his face and went to see Binodini. He found her door closed. Banging on her door, he called: 'Are you asleep?'

'No. Please go away now.'

'I have something important to say. I shall not stay long.'

'I can't bear to listen to your words anymore. Please go away. Don't trouble me, leave me alone.'

At any other time, this rejection would have heightened Mahendra's desperation. But today, he felt extreme contempt. He thought, 'Have I so degraded myself in the eyes of this common woman, that she can assume the right to dismiss me so contemptuously at her own will? This is not her natural right. It is I who have granted it to her, and thereby allowed her to become so arrogant.' After this humiliation, Mahendra tried to remind himself of his own superiority. 'I shall be victorious,' he vowed. 'I shall go away, breaking the ties that bind me to her.'

After lunch, Mahendra went to the bank to withdraw some money. Having collected the amount, he began to wander about in the Allahabad market to buy some nice new things for his mother and Asha.

Once again, there was a knock on Binodini's door. At first, she was too exasperated to answer, but when the knocking continued, she flung the door open in a temper and demanded: 'Why must you come to trouble me, again and again?' Before she could complete her sentence, Binodini saw Bihari standing there.

Bihari glanced into the room to see if Mahendra was there. He saw the bedroom strewn with faded blossoms and tattered garlands. In an instant, his heart turned virulently hostile. When Bihari was far away, it was not as if suspicions about Binodini's lifestyle had never arisen in his mind; but the play of fancy had obscured those doubts, creating instead the glittering image of an enchantress. Bihari's heart was quaking as he entered the garden estate, his mind cringing lest the image of his dreams be suddenly shattered. As soon as Bihari stood before the door to Binodini's bedchamber, he received the jolt that he had feared.

While he was away, Bihari had imagined that the purifying touch of his love would easily purge Binodini's life of all pollutants. Coming close to her, he realized that this would not be easy. But why did he not feel any pity or tenderness in his heart? Suddenly, a wave of disgust engulfed him. To Bihari, Binodini now seemed utterly impure.

Abruptly, Bihari turned around and called out, 'Mahendra! Mahendra!'

Binodini felt insulted. 'Mahendra is not here, he has gone to town,' she told him, in a low, gentle voice.

When Bihari prepared to leave, Binodini pleaded, 'Bihari Thakurpo, I beg you, please stay here awhile.'

Bihari had not intended to listen to any pleas. He had decided to remove himself at once from this disgusting scene, but when he heard Binodini's piteous, pleading tone, for a brief instant his feet refused to move.

'If you turn away from me today, I swear that I shall die,' declared Binodini.

Bihari turned around. 'Binodini, why must you entangle me in your life?' he demanded. 'What have I done to you? I have never stood in your way, nor interfered in your joys and sorrows.'

'I had once declared to you the extent of your power over me, but you did not believe me. I repeat the same thing today, even in the face of your aversion. After all, you denied me the time to communicate my feelings without words, in a modest fashion. You have spurned me, yet I fall at your feet and say, I . . .'

'Don't say it, don't bring those words to your lips!' interrupted Bihari. 'I cannot believe those words.'

'Common people may not believe them, but you will. That is why I ask you to remain here awhile.'

'Whether I believe or not, how does it matter? Your life would continue in the same fashion.'

'I know it will make no difference to you. It is my misfortune that I have no right to stand by your side without injuring your dignity. I must forever remain at a distance from you. All the same, my heart refuses to relinquish this tiny claim upon you: wherever I am, you must think of me with some tenderness. I know that you had developed some respect for me: that will be my only succour. That is why you must listen to all I have to say. I beg with folded hands, Thakurpo, please stay awhile.'

'Very well, let's go.' Bihari prepared to move to a different spot.

'Thakurpo, it is not as you think. No disgrace has touched this room. You had slept in this room one night. I have dedicated this room to you; those flowers were offered to you in devotion, and now lie faded. You must remain in this very room.'

At this, Bihari's heart was filled with rapture. He entered the room. With both hands, Binodini gestured towards the bed. Bihari went and sat on the bed. Binodini settled herself on the floor, at his feet. When Bihari made as if to arise, in alarm, Binodini stopped him. 'Thakurpo, please remain seated; don't get up, I insist. I am unworthy of a place at your feet: it is your kindness that you allow me to sit here. Even when I am far away, I shall retain this right.'

Binodini lapsed into a short silence. Then, with a sudden start, she asked: 'Have you eaten, Thakurpo?'

'I ate at the station before coming here.'

'I wrote you a letter from my village. Why did you send it back to me, unopened, through Mahendra's hands?'

'But I never received that letter.'

'Did you meet Mahendra in Kolkata this time?'

'I met Mahendra the day after I escorted you to your village. Immediately after that, I travelled west, and I did not meet him again.'

'Before that, on another day, had you read my letter and returned it unanswered?'

'No, that had never happened.'

Binodini sat dumbfounded. Then she sighed: 'I understand everything. Now let me tell you all about myself. If you believe me, I shall consider myself fortunate; if you don't, I shall not blame you, for it is hard to have faith in me.'

By now, Bihari's heart had softened. He could not slight the homage that Binodini, bowed down by the weight of her devotion, offered so humbly. 'Bouthan, you need not say anything,' he told her. 'I believe you without hearing your words. I cannot hold you in contempt. Please do not say another word.'

Hearing this, tears began to flow from Binodini's eyes. Touching Bihari's feet, she pleaded, 'If I don't tell you everything, I shall die. You must listen with patience. What you had decreed, I accepted with deference. Although you had not even written to me, I would still have spent my life in my village, putting up with the mockery and blame heaped upon me by the people there. I would have accepted your admonition in place of your affection, but destiny was averse even to that. The sin I had committed did not permit me to survive even in exile. Coming to my village, to my door, Mahendra humiliated me in front of everyone. There was no longer any place for me in the village. To seek your instructions for the second time, I searched for you everywhere, but was unable to find you. Mahendra deceived me, returning from your house with my letter, which had been opened. I thought you had forsaken me completely. After this, I could have utterly ruined myself, but you have the strange power to protect me even from a distance; because I had given you a place in my heart, I could remain chaste. Like the hardness of gold, or of a jewel, the hard self you revealed to me the day you spurned me is inside my heart, refining my life and giving it value. My lord, I touch your feet and declare: that value has not been destroyed.'

Bihari sat in silence. Binodini, too, said no more. The late afternoon sunlight began to fade. At this moment, Mahendra, approaching the door to the room, was startled to see Bihari. The indifference he had begun to feel towards Binodini almost vanished in the face of jealousy. Seeing her seated silently at Bihari's feet, Mahendra's pride was wounded. He remained in no doubt that this union had been brought about by an exchange of letters between Binodini and Bihari. All these days, Bihari had been unwilling; now, if he willingly surrendered himself, there would be no stopping Binodini. Mahendra could relinquish Binodini, but seeing Bihari, he realized that he could not give her up to someone else.

In frustrated rage, Mahendra mocked Binodini: 'Now it's time for Mahendra to leave the stage, and for Bihari to enter. The scene is beautiful; I feel like applauding. But I hope this is the last act, for after this, nothing will be seemly.'

Binodini's face grew scarlet. Now that she was dependent on Mahendra, she could not answer this insult. She only cast an anguished glance at Bihari.

Bihari got up from the bed. Advancing, he declared, 'Mahendra, don't insult Binodini like a coward. If your good breeding does not forbid you, then I have the right to do so.'

'Has your right been established already?' Mahendra laughed. 'Today, let us rename you Binod-Bihari, the playful adventurer!'

Sensing the deliberate provocation, Bihari grasped Mahendra's hand. 'Mahendra, I declare to you that I intend to marry Binodini; so, from now on, be careful what you say.'

Mahendra was dumbfounded. Binodini was startled; the blood pounded in her heart.

'There is another piece of news for you,' Bihari continued. 'Your mother is on her deathbed; there is no hope of her survival. I shall leave by the night train, and Binodini will accompany me.'

'Is Pishima ill?' asked Binodini, startled.

'It is not an illness to be cured. Anything could happen at any moment,' Bihari told her.

Without any more words, Mahendra left the room.

'How could you say the words that you just uttered?' Binodini asked Bihari. 'Is this a joke?'

'No, I spoke sincerely; I shall marry you.'

'To rescue this sinful woman.'

'No. Because I love you, because I respect you.'

'This is my ultimate reward. I want nothing more than what you have just admitted. Even if I receive more than this, it will not last; religion will not tolerate it.'

'Why not?'

'For shame, it is embarrassing to think of such a thing. I am a widow, a woman disgraced. I cannot permit you to be humiliated in the eyes of society. For shame, don't mention such things.'

'Would you abandon me?'

'I do not have the right to abandon you. You secretly work for the good of others: grant me responsibility for one of your undertakings, and in fulfiling it, I shall count myself among your devotees. But how shameful, that you should want to marry a widow! In the greatness of your heart, anything is possible, but if I should take this step, destroying you in the eyes of society, I shall never in all my life recover from my shame.'

'But I love you, Binodini.'

'On the strength of that love, I shall commit a single act of daring today.' Saying this, Binodini prostrated herself and kissed Bihari's toe. Kneeling at his feet, she vowed, 'I shall do penance and meditation so that you may be mine in my next birth; in this birth, I have no claims or expectations. I have caused much sadness, and received much sorrow in return; I have learned a great deal. Had I forgotten those lessons I had learned, I would have dragged you down and degraded myself further. But because of your uprightness, I am able to raise my head again, with renewed self-respect. I shall not destroy this refuge, this support.'

Bihari remained silent, his face grave.

Folding her hands in supplication, Binodini said, 'Make no mistake: marrying me will not make you happy. You will lose respect, and so shall I. You are